'Do you know who I am?'

'You are Guy St Edmond, the Earl of Sinnington. You are to take up residence at Sinnington Castle. People have talked of nothing else these past weeks.'

'Then since we are to reside close to each other, Mistress Lovet, I shall look forward to seeing you again. What else should I know of you?'

'I am to be married, sir—yet even had that not been the case your reputation has preceded you. People say you are the spawn of Satan and that men and children fear you. For years there have been rumours that you enjoy killing—that it was by your order that my brother died, and that you take pleasure in the suffering of others.'

When he didn't deny it, Jane felt her insides cringe.

'Since you appear to know so much about me,' he said in a dangerously soft voice, 'there is little wonder I am *persona non grata* in certain company.' Guy's leisurely perusal swept her as he tried to control his restive mount. 'You should know I am as lucky in war as I am in love, sweet Jane.'

AUTHOR NOTE

I thoroughly enjoyed creating THE DEVIL CLAIMS A WIFE, which is my first Medieval novel. I do like to vary the periods I write about and, inspired after reading several books about the Medieval period, I couldn't resist trying something different. Creating the story was challenging and demanding, but most of all enjoyable.

I hope you enjoy reading THE DEVIL CLAIMS A WIFE.

THE DEVIL
CLAIMS A WIFE

Helen Dickson

First published in Great Britain 2013
by Mills & Boon, an imprint of Harlequin (UK) Limited.
Large Print edition 2013
Harlequin (UK) Limited, Eton House, 18-24 Paradise Road, Richmond, Surrey TW9 1SR

© Helen Dickson 2013

ISBN: 978 0 263 23282 0

Harlequin (UK) policy is to use papers that are natural, renewable and recyclable products and made from wood grown in sustainable forests. The logging and manufacturing process conform to the legal environmental regulations of the country of origin.

Printed and bound in Great Britain
by CPI Antony Rowe, Chippenham, Wiltshire

Helen Dickson was born and lives in South Yorkshire, with her retired farm manager husband. Having moved out of the busy farmhouse where she raised their two sons, she has more time to indulge in her favourite pastimes. She enjoys being outdoors, travelling, reading and music. An incurable romantic, she writes for pleasure. It was a love of history that drove her to writing historical fiction.

Previous novels by Helen Dickson:

THE DEFIANT DEBUTANTE
ROGUE'S WIDOW, GENTLEMAN'S WIFE
TRAITOR OR TEMPTRESS
WICKED PLEASURES
  (part of *Christmas By Candlelight*)
A SCOUNDREL OF CONSEQUENCE
FORBIDDEN LORD
SCANDALOUS SECRET, DEFIANT BRIDE
FROM GOVERNESS TO SOCIETY BRIDE
MISTRESS BELOW DECK
THE BRIDE WORE SCANDAL
DESTITUTE ON HIS DOORSTEP
SEDUCING MISS LOCKWOOD
MARRYING MISS MONKTON
DIAMONDS, DECEPTION AND THE DEBUTANTE
BEAUTY IN BREECHES
MISS CAMERON'S FALL FROM GRACE
THE HOUSEMAID'S SCANDALOUS SECRET*
WHEN MARRYING A DUKE…

*Castonbury Park Regency mini-series

And in Mills & Boon® Historical *Undone!* eBooks:

ONE RECKLESS NIGHT

Did you know that some of these novels are also available as eBooks? Visit www.millsandboon.co.uk

Chapter One

They said Guy St Edmond was the spawn of Satan. They said he was as tall as a tree and that he could slay a man with a single stroke of his sword. There were darker tales still in his shadowed past, rumours that Guy St Edmond was the despoiler of innocents, that he ate the flesh of his victims and that he devoured everything in his path.

Battle after battle he led his troops to victory after victory. The king and hardened warriors granted him their respect and deferred to his opinions, and by the time Jane was seventeen years old he was already a legend in Cherriot Vale. It was said he had never lost so much as a skirmish. His name was a password for victory and it was rumoured he only had to appear on the horizon for the enemy to turn and flee.

The mere mention of his name made little children cling to their mothers in terror and hide their faces in their skirts. But as far as Jane knew, no one had ever dared confront him to find out if all of this was fact or legend.

Yes, she thought as, with a thundering heart and almost suffocating with fear, she peeked through the foliage to look at the demonic spectre who was one of the young King Edward of York's most favoured and most formidable knights, Guy St Edmond might well be all those things, but no one had said how handsome he was, that he was a devastatingly masculine male, with a certain air about him that could not help but intrigue and attract every female eye. How could he be all those terrible things? Was that what the wars had done to him, or just his nature?

Power, danger and bold vitality emanated from every line of his towering physique as he rode ahead of a small entourage of knights and squires. Some wore his red-and-black livery. They had evidently been riding hard for some considerable distance for their clothes were dusty and their faces streaked with dirt and sweat. With a jingle of harness and a noise like thunder, the stately chargers came at a gallop in a swirling cloud of dust and earth, looking unreal in the small clearing—yet Guy St Edmond had the God-given right to be there, for was he not the Earl of Sinnington, the lord of Sinnington Castle, to have and to enjoy the lands and revenues to be reaped from his domain?

There were ten horsemen in all, but Jane felt no inclination to move her gaze past the imposing man astride the black steed prancing in the lead. It was huge, a warhorse, high, wide and broad in proportion, with a hint of wildness in its eyes. It had its ears back, its head well up, its smooth-flowing gait a perfect complement to the proud, majestic bearing of his rider. His leather boots were silver-spurred and he wore a sword and a long dagger attached to his belt.

The earl rode with a purpose that was impressive. Tall and powerful, he was of an age perhaps a score and ten. But it wasn't only the height and the impressive display of bulging muscle and sinew that caused him to stand out from the other horsemen. There was about him an air of confidence and intelligent command that he wore as easily as he did his sword. Everything about him spoke of control. Or so it seemed to Jane, who could hardly judge for certain when she'd never seen him before or heard him utter a word.

As if sensing he was being watched, Guy St Edmond snatched at the reins. Wrenched to standstill, his horse stood up on its hind legs, the following riders wheeling and coming to a jarring stop, metal clanking against metal as they cursed at the sudden halt. They were close to where Jane was hiding. The sun sent shafts of light through the high trees and softly crept through the clearing. At closer range she noted Guy St Edmond's hair was unruly and very dark, almost black, curling round his neck. His skin on his hawk-like face was bronzed above the black beard.

Displaying a coat of arms on his tabard, he was clad in a leather tunic and leggings. It showed his strong limbs and thick torso. He turned in the saddle to speak to his men. He laughed as they shared a joke. It was a deep rich sound that made Jane think of clotted cream. She shuddered. It would seem the formidable Earl of Sinnington had a sense of humour. As he turned back to the light, she made out the fascinating tone of his eyes— could they really be so blue and so bright?

Suddenly the voices of the children she was hiding from as they played their game of hide-and-seek could be heard in the woodland behind her. Ears attuned, his body alert, Guy St Edmond's smile turned from open humour to something more guarded. His thick black brows lowered and his eyes narrowed as they searched for the source of the disturbance. Jane could see he was used to weighing up new situations quickly.

Suddenly the unsuspecting children burst into the open, accompanied by Jane's maid, Kate. Confronted by these awesome, terrifying strangers, the children abandoned their game and clung to Kate, whose protective arms went round them and held them close. Blanche, Jane's ten-year-old sister, stared in mute terror, while Alfred, Jane's thirteen-year-old brother, simply stood and looked with wide-eyed awe, craning his neck up the better to see the man on the horse.

Half in fear and half in concern for her siblings, emerging from the shadows, Jane moved to stand a few paces away from the cowering children, tall and graceful with her long-legged stride. Her skirts of myrtle green moulded her fine limbs, flowing out above her brown leather slippers in soft, yielding folds. The waist gathered beneath the rounded young breasts was caught with dark green ribbons emphasising her shape. Then she raised her eyes, indifferent to all, in morbid curiosity desirous only to look at the man bearing the manner of a warrior about him.

As the daughter of Simon Lovet, an English cloth merchant, and younger sister of Andrew Lovet, who had been killed in battle fighting for the Lancastrian cause and the rightful King Henry and his wife, Guy St Edmond would look on her as a traitor. But Jane, having grown heartily tired of strife, was beyond loyalty to anyone but her family and herself. She stood and waited for him to speak, while terror screamed through every pore of her quaking body.

With the clean, heady scent of spring clover and newly budded flowers in the air, and a blackbird happily singing its heart out, Guy watched the girl watching him as he approached and saw her every thought reflected in her eyes—interest, uncertainty, suspicion, dread—but no fear, thank God.

Unbeknown to him, it was not false bravado that made Jane show no fear. She felt it deep in her bones, but she was a Lovet and a Lovet never admitted fear of any man. She had heard that time after time from her father and her dead brother, and she had adopted their creed for her own.

As he halted his horse in front of her, all the breath suddenly seemed to have left him as he was struck by a jolt of unexpected lust. She stood for a moment in silence, contemplating him. The girl was as ravishing a creature as one could imagine—youth and springtime incarnate.

She had affected him, Jane knew that. Her apprehension increased. Here she was, being stared at by a magnetic, thoroughly compelling man, a man whose direct and confident gaze made her heart beat faster—though that, in small part, might have been due to dread.

For a long moment he gazed right into her eyes with a look that blazed, heating them until they glowed like molten coals in his bearded face. They were hard and inscrutable, as if she knew a secret that he had to know, as if they had known each other for ever. She was unsettled by his look, but she could not look away. A modest woman would lower her eyes, but she stood tall, astonished at herself, staring like an ignorant peasant. She found she could not take her eyes from his, eyes which were burning her where she stood.

Guy was not quite sure what to make of it. Either she had not heard, isolated in Cherriot Vale, that he was the Devil incarnate, or was too starved of male company to care. He found himself strangely moved by her candid look. Fancifully, he thought her like a beautiful half-wild creature of this emerald glade—or a wondrous rare forest animal that did not know enough of the world to be afraid.

She was totally innocent.

Though they were at least twelve paces apart, Jane felt his gaze penetrate her heart. Nudging his horse forwards, he circled her, his smile set in a grim line across his darkly handsome face, examining her like a horse at the fair.

Guy's eyes roved approvingly over her lithe figure, stopping at the swelling breasts and tiny waist, then strayed back to the soft tresses of honey-gold hair that escaped the confines of her green velvet cap. Her nose was upturned, a nose bespeaking curiosity and impishness. Her lips were full, parted and hinted of secret, of a hidden sensuality as her tongue flicked nervously over them. The chin was not weak, not strong, argumentative perhaps, but not intransigent. Her skin was creamy white and glowing. Her eyes green, into which one might wish to dive, to be willingly lost for ever, glowed with an inner light and hinted of the woman hidden beneath the child-like innocence of her face.

She was the loveliest creature his eyes had seen in many a day.

'Well, well, and what have we here?' Guy St Edmond murmured in a voice that was deep and rich and full of unexpected beauty, still looking at her. Her eyes flickered over him, clearly interested, but perhaps intimidated by his size and the bruiser's build that he had inherited from his father. 'I don't bite,' he said with a cynical half-smile.

'No? I have heard to the contrary.'

He laughed, a deep, booming laugh as his horse did a full circle. When he faced her once more, already regretting her impulsive words, Jane stared up at the stranger and despite her efforts a soft flush crept up her cheeks. Without lowering her gaze, she sank into a curtsy as gracefully as she knew how and her trembling limbs would permit. In an attempt to alleviate her siblings' fear, she smiled, showing teeth that were white and even and beautifully shaped. 'I am Jane Lovet,' she said, 'daughter of Simon Lovet, who is a trader in fine cloth here in Cherriot.'

'And the father of a Lancastrian, if I am not mistaken,' he said in such a way that made Jane's blood run cold in her veins. 'And do you and your family follow your brother's inclinations as loyal Lancastrians, Jane Lovet, though much good it did him? Are you loyal to King Henry?'

Jane stared at him. Every merchant in London was Yorkist to a man, throwing their support behind the young, strong and intelligent King Edward. Being an exacting, ambitious man, her father's every thought was directed into making money and the elevation of his family, and as such he had no particular leanings for either side. But he had been unable to forgive Andrew his support for Henry, which had turned the majority of merchants against him.

'My brother's support of King Henry cannot be denied, but my parents accept the rule of King Edward.'

He nodded. 'A sensible move, since Henry can no longer raise a decent army to continue the fight.'

'So we have been told, and since the king himself has recently married an impoverished widow from the enemy camp, a woman whose own father fought against him, we can be assured of his leniency.'

Guy's eyes narrowed as they focused on her upturned face, caught somewhere between anger, amazement and admiration for her defiant courage. 'Your words are boldly spoken, Jane Lovet. But I warn you to have a care what you say in the future. Do you live hereabouts?'

She nodded. 'In the manor house at the end of the village close to the river.'

'So we are to be neighbours.' His eyes did a study of Alfred and Blanche and the comely Kate. 'And are these people kin of yours?'

Jane glanced at the threesome. Alfred was tall like his father, while her younger sister, Blanche, was a few inches less, and still growing. They were similar in looks—both had light-brown curly hair and green eyes with brown flecks.

'Kate is my maid, and Alfred and Blanche my siblings. Are you to reside in the village long, sir?'

'As to that, we shall have to wait and see.' His arrogant mouth softened and, leaning down, he cupped her face with his big hand and looked deep into her eyes. 'Never have I seen a face so fair—or eyes so unafraid. Do you not fear me, sweet Jane?'

Jane knew she should draw back and state her objections at this uncalled-for bold familiarity, but she held her ground and endured the feel of his strong fingers and the warmth of them touching her flesh. 'Do I have reason to fear you, sir?'

'Maybe you do. Do you know who I am?'

'Everyone in these parts knows who you are.'

'And how can they possibly know that when they have not set eyes on me in almost a decade?'

Jane stared at him, temporarily speechless, relieved when he dropped his hand and sat up straight in the saddle. His looks were spectacular, but they were not the most important thing about him. Now she could see that his face had an uncompromising ruthlessness and strength which marked him as an adventurer and gambler. In spite of the fact that he was a nobleman, he was a man free from bonds and ties.

'You are Guy St Edmond, the Earl of Sinnington. You are to take up residence at Sinnington Castle. People have talked of nothing else these past weeks.'

Guy St Edmond cocked a brow and canted his head at an angle as he gazed into her eyes, holding her in his blue depths. Suddenly Jane was the captive of those fathomless eyes and, while those around them went on breathing, Jane felt as if she and Guy St Edmond were alone in the world. Though it was not a feeling she was accustomed to feeling, some feminine instinct deep within her recognised the fiery gleam in his eyes and understood that he felt the same.

'Then since we are to reside close to each other, Mistress Lovet, I shall look forward to seeing you again. I have noted your grace and your beauty and that they are but hints of other talents. What else should I know of you?'

'Sir, I do not know what else I might tell you, except that I am soon to be betrothed and when I am wed I will be leaving the village to take up residence with my husband's family in the next village.'

So taken was Guy by her that her pronouncement dealt him a blow of disappointment he was quite unprepared for, though he gave no hint of it. It was because he was watching her so intently that he saw a change in her. He saw the light of exhilaration so suddenly and utterly extinguished and, for a fleeting moment, it was replaced with a look of total desolation. It was the sort of look that could break even the hardest heart and made him wonder what was wrong with the man she was to wed.

'Married! Then I must congratulate your betrothed on an excellent choice of bride,' he said, his eyes never leaving her face. Her astonishing beauty had struck him at once, but now that he saw her more closely he was impressed by something more, a sort of intrinsic worth which he had not expected to find. However, he did not intend to let her see this and there was more than a suggestion of mockery about his smile when he said, 'He is a truly fortunate man to have claimed such a wondrously fair bride. I cannot but imagine the ardent swains who will be left languishing over their loss. I will think of a gift for the bride-to-be and have it delivered directly to your father's house.'

'Thank you,' Jane said, suddenly shy. 'That is indeed thoughtful of you, but I—I could not possibly accept...'

'To refuse is to risk offending the earl,' the rider

closest to the earl said jovially. Cedric was a big, brawny squire with a wild thatch of bright blond hair in dire need of a trimming, who looked more like a bear than a man. He looked Jane over from head to foot, his voice and eyes lazily good humoured. 'When a pretty girl takes his eye, you will find Guy St Edmond a man of the grand gesture,' he quipped, winking good naturedly at his master. 'Now we must be on our way, Guy. We have ridden far and my belly is demanding food. I haven't had a mouthful since I ate that bacon at breakfast.'

His fellow riders laughed heartily at this, for apparently his appetite was a well-established joke among them.

'The deuce you haven't, Cedric,' the earl chided with mock reproach. 'Come, then, we'll be on our way.'

The men wheeled their horses round and as Guy St Edmond's turned, its forelegs lifted high, he turned his head and looked at Jane once more. Perhaps it was the heat of the day or the sun that filled the glade with its golden light, or the blackbird that continued to sing its delightful song, but in the depths of that gaze she felt time was suspended.

'We will meet again, Jane Lovet. Do not be in any doubt of that. I shall see to it.'

Her mouth went dry as alarm gathered apace, along with wild, wanton sensations she had never experienced before that were beginning to fill her body, taking control of her, making her weak and helpless. Recollecting herself, she reminded herself who he was. They had been told it was Guy St Edmond who had issued the death sentence on her beloved brother when he had been taken prisoner at the Battle of Towton in 1461—just one of almost thirty thousand cut down that day. She took a step back, her heart beating sickeningly fast. As she stiffened her shoulders in an effort at least to appear composed, her eyes were intense.

'You forget yourself, sir. It would be inappropriate for us to meet in the way I believe you are suggesting.'

He flashed her a mocking smile, his tone suddenly taunting. 'Why? Would it have anything to do with me being a barbarian?'

'I have told you that I am to be married, sir—yet even had that not been the case,' she said, unaware that she was plunging lightning-fast into unchartered territory, 'your reputation has preceded you. People say you are the spawn of Satan and that men and children fear you. For years there have been rumours that you enjoy killing—that it was by your order that my brother died and that you take pleasure in the suffering of others.' When he didn't deny it, Jane felt her insides cringe.

'Since you appear to know so much about me,' he said in a dangerously soft voice, 'there is little wonder I am *persona non grata* in certain company.'

'You must have luck on your side in war,' she replied tersely.

Guy's leisurely perusal swept her as he tried to control his restive mount. 'I am as lucky in war as I am in love, sweet Jane. I've been a long time at the wars. I confess there might be some justification in the rumours you have heard about me. Killing makes barbarians of many brave and honourable men. However,' he said, his eyes glowing in the warm light as he gave her a lazy smile, his gaze settling on her lips, 'I doubt that in your case my reaction would vary had I just left the king's court.'

Jane's eyes flared at his boldness. Lifting her nose primly in the air, she coolly glanced askance at him. 'You press yourself beyond the bounds of propriety, sir! As I said, I am to leave the village shortly when I am wed.'

A crooked smile slanted Guy's lips. He had seen her eyes flash and he approved. It was a sign that she had spirit. Mistress Lovet was clearly prepared to reject his further attentions. Where with another woman he would have felt merely challenged, if he felt anything at all, her rejection, delivered with a sweet but dauntless pride, cut dangerously deep. He rarely encountered occasions when he bothered to exert himself to change a woman's mind, but a man like Guy St Edmond got what he wanted, and meet with her again he would.

As he leaned forwards there was a flash in his eyes that Jane could not recognise. It was like a sudden hunger, as when a starving man sees a banquet. Bravely she stood her ground. She was neither afraid nor coquettish, but she was still young and there was something about the power and the energy of this man that she didn't want focused on her.

He stared at her with his head tilted to one side. The corners of his mouth lifted as his eyes left hers and wandered to her feet and back, slowly, slowly appraising, approving, for his smile broadened as he looked back into her eyes. Reaching out, he touched her cheek with the backs of his fingers. When he spoke, his voice was solemn and he held her gaze with an intensity of his own.

'You're very beautiful,' he murmured, both entranced and repelled by what he wanted. 'I remember your father and your mother,' he said equably. 'I have known them since I was a boy, in good times and bad. So know this, and never doubt it, sweet Jane.' He seemed to measure his words carefully. 'My word is my bond and I pledge it to you. You can rest assured we shall meet—and at my instigation. I promise you.'

Jane stared at him aghast, realising he meant every word he said. For a moment the blue eyes looked savage. That this mighty lord should want her both fascinated and terrified her. He was confusing on every level. Unknown and intriguing, he was a new threat that could not be second-guessed. She knew beyond doubt that she was his prey, that he intended to seduce her, to dishonour her, and nothing was going to deter him from try-ing—not even the fact that she was about to be betrothed to another.

Guy St Edmond would have no pity on her and he would damn anyone who stood in his way.

She could not let that happen. Time that had stopped for a moment went on again. Unable to bear his taunting gaze, she dropped her eyes and made a curtsy. With a deep laugh and a touch of spurs to his horse's flesh, Guy turned and rode off in pursuit of his companions.

Not until he was out of sight did Jane turn to Kate, who suddenly found her tongue.

'Well, I never! The Earl of Sinnington! He has a way about him, doesn't he?'

'Oh, yes. He certainly has a way. Come, let us play a game of hoodman blind. I shall wear the blindfold.'

Determined not to let the encounter with Guy St Edmond spoil their game, Jane took the cloth from Alfred's pocket and tied it around her eyes. Having no wish to go home just yet, the frighten-ing interlude forgotten as they became caught up in the new game, the children giggled and erupted into gales of laughter as they darted this way and that to avoid their sister's groping hands. Jane laughed delightedly as she pretended she couldn't locate the giggling children.

Taking a moment to pause and look back, Guy was enchanted by what he saw. Mistress Lovet's laughter rang out like tinkling chimes. It was a delightful scene—a scene of innocence and perfection that would become etched in memory and emblazoned on his heart.

From her seat on a stout trunk of a fallen tree, Kate watched the innocent play of her charges. Kate had watched Jane grow. As a child she'd been headstrong, pugnacious and daring. Surrounded by family all her life, especially her doting mother, she was an imp of a girl, always courting laughter with her japes.

Kate's gaze took in the condition of Alfred and Blanche, which brought a frown to her brow. They had set off from home in their best and she was dismayed to see that Alfred had scuffed his shoes and ripped his hose, and that Blanche had leaves and twigs in her hair. They were in for a scolding from their father when they got back to the house, unless she could smuggle them upstairs and clean them up first. Knowing it was time to go home, she rose.

'Jane, come. It's time we were getting back. Enough play for today. Your mother stressed that you mustn't be late.'

Removing her blindfold, Jane laughed at her maid, her beloved Kate, who knew her like no other, who saw to all their needs with affection and devotion. 'Must we go now, Kate?'

'Do you forget that soon you are to be betrothed? There is much to be done before the event. Even now your mother is sewing her fingers raw in her effort to complete your gown in time.'

Kate's words were a harsh reminder to Jane that soon she would have the mundane affairs of the wife of a cloth merchant's son to fill her days and occupy her mind—soon, but not yet. As hard as she resisted, she could not help wondering what it would be like to be married to a man like Guy St Edmond instead.

Not that she could now seriously entertain the idea of marriage to one other than Richard. She'd committed herself to doing right by her family and was not one to go back on her word, no matter how distasteful she found the consequences.

She had been raised to know her place and knew better than to defy the rules of men and make her own destiny. It had come as no surprise to her and with much bitterness that, as a girl, her worth to her family was her marriageability.

Believing in the inherent wisdom of her parents, Jane was optimistic about her future and had not questioned their judgement—until now, when her betrothal was just days away and she had gazed upon the handsome face of Guy St Edmond.

Guy was staring straight ahead into the distance, a faint smile playing about his lips as his eyes embraced his home. He tipped his head in the direction he was staring and in a quiet voice, said, 'Look, Cedric—the castle.'

'It's a fine demesne. You've been looking at it as if you've not set eyes on it before.'

'Not in a long time, Cedric. Eight years, at least—and not since my father passed on and my brother was killed at St Albans. I kept meaning to come back, but the king always had urgent need of me elsewhere, which may have been for the best. The battles have made me wealthy, which will ensure my sons will not have to earn their living with muscle and blood as I have done.'

'So you have done with fighting.'

'I'd like to think I've breached my last castle wall and fought on my last battlefield,' Guy said, his voice harsh with resolve. 'Dear God, it will be good to be home at last, to have a soft bed to sleep in every night and good food in my belly.'

Guy drank in the incredible beauty of the wide vale of Cherriot. Twenty miles north of London, it was a fertile valley. The hills on either side were covered with forest and fertile fields, the lower slopes clothed with pear and apple orchards and fruit gardens. His vast demesne contained four villages, two visible to the eye. A lazy river meandered its way passed the picturesque town of Cherriot, with its main street, the stone bridge which spanned the river, and industrial premises along the waterfront: leather tanners, sawmills, manufacturers and the abattoirs. Smoke rose from a thousand chimneys and miniature people meandered through the streets going about their business. On a raised plateau overlooking this pastoral scene stood Sinnington Castle, with its soaring turrets and high, thick walls punctuated with six gracefully rounded towers.

Guy could hardly contain his excitement the closer they got to the castle. He was expected. There were sentries at the gate. They clattered over the bridge that spanned the moat.

'I can see this is the ideal place for you to settle down and raise those sons you intend to have one day,' Cedric remarked, appreciating all he saw.

'I must first find a wife who will give me children, Cedric,' Guy said with a fierceness that left Cedric in no doubt about his seriousness. 'It's no matter whether she is pretty or not, so long as she can give me fine sons.'

'Then all you have to do is find the lady.'

Guy stared straight ahead. For months he had been plagued by a deepening awareness of a large hole in his life, an emptiness. He had sensed it vaguely and ignored it because for a very long time it evoked painful memories of Isabel Leigh, a callous, brown-eyed witch driven by ambition and greed. For a time her beauty had bewitched him and, when she had betrayed him with another, he had been shocked to discover how close he had come to losing control. He had vowed that his emotions would never again be engaged by a woman. He wanted none of their treachery and deceit. But his need for sons had sharpened since he had fought his last battle into a nameless hunger, a gnawing urgency.

He had a fortune to rival many of his aristocratic friends, but he had no heir to leave it to. If he died unexpectedly—and there was always a chance of that, the way he lived—everything he'd worked and fought for would die with him. But getting heirs meant putting up with the inconvenience of a wife, a prospect he so little relished that he had been putting it off for years. Where could a man find a woman who would bear his children and otherwise leave him alone?

Unbidden, an image of Jane Lovet came to mind. As Guy recalled the moment when she had smiled at him, a smile that had grown slowly and then shone, his expression softened and his eyes gentled. He had seen Madonnas whose features would pale before her loveliness. It was as though a shutter had been flung open and the sun had rushed in. And the way she had stood up to him! She had looked him in the eye and spoken her mind with a frankness most men wouldn't dare.

With her anything might happen. There was a mark of destiny on her, quite apart from her beauty and the rare and subtle quality she emanated. She made one think of hot, tumbling love and sensual sport. She was a well brought-up young woman with a decent woman's need for marriage which he was not able to give her. It would be social death to consider looking outside his own circle, a penniless girl from the lower orders, the daughter of a cloth merchant…but as a mistress? His eyes narrowed and a calculating gleam glinted in their depths.

He did not stop to wonder why he was so inflexible, it was just so. He was the Earl of Sinnington and he must rebuild. Men of his station married for advantage so that they might be the founders of dynasties. It was a business. Love did not come into it. He had decided long ago that such an affliction of the heart was best left to the peasants as compensation for their miserable lot in life.

'Mistress Lovet is comely enough, Cedric. What was your opinion of her?'

Cedric gave him a knowing look and laughed heartily at his friend's remark, knowing precisely where his thoughts were leading him. 'Mistress

Lovet is no ordinary girl, I grant you, but I imagined your interest to be in the way of finding a little amusement and nothing more. She is a strangely fascinating young creature, but hardly your type.'

Guy felt a moment of annoyance at Cedric's pronouncement, remembering the exuberance of his most recent wild coupling with one of the more rapaciously demanding, hedonistic ladies of the court, who positively encouraged him in his more abandoned pursuits. But he had never lain with a virgin—had never been given the opportunity to discover the pleasures of such unblemished perfection, of making his mark on untouched territory. He imagined the sensation and felt a stirring in his loins.

'You are quite right, Cedric. Jane Lovet is not my usual type at all. But then, one's taste improves with age, I've been told.'

'Aye, but for a wife you have to think about selecting a woman with an eye to forming political alliances and important connections. Mistress Lovet is merely the daughter of a humble cloth merchant.'

'It is the way of things,' Guy replied, knowing Cedric spoke the truth, but the image of Jane Lovet was too fresh in his mind.

Knowing Guy so well that he could follow his train of thought, Cedric smiled. 'Did I not hear Mistress Lovet say she is to wed to someone else?'

'Apparently so,' Guy replied dismissively. 'But I shall not be denied the pleasure of pursuing her if I so wish.'

'Even though her brother was a supporter of the Lancastrians in the past.'

'That no longer cuts any cloth with me, Cedric. Pray to God that after countless battles, the peace holds and Edward will sit on the throne of England for many years to come, leaving me free to enjoy the more enjoyable, gentler pursuits of life—and if I have a mistress as delectable as Mistress Lovet to enjoy them with, it will make life a damned sight more delightful.'

Cedric had seen how Guy had warmed to Jane Lovet, had been aware that his eyes had filled with the soft fire he felt when he'd looked at her. It could be interesting seeing how he dealt with the finer points of luring her into his bed. He had what other men envied. He was well favoured in looks and fortune, and he had any woman he wanted. It was no boast, but the honest truth. Women never turned him down.

Guy was also a fighter without equal, a soldier for whom violence was not indulged, but controlled—whose aggression was directed, not by ambition for personal glory, but by a sense of justice. He was a clear-headed, resourceful planner, a tireless campaigner, an entertaining, cheerful, unpretentious companion and faithfully loyal. But all Guy's virtues were warrior virtues. He was made for war. He thought of nothing else. He was also an integral part of King Edward's council, and as such the powerful barons saw him either as a shrewd friend to look to in times of trouble, or as a man to be wary of if they were involved in anything detrimental to the king.

But of late Cedric could see in his friend that he was, at thirty years old and having been brought low by the death of his brother, growing tired of war and that his thoughts were turning to the softer joys of hunting and hawking, of peace and music and love.

Guy rode into the outer bailey, casting an eye over the castle folk waiting to welcome their lord home, nodding in reply to their welcome. There wasn't a man, woman or child that didn't know of the black reputation he had acquired in France. He took a moment to look around. The main structure of the castle was built around the inner bailey in whose centre was the well that ensured the water supply. On the ground floor were the Great Hall, the stables, the kitchen and storerooms, and the living quarters communally shared by a large collection of human and animal dependants.

Guy and his men dismounted and handed their horses to the grooms who rushed forwards to take them, servants bowing low when they entered the great hall. The warmth and welcome of Sinnington Castle embraced him, along with the aroma of roasting meat from the kitchen. Guy felt himself relax, all the tensions easing out of him. After years of fighting, the need to be forever alert and watchful was being replaced by a sense of well-being.

Lovet House was a substantial family home. It was a long house, half-brick, half-timber, and commodious with glass in the windows. Its airy halls and parlours were decorated with many tapestries and carpets. Between the house and the river were the well-tended gardens which Margaret Lovet, Jane's mother, had filled with sweet-scented roses growing on trellises and where peacocks flaunted their beautiful feathers like vainglorious lords.

Margaret, whose greatest pleasure was cosseting, watching over and cherishing her children, was elegant, charming and composed. She had a sweet, lilting voice and a patient smile. She was a perfect lady, one Jane had tried to emulate all her life. She kept the house in perfect order and the servants were devoted to her. She was the lady bountiful of Cherriot Vale and her hospitality to the poor was well known.

On entering the house, Jane sought her out after glancing into the spacious undercroft where her father carried out his work and stored his merchandise and seeing a happy band of silk women doing their needlework or weaving or throwing or twisting threads surrounded by the many bolts of cloth: brocades from Milan, Venetian velvets, the finest manufactured silk from Lucca—Italian silk being of supreme quality and a significant source of trade. Jane liked nothing better than fingering these sumptuous fabrics, hopefully destined for the wealthy when her father's business picked up, as it surely would when she married Richard.

She found her mother in the parlour. She had opened the windows that overlooked the river shifting endlessly by. Her head beneath her tall headdress was bent over her work as she put the finishing touches to the dress Jane was to wear for her betrothal, her face still and serene as she embroidered her thoughts into the gown.

Looking up from her work when Jane entered the room, Margaret curved her lips in a smile of welcome. 'Ah, Jane! I'm glad you're back, although I do wish you had been home earlier. John Aniston called on us this afternoon.'

'Did he? For what reason?'

'Richard has to leave for Italy sooner than planned, so, as soon you are betrothed, the wedding will have to be brought forwards.'

Jane's heart sank. That Richard was leaving for the commercial metropolis of Florence with a group of cloth merchants had been planned for weeks now. 'I see. How soon?'

'No more than two weeks after the betrothal.'

Jane stared at her mother in disbelief, panic taking hold of her. 'You can't mean that. The wedding is set for six weeks after the betrothal. There is so much to do. It is too soon. We cannot possibly be ready in time.'

'We have to be,' Margaret said, resuming her sewing. 'Richard wants to see you settled in his father's house before he leaves. With you and Kate to help me we can be ready with time to spare.' Looking up, she noted her daughter's pale face and sensed her unease. 'Jane, you do want to marry Richard, don't you? You know I love you and I would understand if you are against this marriage—but...'

'I don't think Father would be so understanding,' Jane said when her mother's voice tapered off. 'Where he is concerned, my opinion counts for nothing.'

Neither, she thought, did her mother's. Her father had not always treated his wife kindly and Jane could not remember him asking her mother's opinion on anything. Docile and submissive, she was not a wilful woman and survived quite well. Unlike everyone else in the household, Andrew had not been afraid of his father. He had believed he knew his tempers, having been on the receiving end of his blows many times. Their father had expected Andrew to dutifully follow him into the business, but Andrew, with his sights firmly set on a military career, had had no such ambitions.

Their father had been furious when Andrew had shown support for the Lancastrian cause and went off to fight. Indeed, wild-eyed and monstrous, he had shouted curses that had rung to the rafters. Jane always squeezed her eyes tight shut at the memory, wishing to banish it from her mind, but could not.

Her father's greatest fear was loss of status and, it seemed, when confronted with that possibility he lost all reason. Despite Jane's sympathy for him, she could not bring herself to justify his treatment. She did not care if he was a man mad with disappointment and resentment or the master of the house and her person. There was no claim he could make great enough to make this right.

'Your father is only doing what he thinks is best for you,' her mother said in his defence. 'You have to marry as your circumstances demand. And Richard does want to marry you so much.' Sighing despondently, she shook her head and went on, 'Circumstances have been—difficult of late. Indeed, as you are aware, the business has suffered very badly.'

Jane knew this was true. No one could do business in a town without belonging to or having the respect of the other members of the guild. Her father's business and his standing among the other guild members had suffered greatly because of Andrew's support for King Henry. They all felt the humiliation of his reduced status and it was like balm to her parents' wounds to have their daughter marrying the son of an important and respected alderman of the guild.

'Far more devastating to your father's pride was the knowledge that you would have to share the grim consequences of his misfortune,' her mother went on in an attempt to justify her husband's strict treatment of his eldest daughter. 'Everyone would realise that you would not have the great dowry formerly anticipated and the most worthy of the men seeking wives, those best able to provide the standing and security you deserve, would turn their attention elsewhere. Which is why arranging this alliance is just as important to your father as winning a battle. Marriage to Richard is a way in which John Aniston intends to honour him with such an important connection. Your father is hopeful of calming the temper of the guild and redeeming both his status and the respect he rightly deserves. Perhaps then the business will prosper once more.'

Jane took a deep, tight breath. That she was being sacrificed for her father's ambition went against the grain, but this she kept to herself. All her life she had hoped she would have the freedom to choose her own husband, but, when it came to it, her father had chosen for her. A good alliance, he called it—but the last person she'd ever have chosen would be Richard. How she wished she could look upon him more favourably. It would be so much easier to welcome this marriage, but he was not her idea of an ideal husband—or lover.

Averting her eyes, she was unable to ignore the picture that entered her mind of the last time she had seen Richard when he had come to dinner with his parents and other guild members, when her father had put on a lavish meal in an attempt to impress the aldermen. Jane did not think she would ever grow to love Richard, not as a woman should love her husband. Would she be able to pretend to do more than endure? When she looked into his eyes she did not see love, comfort, laughter or companionship—in fact, when he had leered at her obscenely and tried to grab her knee under the table, it seemed his thin veneer of courtesy was easily dissolved by brandy wine.

Richard was the eldest son of John Aniston, who could refuse his son nothing. With his second son to run his cloth business, Richard had been free to follow his dream and became a squire in a nobleman's household in Wiltshire, and later doing military service on the field of battle where his skill and bravery brought him acclamation from his superiors. It was his ambition to become a knight—but not all squires became knights.

There had been some kind of trouble at his master's house. The true facts were not known, but Richard's involvement was suspected and he had been dismissed. As a consequence, under great sufferance, Richard had returned home and joined his father and brother in the business. But the manufacture of cloth held no appeal for Richard and his life's ambition, to become a knight, to ride, hunt, fence and fight in battle, was in no way diminished.

When Richard's father had offered a sizeable

stipend to be paid for Jane's hand in marriage to his son, assuring Jane's father that Richard's dismissal from his master's house was a trivial matter and nothing more than a young man's exuberance, Simon Lovet had considered it a good match and seen no reason why Richard should not be considered as a suitor for Jane.

When he told his daughter of his decision, Jane knew she would have to give up all hope of marrying someone she loved in order to save the family. Her stomach twisted into sick knots at the thought of committing her body, her entire life, into the hands of a man she instinctively recoiled from, but, miserably resigned to her fate, she lifted her head and bravely met her mother's gaze.

'Please don't worry, Mother. Everything will work out for the best, and this painful time will soon be forgotten. Of course I will marry Richard. It is already decided,' she said, telling herself that the look of pride and relief on her mother's face made the sacrifice worthwhile.

Chapter Two

It was the following day when Jane found herself alone with Richard. He had ridden over with his father. His stubborn beard was subdued with oil, his crinkled red hair smoothed down and close cut, which gave him an aggressive look. His clothing and accessories were stylish and well made of only the finest cloth.

Jane raised her eyes to his heavy-featured face. Tall and of stocky build, he wasn't unattractive, in a coarse way. Surly and argumentative, he had a belligerent nature which simmered away beneath the surface. He was always in trouble for slovenliness, laziness and greed. The despair of his parents, he was without self-control, and it was his father's hope that marriage to Jane was a way of getting someone else to enforce the restraint he could not impose himself.

Richard was delighted to be marrying Jane and to sit next to her at the dining table. He could stare at her while he ate, at her breasts, and every time she leaned forwards he could peek down the square neckline of her dress. His blood ran hot when he thought of the time not far away when he would command her to take off her clothes and stand naked before him, and he could look at her breasts and fondle them in their magnificent entirety.

When he suggested they take a walk, Jane was hoping her father would refuse his permission, but to her disappointment he obliged most readily.

Before Jane could utter any protestations, with the shadow of a sly grin upon his face and carrying himself with an air of arrogant self-assurance, Richard had taken her hand and drawn her outside. In no time at all they had left the house behind. He told her how happy he was that the wedding had been brought forwards and that he was looking forward to their betrothal party, seemingly unaware of how quiet she was.

Richard talked of his trip to Italy and how she would be cared for in his father's house. When he returned they would have their own house and he would start up his own enterprise—perhaps one day take over his father's.

The sun was hot and much as Jane would have liked to withdraw her hand from his nauseatingly soft, damp grasp, she endured it—as she would have to endure many intimacies in the days ahead. They were walking along a well-worn path in the forest, and when they were no longer within sight of the village Richard stopped and turned to her.

Uncertain about what was to happen, Jane looked at him, suddenly nervous of him and the solitude of the woods. 'I think we have walked far enough, Richard. We should go back.'

'Nay, not yet, not when I have you to myself at last.'

He stared at her with impudent admiration, letting his gaze travel from her eyes to her mouth, then down to the pale swell of her breasts. Instinctively she lifted her shawl to cover her bare neck and shoulders, aware that her cheeks had grown hot beneath his lecherous scrutiny.

He laughed softly. 'You are a witch, Jane, for have you not cast a spell on me so I can think of nothing else but you? Will you kiss me, to demonstrate your affection for your future husband?'

Feeling the heat of his close proximity, she stepped back. 'This is neither the time nor the place to take such liberties. Let us go back to the house,' she pleaded with quiet desperation.

At first Richard was disappointed by her reaction, but then, not to be deterred, he grinned. 'Oh, such a proud one,' he murmured, allowing his fingers to brush her cheek, annoyed when she flinched at his touch. 'And such a beauty…such a beauty. Don't fight me. There's nothing to fear.' He reached out to slip the shawl from her shoulders.

'No, Richard,' she retorted, holding on to it with grim determination.

'It isn't right to tease a man that way, Jane.'

'I don't mean to tease you.'

His eyes darkened. 'Happen you didn't. You don't know the power behind the promise in your eyes. God knows you're a woman to tempt a man to lose his reason. I want you. You drive me to madness with your wanton beauty.'

'Wanton? Is that what you think?' Her pale cheeks instantly flushed scarlet as June poppies with shame. 'Your impatience does not do you justice, Richard. You must not pre-empt our marriage vows. You must respect my wishes and wait until we are wed.'

Reaching out, he held the point of her chin and made her look at him. 'Don't look so worried. I won't hurt you. There's nothing to fear. If we go further into the wood, no one will come upon us.'

Although she was inexperienced, his words were too glibly spoken, as though from practised seduction. 'Please, Richard, let me go. Take me home.'

'I will. Soon.' He took his hand from her chin and caressed her burning cheek.

'Please take you hands of me. What do you think you're doing?'

'Examining the goods.'

'Not until after we're married.'

'We're to have our hand fasting in a day or so, which is as binding as the wedding ceremony.'

'Then I am sure you can wait a few more days.'

He laughed softly, his eyes dark and heavy-lidded with desire. It was as though her resistance excited him further. Smiling with wicked entice-ment, he lowered his head to kiss her, which she averted by sharply turning her head. What he in-tended evoked within her a shuddering revulsion.

Far more difficult to suppress, however, was the sickening feeling in the pit of her stomach that had much to do with the realisation that, once they were wed, she would have no right to withhold herself from this man.

'Come, Jane—the ice maiden—the untouchable one—why so coy?' His voice was low and coercing. There was an evil echo in his soft laugher which escaped her as her mind darted about wildly to find a way to distract him from his amorous intent. 'I can't get you out of my mind. The pain of wanting you is driving me insane.' He moved closer, but as she edged away, he grinned and positioned himself so that she could not get past him.

'Good God, man,' a deep voice rang out. 'The lady said no. Would you force yourself upon her when she is clearly unwilling?'

Richard spun round, furious at the interruption.

Jane raised her head and looked at her rescuer. It was the Earl of Sinnington who came to stand between them, his handsome mouth curled with distaste, his dark hair shining in the sun's rays.

His eyelids drooped over his vivid blue eyes as they always did when he was angry. He had reasons for getting involved. He was more cynic than idealist, but he could never stand a bully, and it was plain to see that if somebody didn't help the girl, the man was going to force himself on her. Though not usually given to damsel rescues, Guy had shaken off his momentary daze, more than happy to make an exception and play the hero in this case—and then when he recognised the girl as Jane Lovet, and suspecting whom her assailant might be, rage had justifiably coursed through him.

He looked at her red-faced, sweaty assailant and spoke in a voice of biting calm. 'Good God, man, can't you restrain yourself?'

His gaze slid to the girl. He watched as she flicked her long mane of honey-gold hair back from her face, his stare following the shining tendrils that twined over her delicate shoulders. Her eyes sparkled angrily. All his breath froze inside his chest, splintering to ice-slivers of pure pain. How lovely she was! How achingly, tormenting lovely. Her beauty was almost blinding and he had a presentiment that Jane Lovet was one of those rare women for whom wars are fought, for whom men kill themselves and who rarely bring happiness to the men who loved them.

When he thought of what this great lout might have done to her, anger consumed him. Then the look of abject rage on his face gave way to something else, something equally dark and dangerous, but in a very different way. The horrifying stories Jane had heard about him no longer seemed so far-fetched. Guy saw the concern on her pale young face and two enormous eyes stared up at him with passionate gratitude. He struggled to control the fury that had gripped him on seeing this oaf's attempt to coax her into the woods.

'Thank you, sir,' she said.

She offered him a smile, thankful that he had been on hand to save her from whatever Richard had had in mind. Her mouth was tinder dry, her heart pounding in her throat. For what seemed to her an infinite amount of time, she remained unable to move. She was glad of the shadow her hair cast over her face because she could take advantage of it and feel less exposed, less readable. When she was finally in control, she adopted an attitude of cool composure.

Guy was touched by her instinctive bid for his

protection and admired her dignified recovery from dishevelment. 'Are you hurt?' he queried.

The best answer Jane could manage was to shake her head in denial. What a handsome man Guy St Edmond was, she thought—his colouring, his strong build, the spicy smell of him, the deep resonance of his voice that made her bones hum.

Guy turned with increased anger to Aniston, and this time, when he spoke, his voice was more terrible because it was so tautly controlled that it hissed with muted fury. 'So you are Richard Aniston—the same Aniston who was a squire in Lord Lambert's household in Wiltshire.'

Richard froze and shifted uneasily, his eyes wary as they surveyed the threatening figure of Guy St Edmond. 'How do you know that?'

'I make it my business to know about the people who live in my demesne,' Guy replied in a low, meaningful voice, trying to keep his fury at bay. 'It is clear the lady does not share your lust. What did you intend? To drag her into the forest and ravish her?'

Had it been anyone else but the Earl of Sinnington, Richard would have replied with equal anger—as it was he glowered at him, his righteous indignation replaced by smouldering malevolence. If he made an enemy of the earl, he could be made to suffer.

'The lady is to be my wife,' he bit back tersely.

'He's right,' Jane confirmed. 'We are to be married shortly.'

'Aye,' Richard said, fists clenched at his sides. 'Mistress Lovet has pledged her troth to me. I can see nothing wrong with kissing my future wife.'

'By the lady's reaction perhaps you should reconsider your situation or learn to treat her with more respect.' Guy looked again at Jane. 'Come, I will escort you to your home.'

'Thank you, sir, but there's no need,' Jane replied, embarrassment colouring her cheeks when she thought of the tousled image she must portray. 'Although I know my father would be pleased if you were to honour him with a visit.'

'There is every need—and I am happy to know I shall be welcomed in your home. Come. Your parents must be told. The fact that Aniston is to be your husband is no excuse for his loutish behaviour.'

Jane looked at him in alarm. 'No—please do not mention this to my parents. It—would upset them needlessly—and what Richard said is true. We are to be wed shortly. He has done me no harm,' she told him, unable to look at Richard, who was openly glowering at her. 'It was an innocent tryst, no more than that.'

Seeing evidence of her dispirited dejection despite her brave words, Guy took pity on her. 'Very well, but in my opinion your future husband doesn't deserve your loyalty or consideration.'

Leading his horse, Guy walked with her the short distance to her home. Jane cast a glance at her betrothed. The look on his face as he glared at the earl told her that he wanted blood. She had seen that look before when he failed to get his own way. It was a look she loathed more than anything. He stared at her in icy stillness.

Fear spiked through her when she read the fury in his eyes, as though he saw and understood just how relieved she was that Guy St Edmond had arrived in time to save her from his lust. Before she turned from him he sent her a look that promised there would be consequences later. From the moment they had met, he had held himself in check, waiting until the time was right, but after today she knew that only his fury awaited her now, and she was afraid. She had an idea what he was capable of—if his rage broke free, there would be no choice but to yield. Then she would be his prisoner for the rest of her life.

The relief that had engulfed her when Guy St Edmond had stormed to her rescue, his face a mask of cold fury, had been immense. She would be forever grateful for his timeliness in coming to her aid and forever in awe of how effortlessly he had dealt with the situation. Her gaze locked in the blue of his and she felt a tingling sensation run over her skin, like the time when she had first lain eyes on him. What was happening to her? Were the distress and despair she felt over her forthcoming marriage to Richard making her mind vulnerable to her basest impulses? Why could she not see Guy St Edmond and feel only simple gratitude?

She looked towards the house. Her father was at the front door. He recognised their illustrious visitor and bowed low. Desperate to regain status among the people of Cherriot, he was prepared to humble himself and ignore that Guy St Edmond was the man behind his son's death. When he straightened she gazed at his narrow face, now creased in a rare smile. His exacting eyes crinkled at the corners.

'Sir Guy. Welcome home. You are very welcome at Lovet Hall.'

Guy's face was expressionless as his brooding gaze settled on Simon Lovet. 'I trust you are well, Master Lovet? It's been a long time.'

'Indeed it has, my lord. We were grieved to learn of the loss of your brother at St Albans. These past years have been hard times for all of us. We still mourn the loss of our son and we have suffered greatly for his support of Henry.'

Guy allowed a wry note to creep into his voice. 'Indeed. In faith, I do not understand how anyone would think ill of you for grieving for your son, but I can for your lack of judgement in allowing his support of the Lancastrians.'

'But I did not—what I mean to say is—'

'Forget it, Master Lovet,' Guy said in quick response. 'And now? Are you loyal to King Edward?'

Simon met his eyes. However cringingly pleased he might secretly be at the earl's visit to his house, he was still a proud man despite his son's misplaced support of the Lancastrians. 'My family history cannot be denied. Andrew was a loyal subject of the ordained King Henry—as I shall be under King Edward. I accept his rule and wish for nothing now but to live in peace. We are all Englishmen. We should not be divided.'

'That is sensible. Those who have fought against Edward will find he can be just in victory.' His eyes shifted admiringly to Jane. 'Your daughter invited me to call on you. How could I resist when I was asked so prettily? You have a beautiful daughter—and soon to be married.'

Her father smiled, relieved that any awkwardness had been dealt with. 'There are few men who can ride past Jane. Her betrothal to Richard Aniston here is imminent.'

Guy's face darkened and his narrowed eyes settled on Jane's assailant. 'So I understand.'

'Indeed,' Simon enthused. 'His father is John Aniston, a respected alderman in the cloth merchant's guild. You have heard of him?'

'The name is known to me, but we have not met.'

'Then please, come inside and meet my wife. Master Aniston has ridden over to discuss the betrothal.'

A young groom approached and took the reins of the horse to lead it to the stables. Guy noticed one of the young servant girls with a pail of water in her hand watching him with interest. A delightful creature, with auburn hair and a comely form. When his stare honed in on her, her eyes widened. She dropped her gaze with a wildly unsettled look and fled, disappearing into the house, regardless of the water slopping about her ankles. He let out a low sigh and pursed his lips. *Ah well,* he thought, *another terrified wench.* His ruthless reputation must have preceded him as usual.

Mindful of his position and the importance of the visitor to his house, Simon stepped back and allowed Guy to enter the hall before him. 'Will you take a glass of small ale? Or we have a very good French wine if you prefer.'

'The ale, if you please,' Guy said agreeably. 'It is a warm day and thirsty work riding. I was familiarising myself with Cherriot Vale when I encountered Jane and—Master Aniston, walking in the forest.' He gave Richard, hovering behind them, no more than a cursory glance.

Jane's mother swept into the hall, followed by John Aniston, and curtsied low. 'Sir Guy, you are most welcome. My husband has offered you refreshment?'

'Sir Guy would like a glass of ale, Margaret. See to it, will you?'

Margaret fussed about while her husband introduced the earl to John Aniston. Richard muttered something unintelligible and, after glowering at his betrothed, disappeared to vent his fury on someone else. Jane's parents failed to notice that something was grievously wrong between Jane and Richard, so dazzled were their eyes by the illustrious visitor and the importance of his visit.

When their visitor was seated in a high chair Margaret handed him a cup of ale.

'It's our finest,' she said, her heart beating with the hope that past differences were forgiven and that their association with the Earl of Sinnington could only further advance her husband's standing in the community and with the guild members. She sent up a silent prayer that things were beginning to look up for them at last.

Guy laughed at her pride and turned to smile at Jane. Their eyes met and she caught her breath. She could think of nothing to say. He had such presence. Nothing in his face indicated the path of his thoughts, yet she felt the weight of that un-relenting gaze as surely as if he were touching her. She told herself it was only natural that being stared at in such a dogged manner would pull her gaze back to his, no matter how diligently she steered it elsewhere. She just stood and stared at him while her parents and her future father-in-law conversed about things in general. When he'd finished his ale he got to his feet.

'Thank you for your hospitality. I must be going.'

'You are most welcome to stay and share our meal,' Margaret offered, hoping he would accept.

'Thank you. Your offer is most generous, but I must be on my way.'

Simon and his wife walked with him to the door. Jane followed, holding back. On the threshold Guy turned and, taking her hand, drew her forwards. He bowed his dark head and pressed a kiss into her palm. His skin smelled faintly of spices. She felt the warmth of his lips on her flesh and saw the softness of the hair that curled at the nape of his neck. Raising his eyes to hers, he folded her fingers over, as if to keep his kiss safe.

'It was a pleasure meeting you again, Mistress Lovet.'

He looked down at her entranced face. When he had first met her, he'd considered making her his mistress—even though deflowering a gently reared virgin who was to wed another violated even his relaxed code of honour. Nothing had changed. Until today, she had merely been the delightful object of his lustful thoughts. But on witnessing her on the point of being attacked in the forest by the very man she was to wed—a man with a distasteful and violent reputation, who was not unknown to him even though they had never met—that had changed. Jane had inspired his compassion for her position. Seeing her distress had touched a tenderness, a protectiveness, within him that he never knew existed.

Guy had seen enough of the world to know that sometimes, out of desperation and despair, people found it necessary to act in a manner they would not otherwise have contemplated. Maybe Jane was desperate. Or maybe she despaired. If, after making enquiries into her situation, what Cedric had told him was true and that she was willing to sacrifice her own happiness for her family's welfare, then he hoped Simon Lovet would refuse to let the marriage go ahead when he had informed him of the true nature of Aniston's character.

The effect this would have on Richard Aniston didn't concern him. The man wasn't worthy of consideration.

He bowed to Jane and her parents and turned and walked through the heavy door and out into the sunlight.

Jane watched him mount his horse and ride away. How quickly, how suddenly she was becoming aware of the violent passions of men. The last hour would always stand out in her mind as the time when she had awoken to the strength of her feelings.

Observing the look of concentration on her daughter's face—and something else she did not dare put a name to, as her gaze followed the Earl of Sinnington's departing figure—with a concerned frown puckering her brow, Margaret moved to her side. 'Sir Guy was very attentive to you, Jane,' she remarked quietly. 'Don't let your head be turned.'

Jane turned her burning face to look at her mother. 'Mother—I hope you don't think...'

She smiled, but the frown remained. 'I don't think anything. But let me give you a bit of pure wisdom. There is more to a man than a handsome face or a pair of broad shoulders. Think on it, my dear, should you happen to meet the Earl of Sinnington again.'

Jane looked again in the direction of the departing figure. There was a lingering scent in the hall, of a spicy cologne, and for an elusive moment the blue eyes flicked through her mind and hinted at what the strong, straight lips had not been wont to speak. Her mind conjured up an image of his dark face all but hidden by his black beard and she shivered at the memory of those eyes as they'd looked into hers.

Today in the woods his eyes had been the angry darkness of a stormy sky—but there had been a moment, when his eyes had settled on her mouth, that the expression in their depths had changed, and that indefinable change had made him seem more threatening than ever. It was his beard, she told herself. Without it he'd look like any other man. Or would he? she asked herself. No, he would still look alarming. It wasn't just his beard. It was his daunting height and build, and his strange, deep blue eyes.

She closed her eyes to banish the vision. When she opened them she chided herself at the meanderings of her mind.

'You need not be concerned, Mother.' She smiled somewhat ruefully. 'With a reputation as black as his, I shall never be taken in by the likes of the Earl of Sinnington.'

Arriving back at the castle, Guy strode into the great hall with long, purposeful strides, his brow furrowed by a deep frown.

Cedric was seated by the fire with his feet resting on one of the logs in the great hearth, a tankard of ale in his hand. He regarded Guy attentively. Without saying a word, he stood staring absently into the fire. His body was tense, the tendons in his neck corded. 'Well?' Cedric said at length. 'It's clear you have something on your mind. Out with it.'

'I have decided. I must have her. I mean to make Jane Lovet my mistress,' Guy said, making no effort whatsoever to conceal his intention.

Cedric stared at him, his tankard, halfway to

his mouth, arrested in his hand. 'And you assume that she will naturally consent and fall into your bed without objection?'

'Why not?'

'Why not, indeed, when the whole district is waiting on tenterhooks and expectation for the wedding between Mistress Lovet and Master Aniston to take place.'

'We both know what Aniston is like, what he is guilty of. He should consider himself fortunate his head remains on his shoulders. Frankly, I don't give a blessed damn.'

'About the gossip?' Cedric persisted carefully. 'Or about Richard Aniston?' When Guy didn't reply, he leaned forwards and asked bluntly, 'What are your reasons for wanting the wench—apart from the obvious?' He chuckled low. 'Heaven forbid your heart's become afflicted and you've fallen for the wench?'

Guy turned a glacial stare upon his friend. 'When has love anything to do with desire?' he returned, deriding his cynicism. 'Love is inconsistent. Desire is an honest emotion, at least. Love is the word given to it by moral bigots.'

Cedric laughed. 'So speaks a confirmed rake—

and I would say bachelor, if I didn't know you were looking for a wife.'

'I want Jane Lovet for myself,' Guy said stonily. 'I've given up trying to understand my reasons for the step I am about to take. I want her. That is reason enough.'

'Forgive me if I find your decision somewhat hasty,' Cedric remarked, taking a long draught of his ale. 'My advice is for you to proceed with caution.'

'I intend to. My mind is focused on not making sudden moves. There is no denying that the slow, gentling approach works miracles on skittish animals. I doubt women are much different,' he said with the arrogant confidence of a man who believes he cannot lose.

With that he quit the hall, leaving Cedric gazing after him in amazement and alarm. After a moment, however, the squire's expression cleared and he began to chuckle and then laughed out loud. 'May God help him,' he chortled. Not since Isabel Leigh had stolen his heart and then betrayed him with another had a woman managed to entrap his friend.

He glanced in the direction Guy had taken

and raised his tankard in a salute. 'To your future bliss, Guy.' He grinned.

Jane loved to spend time in the parish church of St Peter, beaming benignly upon the sleepy town of Cherriot. On her knees she would confide all her hopes and fears and heartaches to the saints she had no doubt guided and protected her. The solace, the scent of incense blending with candle wax and the low murmurings of others in prayer were a great comfort to her.

Today was a working day so it was a quiet time in the church. It held an intimacy which was lacking on Sundays, when it was crowded and filled with the scent of humanity. It was the only time she was allowed out without a companion and she felt safe within the confines of the church.

She went to the statue of the Blessed Virgin and knelt on the prie-dieu before it and bowed her head over her hands holding her paternoster beads, her lips moving in prayer. The prayer in her heart was that some miracle would happen so that she didn't have to marry Richard, but since that was unlikely to happen, she asked God for a blessing on her married life. It seemed a safe prayer and helped her set aside her feelings of frustration of marriage to a man she didn't know well, a man she wasn't sure she even liked.

The church door opened and closed. A shadow moved nearby. Male footsteps moved closer and stopped a few paces away. She didn't recognise them. It wasn't a servant, for the man had spurs that clinked. She didn't look up, but glanced sideways. She saw mud on his boots. The spurs were silver and glinted in the light slanting through the windows.

With a shock, she realised whose boots these were. Her intruder was neither friend nor stranger. Caution and propriety dictated she left his presence immediately, but something else, something far less familiar, kept her on her knees. What strange power did this man radiate that a mere glance or a small curve of his mouth could set her senses reeling this way? The very sight of him should send an unmarried young woman scampering for the safety of her home, but she couldn't move.

He came and knelt beside her. Folding his hands in front of his face, he bowed his head, but she knew he wasn't praying. His head was turned and he was looking at her with bold, unguarded interest. She kept her head determinedly down, hoping he would go away if she kept quiet.

She held her breath. There was a long silence. Unable to endure the suspense any longer, boldly she raised her head and met his bright gaze. She felt it as a shock right through her body. She found him poised, taut and still and dark as ever. But his expression was guarded. Guy was clean shaven. This startled her, for it made him seem much younger, and she saw that his chin was square and had a cleft in it. His mouth, wide, curved and passionate, was drawn thin at the corners and his heavy eyelids seemed as though they would never wholly lift again to disclose the vivid blue beneath.

When the beautiful bass voice murmured, 'Forgive me for interrupting your prayers, but I saw you come in here and I wanted to speak to you', the memory of that silken male touch when he had cupped her chin, the like of which she might never feel in the future closing in around her, was enough to dispel her irritation at being interrupted in her prayers. Her pulses had leaped to the thrill of it, and her body had tingled with a delicious urgency to experience more of the pleasure a man's touch could evoke.

'I beg your pardon, but I fail to understand what you can have to say to me. Indeed, your time must have been so taken up with your homecoming that I imagined you had forgotten I existed.'

He bent his head closer to her. The soft scent of violets that she exuded overlay the scent of incense in the church. 'I haven't forgotten. Nor have I forgotten what occurred in the forest.'

In one easy movement he got to his feet and, taking her hand, raised her up. Her dress was a startling slash of colour in the dim grey church. It was a dark red dress belted at the waist and the fine wool clung to her breasts and hips. She looked like a beautiful statue representing temptation, Guy thought.

He was so tall, way over six foot, that Jane had to tilt her head to look at his face.

'I cannot stay long,' he said. 'Come outside where we can talk.' Without waiting for her to reply, he took her hand and walked her to the door.

Once outside he pulled her into the dark shadow of the church. They were hidden from the road by thick yew trees.

Jane could not tell which sensation had more command of her senses—the horror of embarrassment or the ecstasy of being so close to him. It was as though she had never before been in the presence of a man. Guy St Edmond clouded her mind so that she had no clarity of judgement, no sense of direction.

Lifting her head, vowing she would not let him see how he affected her, Jane frowned in consternation. 'Was it necessary to bring me out of the warmth of the church to this dark, dank spot?'

'I wanted to speak to you alone. There's less chance of being interrupted out here. My lady is displeased over something?' he queried with a slight lift of his brow.'

For a moment Jane debated her answer. For the sake of pride, she could not tell him how well he disrupted her thoughts and that the calm serenity she displayed hid emotions that were well stirred up by the fact of his nearness. Trying not to think of how handsome he looked in his smooth-fitting hose and beautifully cut black tunic with gold embroidery, shielding herself against his mockery, she chose to attack rather than reveal her weakness. Was he playing upon her confusion for his own amusement? That there might be some truth in this stung her pride beneath the suspicion that he had been one step ahead of her all the time.

'Please say what you have to say for I must be on my way. My mother is expecting me back at the house.'

Now he had her alone, Guy was in no hurry to be parted from her. His eyes passed over the shapely figure with warm admiration. The light breeze teased the fair tresses about her face and she paused to tuck the stray wisps beneath her plain headdress. With her arms raised, for a moment the bodice of her gown stretched tight across the slim back, reassuring him of the fact that her waist was naturally narrow. In his far-reaching travels he had seen his share of women and had been most selective of those he had chosen to sample. His experience could hardly be termed as lacking, yet it was hard in his mind that the delectable girl whom he scrutinised so carefully far exceeded anything he could call to mind.

Since returning to Sinnington Castle, as he strolled its corridors and chambers, he was inspired with a most gratifying sense of solid order and security. He was no longer a snivelling boy, sent away from his mother to become a knight. Now he was a powerful man who needed no one. And now that he had made his life just the way he wanted it, he had no intention of handing over to another proud and selfish lady the ability to disrupt his life.

But that wasn't right, he thought. Jane Lovet wasn't proud or selfish. She was lovely and virtuous, and as he'd heard in the woodland glade, she had a laugh so infectious she made him smile—and he wanted her with a desperate ardour that twisted him in knots of desire. These things were in the background of his mind, but he refused to concentrate on them. To do so would have meant that he was more than physically involved with her and that he refused to accept.

Aware of his scrutiny, Jane tilted her head to look at his face. 'Please don't look at me like that. Don't you have a battle to fight or something?'

A smile touched his lips. 'My apologies. I didn't mean to stare. And in answer to your question, unless I am called upon by the king, I am done with fighting. Believe me, Jane, I shall not miss the cut and thrust of the campaign.'

'Forgive me, but since you are a renowned soldier with a reputation for shedding blood and as black as Satan's, I find that difficult to believe. Have you come to church to repent of your sins?'

Chuckling softly, his smiling eyes captured hers and held them prisoner until she felt a warmth suffuse her cheeks. 'If I were to do that, I would be here until doomsday and beyond. But I am not alone in leading a sinful life and there is nothing unusual for a soldier to lay down his sword. A fighting man often decides to abandon his life of warfare and seek forgiveness for his sins. What of your own family, sweet Jane? Your own brother was an ardent Lancastrian fighting his cause.'

Sadness clouded her eyes and her heart was heavy on being reminded of her wild, handsome brother. But when she spoke there was bitterness and accusation in her voice. 'It is no secret that Andrew was a cavalry man and a Lancastrian, or that when he was taken prisoner he was sentenced to death—on your orders, I believe.'

Guy's eyes narrowed and his jaw tensed. He did not deny her accusation. 'War is never honourable, Jane. You brother was a brave man, I have no doubt, who did his duty as he conceived it to be—as did hundreds of others at Towton.'

'Yes, he did. You will consider him a traitor, but he was a beloved brother and my family miss him dreadfully.'

'I, too, lost my older brother, so I can empathise with your loss. But life has to go on and for me the time has come for me to consider my future. I am home to stay and find my thoughts turning to the softer aspects of life—and a woman in my bed.'

Jane's cheeks stung with heat. 'Do you have a lady in mind?'

His eyes locked on hers, implacably he stated, 'I do. You.'

Chapter Three

For a moment Jane's mind went completely blank. 'Me?' She laughed nervously, completely thrown by his remark. 'But that is ridiculous. It cannot possibly be.'

Guy's eyes narrowed and his voice took on an odd note of determination. 'Will you not accept my proposal to become my mistress?' he asked *sotto voce*.

Jane felt like she had been shot with a crossbow at point-blank range. She was shocked into instant reply. 'You insult me, sir. You will not take me to your bed, nor will you take me by force. I will not be your mistress.'

'You shall, Jane. I swear.'

It was a most arrogant declaration and too much to contemplate with all the emotions roiling inside her. She did not move, but Guy saw her face set in a dreadful silent stare and felt the shudder that went through her body as clearly as though she had been touching him instead of separated from him by a full two paces. 'How will you do that? Will you *command* me, as is your right?'

'No, Jane, I ask it. You seem distressed,' he remarked, observing the tension in her face.

'Distressed?' she railed. Her colour mounted high in her cheeks and warmed her ears as her temper escalated to unparalleled heights. 'I am anything but *distressed*, my lord! Can you not understand that I am furious?'

'I understand *perfectly*,' he said in a silky, courteous voice. 'I can imagine that a young woman does not take a step like this without a little apprehension. But there is no need to get things out of proportion.'

He was obviously trying to reassure her, but he was mistaken if he thought he could do that—as mistaken as he was devious. 'Out of proportion? You propose that I be your mistress and you have the audacity to say that *I* have got everything out of proportion!' She spoke bitterly as the full force of what he expected of her hit her with all its hu-

miliating clarity. 'It isn't *your* reputation that will
be slaughtered. It will be *mine.*'

The muscles in Guy's jaw clenched tightly, banishing any trace of softness from his too-handsome face, and in a tone of calm finality he stated,
'People will think whatever they want to think.'

'Why?' Jane cried passionately. 'Is it because
you want me, or to ensure that my father knows
his place—to affirm your lordship's power over
your serfs? What do you expect of me? Do you
suppose that I will fulfil such a bargain? For whatever reason, there is no justifying this. You are a
conniving, black-hearted scoundrel. It is dishonourable behaviour and absolutely unacceptable
and an outrage. I will not be used in this way. I
am disgusted by your monstrous egotism your
actions have revealed.'

It gave Jane a kind of awful joy to hurl the in-
nermost feelings of her heart in wild confusion at
the feet of this unfeeling man. If he were to flay
her alive, he could not hurt her more than he had
done already.

One sardonic brow lifted over mocking blue
eyes. 'I mean to have you, Jane.'

'How? Will you rape me? For that is the only

way you will have me—and I will fight you all the way. You can count on that, *my lord*. I find it insulting to me and dishonourable of you. I had not expected you to stake your claim on me quite so callously. By your actions, were I to do as you ask, the shame and humiliation heaped not only on me, but Richard and my family also, would be complete. Your arrogance is unbelievable! I don't know why you are doing this, but whatever the reason it matters little to me whether you are known henceforth as the least honourable lord in Christendom.'

Guy stepped close—and Jane retreated from those suddenly fierce eyes. 'It was never my intention to insult you—your future *husband* is another matter.'

'My feelings for Richard are my concern,' she said tonelessly. 'I cannot—no, I *will* not be your lover or anything else. What you ask of me is a grave sin. I will not shamelessly dishonour Richard or my parents.'

'I believe your father and I could come to an understanding.'

The bright hue of Jane's cheeks and the flashing of her eyes gave evidence to the effect of his savage, cutting words. 'You beast,' she hissed. 'Am I a serf to be sold or bartered at will? You are frivolous when there is nothing to be lost for you. You would take me for your own pleasure and afterwards you could just as well flee and leave me big with child.' She tossed her head angrily. 'You are just like all men—free to your every whim.'

'Free!' Guy gave a derisive snort. 'Nay, Jane. I am not free.' He leaned close to her and his voice rose as he chafed under the lash of her words. 'And I would not flee from you. Let me assure you I would not. Do you think I would put so little value on you that I would so lightly regard your state?'

Jane stared at him. Guy St Edmond was shameless. 'Is it your desire to see me shamed?' she asked him.

'I hope that won't happen.'

'I fear it will. I would have to live with what you would do to me for the rest of my life. I will be a fallen woman. Impure. You deserve no respect for this.'

'Perhaps not. I'm afraid I might find it hard to find peace away from you. You are very well aware of the effect you have on me—surely you recognise desire in a man's eyes?'

Jane stared at him, wondering that he could speak like this to her, with such assurance, as if he believed she would not be able to resist him. Vaguely disturbed by his words, she felt a strange emotion swell within her breast. His voice was at once brusque and warm, imperious and tender. She must fight against this fascination he was beginning to exert over her.

'If you still require a mistress, then you must look elsewhere.'

'I have no desire to look elsewhere.' He took her hand and traced the lines on its palm. He felt her response and smiled. 'See how easily I touch you,' he murmured, 'how recklessly I make you come to me and then tease you—how I pluck your strings, as if you are but a lute.'

The intimacy of his touch and his voice, the suggestion of playing her like a lute, both excited and shamed her. 'You jest with me, my lord.'

He laughed, a robust sound as mighty as he was. 'Ah, Jane, I never jest on matters as serious as this.

'What an impatient nature you have,' she remarked. 'You certainly have an aptitude for spontaneity. But as I said, you must look elsewhere.'

'Why should I do that when I have perfection right here? My dear Jane, you look like something a lonely man far from home would dream about in the small hours of the morning. Had I been able to store such a memory in my heart years ago, it would have surely given me hope in times of need.'

Jane gave him a scornful look. 'Your words flow like honey from your lips, my lord, that it makes me wary. I am nothing to you. You do not know me. We are strangers and I have certainly not sought your attention or encouraged you in any way. Why are you doing this?'

He shrugged. 'Several reasons—some I do not understand myself. You have attracted my attention. You have excited my compassion for your position, inspired my sympathy for your needs—'

'And for this you want me to become your mistress?' she remarked with a sneer.

'Aye, Jane, and the fact that you remain in my memory long enough for me to do something about it.'

'Then if this is the way you go about trying to woo a lady, you haven't a prayer of success.'

'I haven't?'

'No. Based on what I know of you, I would not be in the least surprised if you were to toss the lady over your shoulder and carry her off, and, if she still refused your amorous intentions, to lay her over your knee and beat her into submission.'

For some reason her words brought a mocking gleam and a narrowing to his eyes. 'Have a care what you say, Jane, lest you give me food for thought. I admit that I have erred, having spent so much time in conquest to bring peace. As a boy I saw little of my parents. When I was seven I was sent to live with a noble family in Hertfordshire. I became a page and had to wait on lords and ladies. I also learned to fight. At fourteen I became a squire and at twenty-one a knight. I've spent so much of my life in conquest that I have much to learn when it comes to the finer points of wooing a lady. One hasn't the opportunity to meet very many suitable ladies on the battlefield.'

'Then perhaps you should turn you mind to seeking a wife, my lord, instead of a mistress. A wife would satisfy your baser needs and provide you with heirs.'

'That is what I intend.'

'Isn't it the practice for nobles to select their wives with an eye to forming political alliances?'

'It is. I am the last of the line. I have no siblings or nephew to leave my inheritance to, which is why I must marry a woman who can give me sons to inherit my demesne and carry on my name. I have to rebuild.'

'And a cloth merchant's daughter would never do,' Jane responded sneeringly. 'It appears to have slipped your mind that my future husband may not take kindly to me being another man's mistress—however noble that man may be.'

'You don't want to wed Aniston. I see it in your eyes. Your life is not yours to order, is it, sweet Jane?'

'What woman's life is?'

It was true. She lived in a fine house and had the love of her family. But the price she paid was that her life was not hers to order. Her father's word was law. He commanded. She must obey.

'Aniston can soon be got rid of,' Guy suggested with ease. 'You can be assured I would not be a poor substitute. Aniston will get over his disappointment.'

'I fear it is you who will be disappointed, sir,' she told him curtly.

'Truly?' He ambled a few steps closer, regarding her with deliberation. 'I cannot think why, when the heavens have seen fit to reward me for whatever reason with a glimpse of the fairest maid that ever graced my sights.'

Though she roiled inside, Jane feigned control, rolling her eyes in seeming humour. 'If nothing else, you were born with a smooth tongue, sir. But since there is no one here you seek to impress, you may as well save your pretty words for another who is willing to listen.'

He took another step and Jane was very aware that the closer he came, the softer and lower pitched his voice became, and, as he moved closer still, she felt a frisson of velvet along her spine. 'Are you so sure you know me well enough to know whom it is I seek to impress?'

'I have no wish to know you, sir.'

'Ah,' he said, with an unmistakable trace of amusement. 'In which case, sweet Jane, I acknowledge my poor judgement and can only wonder at the reason which brings you to an empty church, at a time when most brides would be preparing for marriage and dreaming sweet bridal dreams. Is it God's comfort you seek to calm your nerves of what is to come?'

'I marvel at your intimate knowledge of brides. Speaking only for myself, I often come to the church when it is quiet to pray.'

'For a young woman to spend so much time on her knees, perhaps you should reconsider your future and become a nun instead of a wife.'

'I have often been accused of being wilful and disobedient. I fear I would make a very bad nun. And it is not uncommon for a bride to be nervous as her wedding day approaches. One must cope with one's nerves as best one can and a wedding causes so much happy anticipation…'

The words nearly choked her, but she would not have him know the extent of her desperation. She had no happy dreams of the future and soon more would be taken from her, but she would not surrender the battered remnants of her pride.

Guy arched a dark brow. 'Happy anticipation? Forgive my impertinence, Jane, but I seem to recall that the last time I saw you with Aniston, he was on the point of assaulting you. Is it that which inspires such happy anticipation? Or was my judgement also faulty? Maybe you were not in need of rescuing after all and would have enjoyed the rough and tumble of his lusts.'

Jane tensed as he came closer still, reminding herself it was past time for her to take leave of him, and she told herself she would, but she was reluctant to do so. His closeness was forcing her heart to beat even more rapidly than before, something she would not have thought possible. She asked herself what was wrong with her, for if there was ever a time when she ought to be erring on the side of caution, it was surely now.

She lowered her eyes. 'What happened yesterday was between Richard and myself,' she told him. 'Any differences of understandings we have will be rectified by us.'

All trace of mockery had vanished. Guy's blue eyes were as hard as granite, as was his voice. He was clearly angry and his tone was deadly quiet. 'Differences of understandings? Tell me this. Has Aniston ever threatened you with violence? Have you ever felt yourself to be in direct physical danger from him?'

Jane was determined to maintain her composure, though the effort cost her dearly. She had been disturbed by Richard's behaviour and felt nothing but dread for what he would do to her on her wedding night. But knowing how important this marriage was to her father, she had no choice but to defend him.

She gave a half-hearted shrug. 'No. I think it was a matter of Richard being too eager. He believes that once a couple is engaged, they are considered as good as married. He is not alone in that.'

She could see that the anger she'd heard building in Guy St Edmond's voice had become etched on his face in hard lines as he responded to her words. 'Which is why a good many brides are already pregnant when they make their vows to the priest. There are things in this world that are worth the waiting.'

'Since you have just proposed that I become your mistress, that makes you a hypocrite,' Jane retorted sharply.

He gave her a lopsided grin. 'I've had my moments.'

She gave him a questioning look. 'Yesterday

you implied that you knew Richard—or know of him. I am curious.'

'I know Lord Lambert. He was a good friend of mine. We fought many a battle together. Aniston was a squire in his household. We never met, but I knew of him.'

'I see. And what happened to Lord Lambert— you speak of him in the past tense.'

'He did not live long following the tragic death of his beloved daughter Lucy.'

'I'm sorry,' Jane said, having no desire to pry into what was clearly a private matter. Unless… Her eyes flew to his. 'Was Richard involved in what happened to her?'

He shook his head. 'I can't say. But you must understand my concern.'

'I—I do care for Richard,' she lied in desperation, haltingly, unconvincingly, tears welling up in her eyes which she immediately blinked away. There was a part of her, young woman that she was, that wanted to run home and fling herself on her bed and cry. But she could not do that. She wasn't Blanche, who laughed and cried easily. 'Please do not speak to me like this again. I will not listen.'

'Damn it, Jane. I am no monster. Would you rather take that coarse, unsightly lout and nurture him with the sweet joys of wedlock than consider me? Are you mad? Aniston is to have what I want and silence on the matter will *not* make that fact any sweeter. You forget who you are dealing with. Do you not realise that as lord of this demesne, no man who lives on my land can marry off his daughter unless I allow it? I have the right to forbid your marriage to Richard Aniston.'

Jane paled, her eyes wide with disbelief. 'You would not do that?'

'It is within my power to do so—if I so wish.'

Jane was furious at what he was implying. Her angry eyes held his. 'How could you even think of doing something so base? You may command your soldiers to your will, sir, but you have no such authority over me—and you have much to learn about courtship.'

Guy had to concede that she spoke the truth. The people of Cherriot were not like the knights and squires with whom he had spent the last fifteen years. He was a fighting man. In his world loyalties were clear. Bravery was a virtue and the issue was life or death. No time for courtship. Since Isabel, he had vowed that his emotions would never be engaged by a woman—until he met Jane Lovet. Guy cauterised his emotions. Women had always been attracted to him because he remained aloof, giving only so much of himself. That was the way he liked it, the way he intended to control his life.

But he would be satisfied with nothing less than a satisfying union with a woman whose charm and beauty had entirely seduced him.

'Richard and I *will* be married. It is final—irrevocable.' Jane stepped passed him, her head held high. Guy St Edmond didn't know the wedding had been brought forwards. By the time he found out she would be married to Richard and that would be an end to the matter. 'Now excuse me. I have nothing further to say to you.'

He grasped her arm. 'Come, I will walk with you to your home.'

She shook his hand free. 'No. I cannot be seen with you. People will gossip, which would not be good for either of us.'

Despite the fact she'd only glanced at him before she'd walked on, Jane had registered the odd light in his eyes and the indefinable smile lurking at the corners of his lips. She had no idea what was behind it, she only knew his smile increased her fury until it completely eclipsed her misery.

Had Cedric or any of his knights been present to see that look, they could have told her that it was a portent of what was to come and their explanation would have angered Jane far more than she already was. It was the look Guy St Edmond had on his face when he was about to ride into battle contemplating victory, refusing to be deterred by the opposition. Guy St Edmond, arrogant sensualist, would let nothing stand in the way of his desire.

From where he stood hidden from view by a dense yew tree, Richard seethed. He had seen all of it. He had seen them come out of the church and been watching for the entirety. How he would like to teach Guy St Edmond a lesson. But in a few short weeks after he had married and bedded his wife, he would have driven home the message that he owned her, before man and God, that he alone had the right to touch her, whenever and wherever he pleased, and that no man would ever dare challenge that right.

* * *

Unaware that she was being observed by Richard, Jane left the church in a whirl of emotions. She was more affected by the earl's proposal that she become his mistress than she would have him know. Fleeing from the wreck he had brought about, desperate to be alone so that she might think about this new, incredible turn of events, on entering the house she hurried to her room. Around her the house was quiet.

Sitting on the window seat, gradually she recovered her self-possession. For the first time in her life she was discovering power over a man, sufficient at least to disturb the disagreeable, yet oh-so-attractive Earl of Sinnington. As much as she wanted to give way to the perfectly natural temptation to abuse it, she was wondering if she really could turn it to her advantage.

He had told her he was offering her a lifeline. Perhaps he was, but then, if she were to give in to his demands, was there not a chance that she would be jumping out of the proverbial frying pan into a blazing inferno? In the eyes of everyone in Cherriot Vale she would be a shameless wanton, soiled and used, unfit company for unsullied young women and unfit to mingle in polite society. She would have broken the rules governing moral conduct and not even with someone of her own class.

Richard was an objectionable character, controlling and aggressive, an aggression that was ever present in her father. She made up her mind that she could not live as her mother had done beneath the heel of a domineering man, as a woman who, in her father's strict adherence to his code that a man must rule in his own house and who expected his will to be done at all times, needed rough handling in order to be mastered.

Guy St Edmund was a brutal warrior, and if his reputation was to be believed, with the blood of thousands on his hands. But he was without doubt the more handsome of the two. Wild and wanton sensations she had never experienced with Richard took control of her whenever they were together, filling her mind with thoughts no decent, unmarried girl should think of. She allowed herself to imagine how it would be were she to give in to his desire. A thrill coursed through her and warmed her blood. It seemed far-fetched to think that one man could move her to such extremes, yet when she compared her joy at the feelings he had awakened in her to the strange, inexplicable yearning that presently thwarted her mood, what else could she put it down to?

How could she possibly bear being married to Richard now?

Her brain worked quickly, and when she finally got to her feet, she felt as though she had been born anew as a result of some painful and unaccustomed process of gestation. Slowly the picture she had built up of her life with Richard was finally crumbling away.

Her father's image came to mind. Suddenly her heart was pounding and her cheeks were hot and she tried not to think of him or how angry he had been when Andrew had told him he was to fight for the Lancastrian cause. He would be furious. But he had not arranged her marriage to Richard out of devotion to her but, controlling, cruel and manipulative, to his devotion to his own self-interests. Her mind made up, she heaved a deep sigh. She would be in command of her own fate. As much as she dreaded confronting her father, she knew she had made the right decision. She could not have sustained living with such a man as Richard.

Having no wish to alarm her parents and wanting to absorb her decision and consider what it would mean to her future, wanting to think about it some more and to nurse her secret a while longer, she had kept it to herself.

What she had not expected was that Richard would call on her.

It was mid-morning the following day when he arrived. She was alone in the parlour and with a quiet confidence she watched him approach. There was something different about his manner, something out of character. There was also a strange excitement in his eyes. She felt her hair bristle in the nape of her neck, but forced herself to remain calm. Now the moment of confrontation was at hand, she was strangely relieved. He made no move to approach her. His face was white and he seemed to be struggling with some inner turmoil.

Despite the repugnance he inspired in her, her smile did not falter for an instant. She knew she looked stunning in her snug-fitting gown of emerald green with its flared skirt and a lace cap covering her hair, but it would be lost on Richard, whose thoughts only seemed to focus on what they concealed.

When she rose from the settle by the hearth, Richard could barely keep his lusting gaze from straying from her beautiful face to her softly rounded breasts and tiny waist. But suddenly he seemed to recollect himself and pulled himself up straight, a hard gleam replacing the sexual desire in his eyes.

'Richard! You find me all alone today. My parents have gone to call on my aunt and uncle. But I am glad you are here. I—have something to tell you which cannot wait.'

'How odd,' he said, anger flushing the pallor from his face. 'I have something to say to you— you whore.'

She stared at him as if she didn't understand the meaning of his word. 'What?'

'You whore. I will not be played false.'

Thrown off balance by his callous insult, she stepped back. 'What are you talking about?'

He looked at her accusingly. 'As if you didn't

know? The minute my back is turned I find you consorting with someone else—Sinnington, of all people.' Moving closer, his face having turned a terrible shade of red, Richard fastened his rage-filled eyes on her. 'I saw you with him outside the church yesterday—talking to him, preening yourself for him like a whore, flirting and cavorting with your simpering smiles.'

'I most certainly was not.' Jane flared with indignation, shocked by what Richard was implying.

'He put his hands on you. I saw him—and your wanton response.'

Jane glared at him. 'You spied on us. You should have made your presence known, Richard.'

'What? And spoil your little tête-à-tête?' he sneered.

'It was not what you think.'

'Did my eyes deceive me?' he spat savagely.

'What you saw was what you wanted to see, when in reality the Earl of Sinnington was merely passing the time of day.' Taking a deep breath, she steeled herself as if preparing for battle. 'I have often questioned my acceptance of you as a husband, Richard, so better we end it now. I am calling the wedding off. I will not tie myself to a man I do not love—a man I know I can never love. Before you came here today I had already decided I am not going to marry you. I intend telling my parents when they return, and afterwards I am sure my father will want to speak to your own.'

'So, that's the way of things, is it? I can see Sinnington has turned your head,' he sneered contemptuously. 'If you think he will marry you, then think again. He holds a position close to the King of England. He's not going to wed some beggarly cloth merchant's daughter from the camp of his enemy. If he marries at all it will be one of the great ladies of the king's court.'

Jane paled. 'You have said quite enough. I think you had better go.'

'I will. Do you think I want to remain close to the woman whose hands have been all over Sinnington? Has he told you that he loves you? Is that it? And were you fool enough to believe it? Ha!' he scoffed, eyeing her insultingly. 'As maybe he loves each and every one of the women he's bedded and there are hundreds of them. And when he leaves you and sees another pretty face? What then? He will forget you within a day.'

Jane was beside herself with anger. 'How dare you? How dare you imply that—?'

'I dare, Jane,' he growled savagely, moving closer, making full use of his threatening gaze. 'Oh, yes, I dare—for were you not to be my wife? Sinnington will bed you, then when you have satisfied his needs he will pass you on to one of his men, as he does with all his sluts. Men of his ilk don't marry their whores. If you do this, then, by heavens, you can be assured I will make you pay for what you're doing to me. I will find you when the wall is to your back and you've only one path to go—and that is past me.'

His warning sent icy shards of dread shivering through every fibre of her being, causing her heart to leap in sudden fear. There was something intimidating in his movements that Jane did not like, something almost predatory. She edged back, attempting to put space between them, but he came on, his body a menacing shadow on the floor. Showing him how affected she was would only incite him further.

She had been on the brunt of his lustful nature often enough, but this was a side to Richard she had never seen before, and she knew with a cold, hard certainty that she never wanted to see it again. If she married him, she feared whether she would be able to survive their wedding night, much less their first conjugal mating. The disillusion of her intended betrothal to Richard was complete.

'You have made a fool of me—a laughing stock,' Richard hissed, thrusting his ugly, contorted face close to hers, his lip curling. 'You may congratulate yourself on being the first woman to do that, but you will certainly be the last. Have a care, Jane. You may have been blinded by Sinnington, but if you become his whore then your family will have to bear the brunt of it. You will shame your house and your name. Think of that when you are lying in his bed.'

Richard's accusations and insults brought colour flooding to Jane's cheeks. She turned her head away from the blazing fury shooting from his eyes. He was angry and it was natural that he should be so, but she would not change her mind. She had grown up knowing the shape her life would take and she had accepted it—if not her father's choice of husband—but she was also the daughter of a businessman who had taken her with him to the London markets, where every merchant's worth was measured in gossip. She knew how easily people could be destroyed by rumour.

But there would be no shame, for she had no intention of giving in to Guy St Edmond's demands. Feeling a constriction in her throat, she raised her head, resplendent with a rage which made her eyes flash.

'You are mistaken. I have no intention of becoming the Earl of Sinnington's mistress. I have nothing further to say to you, Richard, except I am sorry things have turned out this way.'

'Sorry? You are *sorry*?'

'Yes—yes, I am. It was not my intention to hurt you, but I have made up my mind. And now I think you should go,' she said calmly, but firmly.

Jane expected further argument and was surprised when he turned on his heel and left. She was left shaken by the encounter, but she was glad it was over and she could look to a future without him.

Jane had waited for her parents to come home, her heart filled with dread in anticipation of the condemnation she would ultimately receive from her father. They returned later than expected. She was walking in her favourite part of the garden where the river meandered its way through the trees. When her mother came to join her, she looked at her anxiously, drawing her down on to a bench beside her.

'What is it, Mother? Are you feeling unwell? You are very pale.'

'We—your father and I—have just seen Richard. He told us he had called on you—and that you have decided to call off the betrothal. He said that you no longer wish to marry him. Jane, tell me it is not true, that it is a mistake.'

Jane hung her head for a moment, then looked at her, unable to hide the truth from her mother's questing, unhappy eyes. 'I can't. It's true. I have changed my mind. Forgive me, Mother, but I cannot marry him. I will not be beholden to a man I cannot honour.'

'But—why? None of this makes sense. Everything is in readiness for your betrothal. Your… father has taken it very badly. He…is extremely angered by your actions. This is not a good time for him. Things are bad—they couldn't be worse.'

'I know and I am sorry. Truly I am. I am aware of how much you will suffer because of this, but I cannot marry him.'

'The consequences of your decision will be immediate and unavoidable,' her mother said quietly. 'John Aniston will be bound to distance himself from your father. At the guild meetings he will be met with hostility from the other members, which will affect him deeply. They will be speculative, curious and even grimly amused, as if his woes serve only to mark another tragedy that one can relate to the next gossip avid for another's misery.'

'I sincerely hope it won't be like that,' Jane said, wishing she could ease her mother's anxiety.

Margaret heaved a pensive sigh. 'The fact that your father is facing ruin will soon be known to all. Without the occurrence of some miracle, there is nothing we can do to ease our present unfortunate state.'

A lump formed in Jane's throat and she felt as if she would never swallow again and her eyes, so strangely dry one moment, stung painfully the next. 'I understand how troubled you are, Mother,' Jane said in a quiet voice, no less distressed as she sought to find some ray of hope in a painfully dark future. 'I truly wish there was something I could do to alter our present unfortunate state.'

She looked up when her father entered the garden and came to join them. His lips were pursed, his eyes angry and accusing, and for the next half-hour Jane listened to his angry tirade, telling her over and over again that she was a wretched girl, ungrateful and a fool.

Jane sighed as she left his presence. He did not profess concern for her well-being and happiness at all. By now she should expect nothing less.

And then the worst, the very worst, happened. Richard told everyone that he was the one who had called off the betrothal, claiming that Jane had attracted the Earl of Sinnington's amorous attentions and that he had bedded her.

Jane could not contain the shock of Richard's accusation. It spilled over on to her cheeks in a torrent of hot tears as she regarded her mother. They were alone in her chamber.

'How can he say such wickedness? I was the one who refused to become betrothed to him.' Her shoulders quaked with sobs. 'What reason can possibly justify this?'

Jane thought her father was going to have a seizure when the news that was spreading throughout Cherriot Vale and beyond reached him. His eyes never moved from her face. He seemed unable to speak, to form any words, from between his rigidly clamped lips. Even though Jane denied Richard's accusations most adamantly, his thin face was drawn, his eyes cold and accusing. He was convinced there had to be some substance behind the rumour and just came short of calling his daughter wanton and a whore.

Jane felt as if she were being swept along by a tidal wave, as if there were no way to save herself from drowning. Her thoughts turned to Guy St Edmond and she found herself in the vexing position of wondering how he would react to Richard's indictment and how furious he would be. She dreaded the moment when she would have to confront him and see what she knew would surely be contempt written all over his features.

She was not wrong. The man who arrived at the house and strode into the hall, his tall frame clad entirely in black, bore little resemblance to the amorous earl she had met at the church only five days ago. Today he was an aloof, icy stranger who gave her no more than a cursory glance before focusing all his attention on her father.

Chapter Four

When the rumour had reached him, a white-hot fury unlike anything he'd ever experienced had consumed Guy, turning his mind into a fiery volcano of boiling rage. Parading before his eyes were visions of a bewitching girl with the face of an angel, laughing as he'd seen her do in the woodland glade. Because of his own gullibility of wanting to bed her, he'd fallen into a trap of his own making.

Aniston had done his worst and disappeared. Which was as well. Had Guy been able to get his hands on him, he would have slit his throat gladly. At that moment he'd been so infuriated, too incensed to care, but now his fury had reduced to a dangerous calm.

His gaze settled on Master Lovet. 'You will know why I have come,' he remarked coolly.

'Indeed, my lord,' Simon replied stiffly, knowing there was something in this for his own gain if he played his cards right. Having considered the situation at great length, he realised he would be a fool not to take the opportunity to turn what had happened to his advantage. The Earl of Sinnington was a wealthy and titled man; one of the most powerful men in the land. The position as Countess of Sinnington would sit very well on his daughter's shoulders. Better by far that she married an earl than the son of a cloth merchant. But he must not forget that the Earl of Sinnington was a proud and noble man—a warrior, a man who had earned the confidence of the king. It was dangerous to question the honour of such a man. 'However, you could have spared yourself the trouble of this visit. I had every intention of calling on you at the castle.'

'Then I have saved you the trouble.'

'Can we offer you refreshment?'

'No, thank you. I have not come here to make polite conversation,' Guy stated ominously, looking at Jane intently.

Jane's entire being was engulfed in mortification, her misery increasing a thousandfold as she stood beside her parents, her eyes settled on the set of Guy's proud head, and again the awakening of pleasure deep within her was strong and disturbing, a long slither of longing sliding down her belly. Her eyes found his face and were trapped there by some satanic seduction. He looked hard at her, seeing through her, in the way he had of judging men. It was a moment of testing and she knew it even then. His eyes were bright, but they pierced like a sword thrust and felt like cold steel.

It took every ounce of courage she possessed to meet his gaze and hold it. There was no tenderness on his face. It was as if he knew everything, that he could judge a man's character to a hair's breadth and from whom few could keep secrets.

He had the look of a conqueror about him and appeared most confident. It frightened her, especially when those thoroughly blue eyes locked on her and slowly raked her. She had almost forgotten how brilliant and clear they were. In some magical way they seemed capable of stripping her mind bare of all thought. It was all she could do to face his unspoken challenge and not retreat to the safety of her room.

'My wife and I recognise that we must lend all

our support to our daughter at this time,' Simon went on, his expression the quintessence of slyness. His eyes were narrowed, his lips twisted into a sardonic smile—he was like a fox about to pounce. 'She has told us of everything that has transpired since the two of you met—how you intended to dishonour her by making her your mistress and how she broke off her intended betrothal to Master Aniston, and that as a consequence he has turned the tables and put the onus on her—and you. I do not like primitive behaviour, sir, when it threatens the stability of my family.'

Guy flicked his brows upwards mockingly. 'Primitive behaviour,' he stated quietly. 'By that remark I sincerely hope you are referring to Aniston, Master Lovet.'

'Forgive my boldness, but by my reckoning the accusation can be applied to a man who approaches a young unmarried girl with seduction in mind. I expected better of you, my lord. Your actions were those of a feckless youth, not a distinguished knight of the realm.'

'I agree absolutely. And for what it's worth I regret what I did. I should have approached you over the matter.'

'Yes, you should—even though as a father I would have refused your request outright. In the light of Richard's announcement, the whole of Cherriot Vale and beyond despise my daughter for things she has not done. In their eyes she has done the unforgivable—giving herself to a man who is not her husband. I have a moral code, sir, and you publicly breached that code by exposing her to scandal.'

'If anyone can make a scandal out of a woman speaking to a man outside a church, then they need their minds examining,' Guy said coldly.

'Not when that young lady is my daughter. I have considered the possible repercussions that may occur because of it. By your actions you have compromised my daughter.'

Abandoning his nonchalant manner and stepping forwards, Guy sounded ready to explode. 'I have done what?' he ground out ominously.

'You attempted to seduce a young woman of a decent, respectable family outside the church.'

'I did no such thing. Jane spoke to me of her own volition—is that not so?' Guy reminded her forcefully, preferring to ignore what her father said about seduction since it was true. Before he had come here he had given little thought to how Jane must be suffering the gossip. He didn't try to defend himself. How could he? But the whole sorry affair brought home to him his own callous treatment of this beautiful young woman.

'Jane had high hopes of making a good marriage and because of this she is ruined—an outcast among her own people,' Simon stated forcefully.

'You know, Master Lovet,' Guy said stony faced, 'I find it amazing that almost everyone who knows me is half-afraid of me, except a handful of my friends, you, sir, and your daughter. I can only surmise that courage—or recklessness, call it what you will—is passed through the bloodline to her. What is it you want from me?'

Believing he knew exactly how to play this game, Simon looked at him, his piercing eyes alive with anticipation. 'You may not like what I have to suggest. Indeed, I am uncomfortable with it myself, yet I can think of no other way at present to stop the gossip that will surely ruin my daughter. There are many kinds of persecution that are not readily apparent, such as the whispered conjectures, the gossip and subtle innuendoes that can destroy a reputation and inflict a lifetime of damage. I believe I am justified in asking reparation from you in every conceivable form. I can think of only one possible arrangement that can hold sway over that to be adequate enough to protect her and avoid having her shut up in a nunnery.'

'And that is?'

'That a marriage between the two of you will be an excellent compromise.'

Having fully expected this—indeed, he had tossed the idea about himself for a time before discarding it in the hope of arriving at another solution to the dilemma—his face a taut mask of controlled fury, Guy stared at him before jerking his gaze to Jane and then back to her father. 'That is a bold suggestion you make, Master Lovet. But to wed her would only broadcast throughout Cherriot Vale the very scandal you find so damaging to your daughter.'

Pushed beyond the bounds of reason by her father's words and knowing how his devious mind worked to manipulate the situation towards his own gain, shamed to the depths of her being, Jane stepped forwards, her body rigid, her hands clenched by her sides. Did he care so little for her that he would see her wed to the man who, by all accounts, was responsible for the death of his own son for no other reason than to elevate himself financially and in prominence no matter what?

'No,' she cried, managing to drag her voice through the strangling mortification in her chest. This was worse, much worse than she had dreamed it could be. 'Please believe me. I knew nothing of this. The idea of our marrying is ludicrous. I don't want to marry you.'

Guy looked at her and his face became a cynical mask. 'You're absolutely right,' he mocked sarcastically. 'It is ludicrous.'

Jane heard the insult in his smoothly worded remark and she almost choked on her chagrin. 'And quite unthinkable that I should even consider marrying the man on whose authority my brother lost his life. I think I would rather be ruined in the eyes of everyone than consent to be your wife.'

'Jane,' her mother said, speaking for the first time. Observing how the earl's eyes narrowed ominously, she was afraid of this dangerous twist in the proceedings. 'The manner of Andrew's death is unproven. Now is not the time.'

Simon subjected Jane to his hard, angry gaze.

'Your mother is right. This is not the time to speak of it and the reports of your brother's death were confusing at the time.'

'But *I know*,' Jane said with emphasis, wondering how her father could possibly insist on this marriage while knowing he might be marrying her to her brother's murderer. 'I cannot wed the man whose hands are in all probability stained with Andrew's blood.'

The eyes Guy turned on her were hard and a jeering grin showed startling white teeth against the swarthy skin. 'I am glad we are of accord, Jane, and you should heed your mother. Now is not the time to speak of your brother. I always said that when I decide to take a wife it would be in my own way, with the woman of my choosing, and not when a woman is holding an axe over my head—which is precisely where all my manly instincts rebel.'

'So you do not intend to right the wrong you have done,' Simon said coldly.

Guy look at him long and hard. He was a man who had made his own choices for most of his life. As much as he yearned to appease his manly appetites with Jane Lovet, how could he blandly accept this sly, ambitious cloth-merchant's will without yielding his mind?

'No, he does not,' Jane said quickly, her small chin lifted and her spine stiffened with pride. 'I can understand your reticence to marry me, sir, as much as my own not to marry you.'

'Be silent, Jane,' her father ordered with icy calm, turning his determined gaze on the earl once more. 'And I would appreciate you addressing my daughter with more respect, my lord.'

Guy allowed a meagre smile to convey his apology. 'After many years as a soldier, Master Lovet, I'm afraid I shall have to relearn the art of gallantry.'

'I dare say there was not much call for it in your encampments,' Jane bit back, falling silent when her father shot her a withering look.

'You are quite right. The ladies who infiltrated the ranks were not the kind you would wish to associate with, Mistress Lovet.'

Incensed by his callous reply, Jane faced him squarely. 'You are not blameless in all this. You sought me out. I did nothing to encourage you and I did not agree to your bargain, but because of it I am despised. Now tell me I was wrong to refuse you.'

She was right. The undeniable truth of her accusation hit Guy with more force than he wanted to acknowledge, but his guilt was lessened by the knowledge that the life with Aniston was lost to her now, which would not have been much of a life for her at all. Thoughts of his military training came to mind and how his superiors had sought to share their wisdom he had gleaned from their own experiences, teaching him not merely with words but through example. Above all they had shown him the true meaning of duty and honour, which Guy had put into practice many times in his military career—the same duty and honour that had been absent in his treatment of many of the women who had shared his bed in the past, but which he must now apply to dealing with this situation of Jane. He had done her a great disservice when he had suggested that she become his mistress. He had no choice except to rescue her from what she was suffering now.

The people of Cherriot Vale would still see her as a fallen woman—someone who has erred, not a victim, and she'd spend the rest of her life paying for it. This fact alone, added to the knowledge that she would suit him in bed more than any other, were what permitted him to make his decision. Having arrived at it, he acted with typical speed and resolve.

'No,' he said in answer to Jane's question, 'you were within your rights to do so and I apologise for any distress I may have caused you and your family. In order to rectify the wrong, I agree to a marriage between us. Whether or not it is the right course to take remains to be seen.'

'No. I will not marry you,' Jane cried furiously, mentally circling for some way out. 'I don't want to marry you.'

Her father shot her a warning glance. 'Jane, control yourself. You are too impertinent. You would do well to watch your manners. The earl is taking the honourable course by agreeing to make you his wife and I agree to it. It's final. You will marry the earl so let that be an end to it.'

Jane despaired. Why did she have to do this? Her heart was racing. She wanted to scream in protest, but knew it was futile. Her father was adamant. His rule was law.

Guy turned his frigid gaze upon Simon Lovet.

'And of course you insist on a hasty betrothal,' he growled.

Simon faced him with an unwavering stare, already gloating on his success. 'Yes, I do,' he said calmly.

A muscle twitched angrily in Guy's cheek, but he said nothing, not even when Simon asked Jane and his wife to leave them, that they had matters to discuss.

With her mother following in her wake, Jane turned on her heel and went out.

When they were alone, still Jane could not help but ask, 'Why is Father doing this? It is exactly the same as it was with Richard. I am beginning to regret my decision to call off our betrothal.'

Margaret bowed her head. 'I'm sorry, Jane, but it is done. It's all settled. You must understand why your father insisted on the earl doing the right thing by you. What has happened has become a joke among everyone in the vale. Your father has become a laughing stock. He will be indebted to you for this sacrifice you make on behalf of the family. You are an honour to the Lovet name.'

Was there an emphasis on the word 'sacrifice'? Jane wondered. Her heart wrenched with pain and bitterness. Her father could rally no hope for the future, knowing his family faced nothing but bleakness unless she married Guy St Edmond. She clearly understood the importance her father set by the alliance to be forged with this union.

She swallowed hard as she faced her mother, unable to still the quavering weakness that hindered her voice. 'You are right. I have no choice but to wed him. I will do what I must to help us all out of this dire situation. I will not allow my family to live in poverty—not when I have it in my power to put things right.'

Solemnly her mother embraced her, kissing her cheek. 'Thank you, Jane. God bless you. I know you are thinking of the good of the family.'

Jane bowed her head. Her mother was right. She was thinking of the family—but most of all she was thinking about herself.

Guy asked to speak to Jane in private before he left. With his narrow gaze trained on her, her father watched her go into the parlour and close the door. When she entered Guy made no move towards her. The impact of his gaze was no less potent for the distance between them. She returned his stare as boldly as he gave it. The lean planes of his cheeks looked harsh and forbidding, his jaw was set and rigid, and she was close enough to detect the underlying currents in his body. He was seething with anger and that anger was directed at her.

He didn't want this betrothal any more now than he had when he'd asked her to be his mistress, she knew. He was simply being chivalrous. She hadn't expected him to rescue her from a scandal that was greatly of his own making.

In a way that Jane considered to be insulting, his eyes coursed down the fine curves of her body, from the slim erect column of her neck to the beckoning fullness of her hips. The all-too-apparent womanliness of her evoked a strong stirring of desire and he felt a familiar hardening beneath the snug fit of his hose. Her innocence was new to him. It made a man feel whole and clean, yet her innocence and vulnerability were weapons against which he had no defence, not for all his swords and fighting skills. Devil take her, all of this was utterly foreign to him. It was a most unsettling sensation.

'Well, my lord?' she said coldly. 'Do you have

to inspect me as you would a filly to be sold at market? If the lust in your eyes is anything to go by, I would say you like what you see.'

'Aye,' he replied, 'but the hostility I can do without.'

She glared at him. 'Were I a man I would not smirk so easily,' she retorted coldly.

He raised a finely arched eyebrow. 'Were you a man, Jane, you wouldn't be in this situation.'

'No,' she agreed. 'I wouldn't.' Infuriated and seething with humiliation, she averted her gaze.

'It is settled, Jane. Accept it. We are to wed.'

'So it would seem. I dislike force of any kind. I loathe it, but I could do nothing to stop this. You are displeased because my father found out about what you proposed and now you are angry because you're having to pay the piper, yet you did not think what it would do to me.'

Guy's face hardened and his eyes took on a malignant expression. 'I would advise you to have a care, Jane. I did not have to come here today. It is your reputation that has been torn asunder— which, I admit, is partly down to me, but for the most part Aniston. My reputation is already as black as pitch. A scandal such as this will not dent the surface. Had you agreed to be my mistress, you would have been well cared for.'

Jane's lips curved in what resembled a sneer rather than a smile. 'As your mistress? No, thank you. I'd have slit my throat before consenting to that proposal.'

A tic appeared in his cheek and he stared at her for such a long time she stood transfixed like a bird before a snake, the lids lowered slightly over mocking eyes.

'A woman who is kept by a man is usually better tended than his wife—as a queen. I would have been kind and more than generous with you.'

'Meaning you will not be now,' she said with sarcasm.

'You've caught on quickly, Jane.'

She glowered at him. 'Why was I so unlucky to meet you that day when you were returning to Cherriot! You're—you're abominable.'

He laughed softly. 'Some women wouldn't agree with you, my love.'

'I am not your love,' she hissed. 'Considering who you are and that you planned to marry someone of your own rank, to agree to marry me merely to appease my father was reckless indeed.'

She was pale—her eyes seemed bigger than usual and the small scattering of freckles across the bridge of her perfect nose stood out dark against her pallor. For a moment they simply stared at each other. Apart from the few angry words they had exchanged earlier, they had not spoken since she had left him at the church. Now here they were, standing on the edge of a very different future than either of them had planned.

At last Guy squared his shoulders and stepped towards her. The muscles in his jaw clenched tightly, banishing any trace of softness from his too-handsome face, and when he spoke, the softness in his voice was far from soothing.

'I am never reckless and I never retract words spoken sincerely.'

She tossed back her shimmering head and said, 'I told you I didn't want to marry you. I still don't—however, circumstances have changed. But I cannot help feeling that I am being traded for a stake in the eminence of your earldom. I am nothing. I have nothing. I have no doubt you know just how close my father is to ruin and just how advantageous our marriage will be to him.'

He nodded. 'I am aware of that. I will offer a

sizeable stipend to be paid for your hand upon execution of the agreement,' Guy informed her, his voice so matter of fact it might have been a business proposition he was talking about. 'I will also guarantee in writing that upon my death you will inherit most of what I own. As rich as I am, I can help shore up your father's financial situation.'

'Oh, yes,' she replied, her voice laced with sarcasm, 'I am sure you can.' She moved to stand in front of him, looking calmly up into his eyes. 'But think about this, Guy St Edmond. I am in exactly the same situation as when I agreed to marry Richard. I will be marrying you to save myself and my family from ruin and for no other reason.'

Contemplating her flushed cheeks, he placed his finger beneath her chin and tilted her face to his. 'You are wrong, Jane. As my wife our situation will be far removed from that which existed between you and Aniston.'

'And no doubt you are hoping I will present you with first-rate sons.'

'It is my wish, and if they are to take after their mother, confidence, robust health, keen intelligence and courage will not be in short supply. My observation has also told me that you will be a good mother, for it is clear that you take after your own. My future wife's ability to love my children is of paramount importance to me.'

'So in practical terms, by all visible measures I fit the bill,' Jane said coolly. 'Are there any more attributes to my character you would like to tell me about?'

At any other time he would have told her she was caring, capable—a woman he could trust, one who could stand on her own two feet—and not one of those irritatingly helpless, empty-headed women who hung about at court, whose response to danger would be to faint clean away. He also thought that one day she would further mature into a formidable countess who could hold down the castle when he was away, probably for long periods at a time, attending to the far-flung reaches of his demesne. Recollecting himself, Guy felt an ironic smile curve his lips. Good Lord! He was making her out to be the ideal wife.

'I could end up being more trouble than I'm worth,' Jane said. 'Would it not be sensible to choose someone who is not altogether her own person? Someone who is more docile? Someone tame? Someone who would never dare question you, but would follow your orders as assiduously as if she were an extension of yourself?'

'I agree,' he replied mockingly.

'Although you might very well die of boredom?' she remarked sarcastically.

He looked at her calmly, a frown wrinkling his brow. 'Before Aniston, was there ever a youth in your neighbourhood you were fond of?'

His question surprised her. She stared at him, thinking of the faceless number of admirers who had looked her way, men she had put out of her consideration. They could strike no fire in her blood, yet when in the midst of those faces Guy St Edmond's visage appeared in her mind, a sweet wildness stirred her very soul.

'No,' she replied sharply, lowering her eyes lest he saw the truth.

The frown vanished. He ran his finger across her cheek and smiled. 'I'm sure there were many who were smitten with you.'

She stepped back, causing him to drop his arm. 'There may have been a few, but none worth considering.'

'I'm not worried,' he answered easily. 'You were well guarded by your father.'

'Yes,' she retorted sarcastically. 'That is, from everybody but you when you and your marauding band of knights happened to come across me in the woods that day. You *are* a devil, Guy St Edmond.'

His anger returned with frightening speed. 'More myth than man, Jane. I may be feared by my enemies, but you have no need to be afraid. Do you imagine me a cruel tyrant?'

'If you are about to tell me you are the kindest man in all the kingdoms, I shall take some convincing,' she scoffed.

'I shall endeavour to do so and shall make a point of telling you until your ears ache.'

'I may not listen.'

'You haven't heard me roar.' He grew instantly grave. 'I am not a monster, Jane. Your doubts disturb me. How a man treats his enemies is one thing. How a man treats his wife may be quite another. If ever I do make you feel threatened or intimidated, you can be certain you are misunderstanding my concern for your welfare. So protest if you must, but I told you in the beginning that you would be mine.'

'Aye, my lord, but not honourably—not as your wife.'

'But either way, you know you will, don't you?'

She closed her eyes and nodded. Guy St Edmond had defeated her as he had said he would from the beginning. She could not fight it and was not sure that she wanted to any more. Opening her eyes, she looked at him, aware that this thing with a man so confident in his own abilities was only just beginning.

'Yes,' she conceded. 'You did. Please excuse me now. I am sure there are further matters you must discuss with my father.'

She turned her back on him, not wanting one more smile or head tilt or glimpse of his overwhelming male presence to complicate her already muddled feelings. She assumed he would allow her to leave, but suddenly she felt his breath caress the back of her neck, causing gooseflesh to prickle along her skin. Before she could move away, his warm hands curled over her shoulders, gentling her in place.

When he traced his finger along the flesh on her neck, she closed her eyes, awed that a hand which dealt death so skilfully with a sword could be so infinitely tender.

'What your father and I have to discuss can wait,' he whispered, his lips dangerously close to her ear. 'I have a more pressing matter to discuss with my future wife. I have yet to taste the sweetness of your lips. Do not withhold them from me, Jane.'

She refused to turn around, refused to look into his eyes and be swayed by what he wanted her to feel, childishly wanting to cover her ears with her hands against this seduction that was proving too potent. The air was charged between them. She heard him sigh as his mouth touched her hair with a brief and tantalising lightness, and her response was immediate. She felt a shifting, an upheaval deep inside her. A shivering shudder went through her as she felt his warm breath caress her flesh, heard her name hoarsely whispered.

'By the way,' he murmured, drawing her back against his hard chest, 'when I listed your attributes, I failed to tell you that you are very lovely—but then, you must know that.'

She could tell by the harsh sound of his breathing that he wanted her to turn round so that he could kiss her—she could feel the pull of his masculinity, almost hear his body begging for her to turn round—but she didn't dare. She caught her breath as strange sensations leaped through her, setting her whole being on fire.

Guy left her with no choice when he forcibly turned her within the circle of his arms, crushing her breasts against his steely warm chest. He looked down at her, letting his eyes sweep the flushed cheeks.

Tilting back her head, Jane gazed up into his eyes. They had darkened to a stormy dark blue. A tremor went through her as his hand claimed the softness of her nape.

'A kiss, Jane—to seal our bargain. I refuse to leave without a taste of my future wife's lips.'

His fingers caressed her nape as he brought his face closer to hers. And then, before she could even react, his mouth swooped down on hers, hot and hard, plundering her lips in a brigand's kiss. In his unyielding haste it was rough, bruising the flesh of her lower lip, his jaw scraping her tender flesh, but the instant she whimpered, trapped in his arms, his kiss softened, deepened.

Pleasure unfolded inside her like a butterfly

opening its wings to fly. Never in her imagination had she experienced anything so piercing or so sweet as this. Their mouths melded in warm communion, turning, twisting, devouring. His mouth slanted over hers in hungry demand, her hands clung weakly to his broad shoulders. His tightening embrace crushed her. But though he held her firmly, inwardly Jane was falling, falling from the highest point, spinning weightlessly to earth. She was totally in his power and the pleasure in this sudden helplessness alarmed her. Her body came keenly alive, all her senses heightened and focused on him and herself and the touch of his mouth until nothing else mattered. Everything else receded into insignificance. She breathed in the scent of him. He parted her lips with his own, a lush, full openness that tasted her, that enabled her to taste him. Oh, how could anything as simple as this bring so much pleasure?

He continued kissing her for several seconds more, as though he had forgotten this was an untried virgin in his arms. But then he broke the kiss, his breathing uneven as he pulled away a little. He trailed kisses up her throat, along her jaw and over her chin and back to her mouth, recapturing her lips. This time they parted at once, all her token resistance gone.

His arm around her relaxed. He bent his head to rest his forehead close to hers. 'You see how much power you have over me when you choose to wield it.'

She did see. It awed and frightened her. It excited her—that she, who had convinced herself she had no influence over anything in her life, had power over the very man who was offering her and her family a lifeline. Suddenly she felt as captivating and alluring as Cleopatra.

For all its intensity the kiss was brief. She stood back from him, averting her gaze. 'I would like to leave. My parents are waiting to speak to you. Our betrothal. When is it to be?'

'A few days—no longer.'

She left him then, her mind spinning with a welter of thoughts. She did not fool herself into believing that Guy St Edmond would be marrying her for any other reason than necessity and to beget himself an heir. He had told her that he desired her, but she knew he would never love her. He belonged to a breed that did not marry for love. They married for advantage, so that they might be founders of dynasties. Marriage was a business to them. She supposed it didn't matter who she was as long as she was a good breeder, and the Lovets had proved that—her father was one of twelve and her mother the oldest of nine, and all in good health.

What better testimony did the Earl of Sinnington need to make her his wife and the mother of the brood of children she would eventually present him with?

Simon Lovet, eminently pleased at the prospect of the powerful Earl of Sinnington becoming his son-in-law, proclaimed the day of their betrothal a cause for celebration. He spoke of good will among the people of Cherriot Vale, and many who had moved on from Jane Lovet's ill-fated association with Richard Aniston, and eager for fresh gossip, seemed interested in his optimism—although there were many who believed Richard Aniston when, bitter and apparently broken hearted, he had said Jane Lovet had been bedded by the Earl of Sinnington and that the earl was doing the decent thing by marrying her.

Generally, people responded in various ways—

some saying that the family had leaped above themselves—but all showed astonishment. They could not believe that the powerful Earl of Sinnington should take for a wife a dowerless daughter of a cloth merchant, and the cloth merchant of such little account following his son's support of King Henry.

Particularly it was being asked by the wives how a young girl was going to manage such a large household and servants and adapt herself to living at court with all the noble lords and ladies. And that same question was being asked in the castle itself—though not too loudly. For a servant to be heard speaking out against the future wife of the earl would be certain to result in immediate dismissal.

Yet it was not so long ago that Simon Lovet had sung a different tune. Did the marriage of his daughter to the Earl of Sinnington so easily satisfy his sense of honour? Would that Jane could be so easily reconciled to her fate. She would only be a brood mare to Guy St Edmond. That would be her foremost duty—bear his children as fast as she could and see that they were all sons.

Jane's one regret was that John Aniston and his

wife had taken the cancellation of their betrothal very badly. Master John had not left the house since, and his wife, who had felt a blessed relief that Richard had found himself a woman to wed, had taken to her bed. Jane was full of remorse when she heard this, for she could not help but feel responsible. But there was nothing to be done.

Preparations for the betrothal were under way. There was to be a small celebration with a few close relatives and friends at the Lovet house, whereas the wedding ceremony was to be held at Sinnington Castle one month after the betrothal. The house was in upheaval, the smell of suckling pig and venison permeating every room.

As loath as she had been to marry Richard, Jane dreaded this union with Guy, even though she knew she would want for nothing. There was no denying or escaping the fact that he could make her feel things she ought not to want to feel, and feel them far too easily to be safe or to protect her heart from him.

She did not know what her life would be like married to him and tried valiantly to think of something to look forward to. Her parents wouldn't be far away, she reminded herself. And some day, with the little knowledge she had of Guy's lustful nature, she'd have children to love and care for.

Closing her eyes, she drew a painful breath, feeling the tension slowly lessen. A child to hold would be something to look forward to. She'd cling to that thought, she decided.

It was a beautiful day and the whole town was in festive mood.

Jane's mother and Kate dressed her and exclaimed how pretty she looked. Blanche, alternately giggling and gasping, was more excited than Jane as she watched her big sister put on her gown. It was green velvet with a fitted bodice and a slashed skirt that parted at the front to reveal a shining pale-gold undergown. A matching velvet mantle was draped over her shoulders and held in place with a gold chain inset with emeralds and an embroidered heavy belt of gold was slung low over her slim hips. Her hair hung loose, drawn from her face by a slender gold filigree headband.

'You are so beautiful. You look perfect,' her mother declared as her fingers fumbled with the small buttons and loops that had to be tugged together on her sleeves.

Jane stared into the polished mirror on the wall and saw her own face stiffen for a moment. A girl's betrothal should be a bittersweet time, but she found no pleasure in these compliments, until her mind conjured up those blue eyes whose inscrutable calm she had disturbed. Her eyes softened when she noted her mother's eyes were red. She had been crying—tears of happiness and pride. Jane hugged her mother close.

'Yes,' she whispered. 'A picture.'

Dressed in a lovely gown of dove-grey satin and a gauzy white wimple completely swathing her neck and part of her face, and a silvery veil trailing down her shoulders, her mother held her at arm's length, noting her ashen face. 'And you are nervous, I can tell. Which is quite normal. I have no doubt that the earl is just as nervous as you are.'

Jane didn't think so. Guy's life wouldn't change. He would continue to live in his castle and enjoy his country pleasures and his occasional journey to court. For her, everything would change. Nothing would ever be the same again. This was the day when she would cross into adulthood, when she would climb a precipice so steep and so treacherous that if she stumbled she would be sent tumbling into the abyss.

The sudden lift to Jane's heart when Guy arrived with Cedric and four of his fellow knights by his side was quickly followed by nervous dread. For reasons she could not name, seeing him gave rise to thoughts she'd been valiantly struggling to avoid. He was most splendidly attired in scarlet and gold and jewels. He lit up the hall that was tense with expectancy like a beacon of light.

He smiled graciously, his gaze sweeping over the small party of guests, who, after much curtsying and bowing, now stood silently respectful, eager to feast their eyes on the Earl of Sinnington, who, as it turned out, was such a devastatingly handsome, devastatingly masculine male.

'We're deeply honoured, my lord,' Simon Lovet said, his face pink with gratification. He was so puffed up with pride he was unable to contain his pleasure.

After greetings and compliments all round, now the moment had arrived for her to plight her troth,

Jane felt ill prepared. Though she had agreed to marry Guy St Edmond, she had thought little of what marriage to such a powerful man and living at Sinnington Castle entailed. But as she became snared by Guy's gaze, his eyes drawing her in, all other thoughts fled her mind.

Sensing her trepidation, Guy reached out a hand to her, a large hand, his long fingers encrusted with bejewelled gold rings. 'Jane? Are you willing to plight your troth to me?'

With the eyes of everyone upon her, she took his hand and let him draw her towards where the priest stood, waiting to hear them make their solemn promises. Just as she was about to reply, the sun came out and shone through the open glass windows. For a moment she forgot what she had to say. There was a circle of light on the stone floor beneath her feet—a good omen, surely, she hoped.

'Yes,' she answered at last. 'I do.'

Everyone in the room took a deep breath and the tension receded.

'And I pledge my troth to you.' He squeezed her hand. His expression softened a little. 'Give me your hand.'

The fingers on her left hand were stiff and he had to prise them open. The warm grasp sent unwanted shivers up her arm. With his free hand he took a jewelled box from his doublet and flicked it open. A magnificent gold ring encrusted with emeralds rested on a bed of white velvet. It was the most beautiful ring Jane had ever seen. Unaware that she was holding her breath, she watched as he took it out and placed it on her third finger. Perhaps it was all that the ring implied or the combination of gentleness and solemnity in Guy's deep-blue eyes as they gazed into hers, but whatever the cause, Jane's heart rate doubled and her eyes misted with tears.

'It belonged to my paternal grandmother,' he commented as if she had asked. 'I want you, Jane. Not as a countess and not as a mistress. I want you just as a woman—as *my* woman. As my wife.'

Jane was strangely warmed, but not completely assured by the endearment, believing his statement was directed at her family and guests. And yet she was caught for a moment by a yearning so strong and physical she found it hard to draw breath. How easy it would be to let appearances slip into reality. Guy was handsome, the most handsome man she had ever seen. Even if none of the gentler emotions such as love were present, they could still have a marriage. Who could predict what miracles the future might bring?

'And now,' he said, 'a kiss to seal the bargain.'

Favouring Jane with that slow, careful scrutiny that made her feel devoured, he drew her into his arms and kissed her slowly, deliberately, on the mouth. Fire shot through her and, as she gasped, her lips opened under his. His lips moved gently, but insistently against hers, as if he were determined to remember the moment. In that instant she felt the hardness of his body under the scarlet surcoat and melting sweetness flower through her bones, depriving her of strength. Guy, feeling her yield, tightened his arms to support her. Then he released her and laughed.

'Your daughter's lips taste as sweet as honey, Master Lovet.' He was impatient for the day when he could drink his fill. 'She will make a beautiful bride.' He laughed lightly to hide a perplexing emotion he had felt as Jane's lips opened under his. Not desire, nor surprise that her body should be so supple, so tender, so soft, though all these thoughts had come to him, but a strange new impulse to protect—to possess for himself all she had to offer.

'This is an excellent day's work,' Simon said. 'To a happy and rewarding marriage. May God grant the two of you a blessed and fruitful life together, and may your firstborn be a boy.'

He clapped his hands for wine to be poured to toast the match and their firstborn son. Jane lifted the goblet to her lips, but she did not drink. She would not hope for a boy and give her betrothed more confidence in himself. She noticed, however, that he drank the wine down quite easily and she eyed him distastefully. His taunting smile seared her and brought a rush of angry colour to her cheeks. He was laughing cruelly at her and her pride was stung. Jutting her chin defiantly, she glared at him before looking away.

Lowering his head to hers, his warm breath fanning her cheek, seeming to enjoy her distress, he murmured, 'We do not fool each other, do we, Jane? Neither of us wanted or asked for this marriage, but now we have plighted our troth we are stuck with it. You cannot escape me. I have a very possessive nature. In a short time you will be mine in every way, so smile and let everyone see how happy you are.'

Chapter Five

With little left to be proud of, Jane sat beside her betrothed while family and friends clustered round and offered enthusiastic congratulations and drank to their health. Despite the conversation between Jane and Guy being limited and stilted, it was a happy, lively meal with banter and descriptions of the latest tournaments and feasts at court.

When everyone had eaten their fill and the minstrels began to play, Guy stood up and held his hand out to Jane.

'May I have this dance, Jane?'

She hesitated, her eye catching three of her pretty female cousins gaping like astonished fish at the handsome earl. Having no wish to dance with him and knowing he was only asking her because it was expected of them and to needle her ire, keeping her voice low, she said, 'You honour me with your request, but would you not enjoy dancing with another choice of partner?'

'Since I know no other lady here but you, Jane, and your mother,' he said equally as quiet, 'I asked you hoping beyond reason your kind heart would take pity on a clumsy soldier and keep him from appearing a total oaf amongst the locals.'

Jane scowled at him. How cleverly he'd turned the tables. Guy St Edmond might not have a talent for dancing, as he claimed, but his persuasive skills were of the highest order. 'How clever you are,' she murmured. 'Clearly you have been born to be a diplomat.' When he held out his hand to her once more, he left her with no choice but to take it. Everyone faded into the background. All she was aware of was her betrothed's eyes holding hers until she felt her own cheeks flush beneath his regard. She was conscious of an unwilling excitement. In fact, much to her annoyance, she was very much aware of everything about him.

The moment she took his hand, Guy was leading her into the quickly forming circle as couples young and old merged together. To her surprise, caught up in the music and merriment, Jane found she was laughing—a laugh of pure animal joy as, floating like thistledown, her feet matched his in the simple steps of the dance. They separated as the pattern of the dance required, coming together and joining hands repeatedly. Her face glowed as she danced and romped her way through first one dance and then another—a lively farandole, doing a sprightly jig or a tapping of a toe and heel. Guy watched as she skipped round the room in spirals, joined him to pass under arches of hands and weaving in and out, all the while their eyes darting to each other.

Guy was fascinated by her lightheartedness. Her hair tumbled freely as a maiden's should—for until she had been bedded that's what she was. Her pink lips cried out to him for kisses, her smooth, creamy skin glowing beneath the softness of the candlelight, beckoned his trembling fingers to touch and caress. Never before had he felt such a response on merely looking at a maiden.

At one point his strong arms lifted her high and with such ease she might have been made of thistledown, his big hands spanning her fragile ribcage. It was as she hovered over him, looking down into his eyes, that he saw the flush on her face and sensed her breathing stop and felt a momentary wonder.

The festivities over, people began making their farewells and wending their way home. With a long ride ahead of them, Guy and his companions bade them all goodnight. Cedric went outside to prepare their horses. Taking Jane's hand, Guy led her through the large hall to the darkened doorway where they were hidden from view.

She looked up at him to bid him farewell. Perhaps it was the wine she had consumed or the fact that her head was still in a dizzying whirl from dancing too much, for she misjudged the distance separating them and collided with his chest. His strong arm encircled her, steadying her. She could have drawn away, but instead she stood there, her heart beating hard as his blue eyes slid to her lips, lingering on them for an endless moment. Then he purposefully lowered his head.

His mouth opened boldly over hers, his hands sliding intimately over her back and then her hips, moulding her tightly to his muscular frame. Taken by surprise by his sudden ardour, Jane stiffened, but then slid her arms shyly about his waist and returned his kiss, glorying in the feel of his lips on hers and his hard body pressed to hers.

Dizzily, she finally pulled away, and then was disappointed that he released her so readily. Her traitorous body was already throbbing to experience another kiss. Unable to trust herself, she stepped back. She must learn to fight these wanton urges, bring them under control, for she could not, must not, risk her heart. Guy raised one well-defined brow, watching her. He seemed to know exactly what was going on in her mind.

But Guy would have none of it. His freedom was of the utmost importance to him—he had no time for affairs of the heart. A man who loved too well was vulnerable.

Life passed quietly for the next four weeks. Wrapped up in his work on the estate, Jane saw nothing of Guy. In the meantime she busied herself preparing for her new role in life as the wife of a powerful man. There was much to learn and, in truth, more responsibility involved than she had expected. Guy knew it was important that she understood how the castle was run and to get to know the people who worked there. Thinking about it too much started panic boiling in her veins, so she shoved all her fears aside with a will. Her mother laughed at her, telling her she was more than capable and that she would learn as time went on.

Jane desperately hoped so. She would try to be a good wife to Guy, a good mother to his children. She would be his helpmate, if she could. At the very least she would learn to manage his house, and perhaps, she thought wistfully as she brushed her hair, they might, in time, deal well together. They were not much alike, yet many couples began life together with less in common that she and Guy shared. And he had a sense of responsibility. The way he had leaped to the defence of her reputation to save her from disgrace proved that. He was honest as well—to the point of bluntness—and his intelligence she had already noted. Even his rugged vitality was something she found attractive.

Perhaps if she worked at it, theirs could still be a good marriage.

By the time she had arranged her silken tresses

into a braid and gone down to the hall, about to seek out her mother in the undercroft, on hearing a soft footfall, she turned quickly to find the imposing figure of Guy stood just behind her.

He was a towering, masculine presence in the low-ceilinged hall. He wore the same grim expression she had seen when he had agreed to marry her. His rugged features were a mask of stone.

'Why—G-Guy,' she stammered, extremely uncomfortable with the dark way he was regarding her, his gaze narrowed and assessing.

The corner of his mouth twisted wryly in a gesture that was not quite a smile. 'I presume our engagement gives me the right to speak to you privately.'

'Of course. My father is not at home and my mother is busy in the undercroft.'

'I'm here to escort you to the castle. I trust that is in order?'

'Yes—yes, of course.'

'It's about time you saw where you are to live. And don't look so worried, Jane. I don't intend to ravish you. That's what precipitated this mess—my desire to bed you—and I'm not fool enough to repeat it.'

Jane didn't know what to say to his declaration, so she excused herself to inform her mother what she was about and to order one of the grooms to saddle her horse. She wore a cape for the day was cool and overcast. They spoke little as they rode.

As they neared the castle the road traced the crest of a hill for a space of time. The exterior of Sinnington Castle was familiar to Jane, who had ridden this way many times, but she never failed to gaze in awe at the sight of it. An aura of the rosy light of early morning still settled upon the western sky and in the distance the silhouette of the castle stood in stark contrast against the soft, billowing clouds that clustered close over the horizon. With its turrets and high ramparts and the sinister rooks perched above the gatehouse, it was a forbidding structure.

Guy pulled his horse to a halt. 'There it is, Jane—soon to be your new home. What do you think?'

Her eyes were alight with pleasure as she turned to look at him. 'It is a wondrous place, but then, I always thought so. It must seem strange to be back after being away so long.'

'Eight years is a long time. As you will see for yourself there is much to be done—although I suppose we must be thankful its crumbling walls are due to neglect and not warfare. I am enthusiastic and committed to make changes. I intend to have an architect and builders working on it very soon.' He looked at her. 'I'm sure any ideas you can come up will be appreciated.'

Jane studied his chiselled profile, realising she scarcely knew him at all. 'I wouldn't be much use. I know nothing about building castles.'

He smiled. 'Neither do I. But we can learn together—after the wedding.'

'Is—is it to be a large affair?' she asked, hoping against hope that royalty had not been invited.

Seeming to read her mind, he shook his head. He was smiling no longer. Jane saw before her the firm features and hard eyes, which the sunlight had turned to steel. A frown darkened his attractive face and his eyes looked on hers with a cool cynicism.

'Worry not, Jane. Let us not fool ourselves. This marriage is not what either of us wanted. It will be a small affair without fuss. Friends and gentry from around Cherriot Vale, and your own family, have been invited. The only family I have is my mother.'

Jane's surprise deepened. This was the first hint she'd had of any living St Edmond kin and she lifted a wondering brow at him. 'Your mother?'

'You will meet her in good time.'

'Will she be at the wedding?'

'It's most unlikely.'

'Why not?'

'She does not travel well. When my father died she remarried a gentleman by the name of Lord Courcy. His house, Rosemead, is close to London. My mother had a place at court and used to flit between one and the other, but since Lord Courcy died and she is no longer able—having taken a nasty tumble from her horse some time ago—every saint's day and holiday she invites the court to go to her at Rosemead. You see, her desire for enjoyment has not diminished, which is why she surrounds herself with her friends and entertains on a regular basis.'

'She seems an interesting lady. I'm looking forward to meeting her.'

'You will, very soon, I promise you.'

'Is she aware of our marriage?'

He nodded. 'I have written informing her. She'll be happy that I've decided to settle down at last and provide the St Edmonds with an heir.'

His careless reminder of her role in his life and what was expected of her diminished Jane's spirit, but she gave no sign of this as she fixed her gaze on the castle. Considering the distance and reserve between them at this time as both entered warily into this new phase of their lives, she dared not tweak his temper any more than she had possibly done already. Though she had glimpsed his unyielding tenacity only once, and that during his confrontation with Richard, she had nevertheless been left with the impression that there were definite limits to what Guy St Edmond would tolerate.

'I can't believe I'm going to see inside the castle at last—or that I'm going to live there,' she remarked. 'It's like a fairy tale.'

'Believe it, Jane. It's no fairy tale. You will find plenty to occupy your time at the castle.'

She glanced at him, observing how a muscle flexed in his jaw and how his eyes had darkened. A frisson of fear trembled through her and she hastily turned her head towards the castle, lest she start to weaken, but she was no test against the beauty of what was to be her new home.

On entering the courtyard, Guy dismounted, then came around to help Jane down. With her hand upon his arm, he escorted her into the great hall. It was cool and dark after the bright sunshine. Drawing a long, steadying breath, she paused in the doorway, for the sight that greeted her made her blink in momentary confusion. It was immense, with a soaring, timbered roof and stained-glass windows set high in the walls. Above, a wide gallery, supported by richly carved stone arches, wrapped around on three sides. A smooth stone floor was swept clean of rushes and two big dogs slept on the stones of a hearth so large a man could easily stand in it.

Around two dozen men were present. Some were standing, drinking ale, some seated and dining at trestle tables. They rose to their feet at the sight of her and pulled off their caps. She glanced at them shyly.

Guy said not a word, but his eyes flicked over them, and immediately, with knowing smiles on their faces, they began to disperse.

Jane found the situation amusing and rather touching. 'Is this how it's to be—all these men in the castle at all times?'

'I told you there are changes to be made—not only outside, but inside too. There have been no women here for a long time. Not since my mother. You are the first. You will get used to it in time. There's a lot going on. Knights and squires coming and going. Some to offer service, some riding out to adventures. The castle is large enough to accommodate all of us without getting in each other's way. I'll sort something out before the wedding.'

'Please don't. This large hall is ideal for them to socialise. If I have quarters of my own to escape to, I won't mind.'

'Escape?' he remarked, a steely edge to his voice and one dark brow elevated to a lofty angle. 'I hope you never feel the need to escape me, Jane.'

'Of course not. It was just a figure of speech. Anyway, I like them being around. It's a relief to me that I've been accepted—at least that's how it appears.'

'You have. They already adore you.'

'But will everyone else?' she said quietly, her eyes taking on a worried look.

'And what does that look mean?'

Sighing deeply, she shook her head. 'Nothing really. You'll think I'm being foolish.'

'Try me,' he prompted, staring down at her stiff shoulders. 'Are you concerned about how you will be received as my wife or the Countess of Sinnington?'

'Both, I suppose. The two go together. I can't pretend otherwise. I tell myself that I don't care what people think of me—but I confess I am filled with nervousness and hope that they will accept me. Whatever happens, your friends and the people you know are going to be my people. I'm going to live all my life among them and I do so want them to like me.'

'Try not to worry. Things will work out. You'll win them over,' he assured her.

'I hope so,' she murmured, wishing he'd been more concerned about how she'd fit in. 'Now, are you going to show me your castle? I am impatient to see where I am to live.'

'It will be my pleasure, my lady. Come this way. We will begin downstairs.'

From this central point were branched hallways with a labyrinth of spacious rooms, some of them somewhat gloomy and depressing.

'As you see, some of the rooms are less than cosy. You are free to make any changes that you care to make. Expense,' he added generously, 'is no object.'

Her own quarters were somewhat more elaborately furnished—as Guy explained, they were unaltered since his mother's time. Dropping her cloak on to a chair, she took her time looking around, showing a great interest in all that she saw. There were sitting rooms with a maid's chamber and her sleeping chamber overlooked the countryside beyond. The bed was large, the coverings in light blue and the walls hung with silks and imported tapestries in gentle shades of cream, blue and gold.

There was one other doorway. Watching her intently, Guy stood back as she opened it tentatively and went in. It was another bedchamber. *His* bedchamber. *His* bed. There could be no doubt of it and it spoke to Jane about the man himself. It was a soldier's room, bare of all ornament except the essentials.

The decor was plain. A large bed stood in the farthermost corner of the room, opposite the windows. It was entirely hung with purple velvet, unadorned, save for the gold cords which held back the heavy curtains. The St Edmond coat of arms was emblazoned above the bedhead. There were a few pieces of furniture in the room, whose stone walls were hung with tapestries depicting battles fought. There were two ornately carved chests against the wall and a small table standing between two chairs drawn up near the window, on which a chessboard of amethyst and silver sparkled in the light from the sconces.

Guy's voice behind her invaded her thoughts.

'Do the rooms please you?'

He was standing in the doorway, his shoulder propped against the frame. 'Please me?' Jane repeated, distracted by the way his gaze had drifted down her hair and stopped at the neckline of her gown. Instinctively she clutched the fabric together with her fingers. 'Yes—they please me—very much,' she replied, trying to take refuge in conversation and scrupulously avoiding looking at the bed. 'Are they all for me?'

'All except this one.' A faint mocking smile

touched his lips. 'I would advise you to loosen your grip on your gown before you strangle yourself. I've seen men dangling from ropes no tighter than that. Relax, Jane. I am not going to ravish you, tempting as the thought might be. Unlike Aniston, whom I am certain would have ravished you in the woods that day had I not come upon you, I fully intend waiting until our wedding night, where our marriage will be consummated here, in this bed.'

For some reason, that admission, made as it was with a tinge of regret in his voice, did much to damage Jane's resistance. The hand she clutched at her throat trembled slightly, in part from an inexplicable excitement that his presence never failed to evoke within her, and, perhaps in similar degrees, from a troubling suspicion that she was weakening to her betrothed's subtle wiles.

'Does the idea of sharing a bed with me frighten you?' he asked, taking a step towards her.

Jane's mouth went dry. 'Yes—I mean, isn't every woman apprehensive about her wedding night?' she amended quickly. 'I cannot be at ease with a man who is a virtual stranger to me.'

'We won't always be strangers.' He moved even closer, his eyes intense.

'No,' she whispered. He seemed enormous and very near. His shirt was open at the neck and she could see the corded muscles of his throat and the pulse that was beating furiously there. His powerful body emanated heat, matching the heat that was rising in her cheeks. 'Just one week…'

'Just one week,' he repeated. His biting tone carried frustration.

Raising her eyes, Jane eyed him warily. She had the feeling that something was terribly wrong. He wasn't merely objecting to the timing of their wedding. 'You—hardly looked overjoyed at the prospect of becoming a bridegroom. You—don't want the ceremony to be held yet—is that it?'

'I don't want it to be held at all,' he bit back. 'Devil take it, I don't want to marry you.'

Jane stared at him in shock, her eyes wide in her pale face. 'I don't want to marry you either,' she returned with frozen civility. 'It would have been better if we had never announced our engagement. You should have left me to weather the scandal alone. I might have been branded an outcast in Cherriot, but at least I would have had the protection of my home, where I could weather the slights and slurs, the whispers and the jeers. The last thing I want is a barbarian for a husband.'

His eyes blazed. 'Barbarian? Lady,' he warned, his voice rumbling softly above her like distant thunder, 'I haven't begun to act the barbarian. You don't want to be my wife, I assure you.'

'Then you shouldn't have agreed.'

'I was saving your reputation.'

'I didn't ask you to.'

They stared at each other for a long moment. Finally, Jane broke the tense silence. 'Please don't look at me like that. You're frightening me.'

He laughed mockingly. 'That's right. Cry foul. Plead feminine frailty.'

'Well, I can't fight you! You're much too big and stronger than I. I think you should take me home.'

Guy cursed silently. She was so lovely and de-mure. He could feel himself responding, a fact that only inflamed his anger. When she would have moved past him he gripped her arm. Slowly, with menacing deliberation, he drew her towards him, but the casual strength exerted in his fingers startled her.

'Please…don't hurt me.'

Guy stared down at her. He hadn't missed the flare of temper in her eyes, or the fright. 'I am not going to hurt you. I've never hurt a woman in my life. But surely you know that as my wife, you will have to accept my attentions.' He bent closer, his face dark and threatening. Impatiently he released her arm and gripped her chin, his fingers unintentionally brushing her breast. He was instantly aware of the contact. And so was she, he could tell by the furious blush that rose to her cheeks. 'Shall I show you how I would assert my husbandly rights?'

Stunned, poised to resist, Jane focused on his lips. His hands came up and framed her face, tilting her lips up as his descended. Of their own volition, her eyelids fell, then his mouth settled on hers, assaulting her lips with a controlled expertise that left her gasping. His tongue plundered her tender recesses, thrusting deeply, shocking her with its arousing warmth. Jane couldn't have quelled the shudder that passed through her had her life depended on it.

When Guy finally raised his head, Jane's breasts were heaving in outrage and something else. Something very much like desire.

'Did you enjoy that, Jane?' Guy goaded, his palm gliding down her throat to lie against the rapidly beating pulse at its base.

Still reeling from his devastating kiss, Jane hardly understood the question. Before she had time to recover, he bent again to let his lips hover over hers.

'You will have to get used to this when you're my wife,' he warned, his breath warm and dangerous against her mouth. 'You'll have to be available to me whenever I want you.'

Helplessly, Jane stared up at him, two bright spots of colour staining her cheeks.

His eyes smouldering, Guy stared back at her. 'Consider it,' he provoked, his fingers cupping her face. 'As my wife, you'll be at my beck and call. I could take you any time I please.'

If he was trying to destroy her resistance, he was succeeding. His voice had suddenly grown husky with sensuality, gliding through her like a hot knife through butter. He fitted their bodies together from chest to thigh. Feeling the male part of him vital and pulsing against her thighs, Jane tensed with a mingling of dread and wanton longing.

Her rigidity only encouraged Guy to pursue his course of persuasion. Again he bent his head, only this time his kiss was subtle, his tongue flicking out to touch the corner of her mouth, sending a flame flickering through her to gather in the deep recesses of her body. As his lips trailed down the sensitive skin of her throat, Jane let her eyelids flutter closed.

'I would do this to you, for instance…' His large hand moved down her throat to cup the soft full-ness of her breast, his thumb brushing her nip-ple, stroking until it stood rigidly erect. Jane was scarcely aware that the sharp gasp came from her own throat. 'And this…' Guy murmured. 'I would take my pleasure of you at my leisure, whenever I wanted.'

A shudder shook Jane's body. She had never willingly yielded her lips to any man, but her pas-sion, her desire, sweet and virginal, answered his call. Strong, sure, his lips moved slowly, languor-ously over hers once more, as if savouring her taste, her texture. There was nothing threatening in the unhurried caress. Indeed, it lured and be-guiled her senses, focusing them on his cool lips, which seemed to instinctively know how to soothe the heat rising in hers.

After the long, lengthy, satisfying kiss, his lips slid from hers to trace the curve of her throat, to heat the blood running just beneath her skin. Jane tipped her head back to give him better access. She had to grasp his shoulders to steady herself. His hands tightening about her waist, he took full advantage. He held her steady as his lips drifted lower, over the ripening swell of her breasts. She sucked in her breath, gasping when the movement pressed her flesh more firmly to his lips.

As Guy raised his head, his heated mouth found hers once more, his tongue sliding between her lips, which resulted in a kiss so intimate she could barely cope with the shattering sensation.

Guy held the reins of his desire in a grip of iron and refused to let his demons loose as he deepened the kiss and felt her lips pliable beneath his. He was satisfied that he could reach her— she would be his, in time. He would savour her slowly as she surrendered herself—all the more sweet because the end was never in doubt. She was untouched, unused to the demands of a man's hands, much less a man's body. As he claimed the softness of the lips she offered him, he laced the heady sensation into every caress and let it absorb into her senses, to lay dormant, until the next time he touched her and called it forth.

Distant voices reached them—inwards, he sighed, bringing the kiss to an end.

Jane opened her eyes and blinked up at him. Her face was delightfully flushed, her lips soft and swollen. Guy couldn't stop his wolfish grin. Nor could he resist the temptation to brush his lips over hers one last time.

'What are you doing?' Jane whispered, feeling somehow that the intimacy of moment had diminished his anger.

'Making sure.'

'Of what?'

'You.' The curve of his lips deepened. He raised her chin with his finger. 'I know I can waken all the passion in that lovely, untutored body of yours—' He broke off suddenly, realising his mistake. He could feel his body throbbing at the image his own words were arousing. He looked at her standing there, wide-eyed and vulnerable and trembling. And lovely. By God, she was lovely. He wanted her with a fierceness that took his breath away. But he couldn't have her until he married her, he reminded himself as he mentally flayed his thoughts into obedience, trying to regain some semblance of control over his throbbing body.

'Don't be concerned that my barbaric display will be repeated—at least, not until after the wedding.'

'So—you are going to marry me?' she whispered. A dozen conflicting emotions warred within her: anger, humiliation, wounded pride, regret. She had truly wanted the opportunity to make this ill-fated marriage work. Her feelings were nebulous, chaotic, yet one stood out clearly: frustrated desire. She hadn't wanted Guy to stop kissing her.

'We have plighted our troth. I shall honour my vow. You're very lovely, Jane—more beautiful than any of the bird-witted creatures who preen and saunter about the court.'

She forced a smile. 'You flatter me.'

'It's not flattery.' His face was serious. A lock of dark hair had fallen over his brow and the light from the window softened his angular face. There was an intensity in his eyes which held her own, and when he spoke his voice was low and husky.

'The gentlemen of the court will be enchanted by you. What chance has a common, hard-bitten warrior with so many elegant lords as rivals?'

Jane refused to take him seriously. 'It's what lies beneath the elegance that counts. And you're not a common soldier. You're an earl, which is a high rank indeed.'

'You have an uncommon honesty in such matters—unlike most women.' There was a gleam of battle in Jane's eyes. He gave her a hard look. She might look fragile, but he was beginning to suspect she was as strong as steel inside.

'Many men see independence in a woman as a threat. You could have any woman at court.'

'Because I'm an earl?'

She chewed her lip in contemplation, for his remark had not been a flippant one. 'Certainly not for your graciousness or your charm. But a woman would be a fool if she saw only the hero and the glitter of your title,' she answered with a smile and an inclination of her head. The wariness left his eyes and a warmth kindled in their depths, striking like a burning arrow in her heart.

He gave her a long, silent look which surprised her, for he was not usually at a loss for words. His expression was unreadable as he glanced beyond her and then back to her face. His stare was admiring. 'You're a strange creature, Jane Lovet. Just as I think I'm getting to know you, you say something that surprises me.'

'May the Good Lord spare me from becoming predictable.'

'I doubt you'll ever be that. That's your charm,' he replied, returning to his carefree manner. 'Now I am reminded that you have not yet eaten. Come—dine with me. It's your first visit to your new home. I cannot send you away without refreshment.'

Jane laughed as they retraced their steps. 'You don't intend for me to starve?'

'You're determined to think of me as a barbarian,' he retorted with a quirk of his lips.

'Many have said so. And then there is my—'

Her words brought him to a halt. He turned and gave her a dark look. 'Your brother. And upon that you condemn me.' His mood when he walked on was once more cold and forbidding.

She hurried after him. 'I don't condemn you, Guy. People can say what they want. I prefer to make up my own mind—but there are some things that will always be between us.'

'That's true,' he bit back.

Jane forced a laugh in an attempt to dispel the seriousness of the moment. 'Besides, don't they say that women are drawn to men who have a mystery about them? Now, to begin proving yourself to me—unless it really is your intention to starve me to death—you had better feed me. I am ravenous.'

She reached down to retrieve her cloak, which had slipped from the chair on to the floor. His gaze was drawn to the low neckline of her bodice, which displayed a generous view of her breasts. When he swallowed and his fingers tightened upon the door-latch, she put her hand to cover her décolletage.

'Devil take it, Jane!' His lack of composure showed in the depth of his voice. 'How am I ever going to restrain myself until our wedding with so much temptation before me?'

'Restraint is good for the soul, my lord,' she challenged with a wicked smile, dancing out of his way when he would have caught her to him once more.

'Heathen!' He gave a hearty laugh and followed her out of the room.

* * *

Arriving at the castle where a small contingent of guests had already arrived to celebrate the wedding, Jane, her mother and Kate were shown to her quarters. Jane would remain here until the ceremony, which had been arranged for midday the following day. She would not see Guy until then.

In the strange bed, Jane lay awake for most of the night, listening to voices raised in ribald laughter from the hall below. Around midnight she was aware of someone moving about in the room beyond the connecting door. She heard voices softly spoken, one of them Guy's. Eventually they fell silent, but lamplight shone from the crack beneath the door, and she listened, until she fell asleep to the steady sound of a measured tread on the bare floorboards.

The wedding day dawned bright and sunny, with a slight breeze that fluttered the flags on the castle's turrets. A maid brought Jane bread and meat to sustain her through the long day, but her stomach was fluttering with nerves so badly she couldn't eat a thing. A great wooden barrel of a bath was rolled in by two serving men, following close behind by maids carrying jug after jug of hot water.

Jane's mother and Kate washed her hair and helped her to bathe and assisted her to dress and tie the laces of her gown, exclaiming how pretty she looked. Blanche, alternately giggling and gasping, was more excited than the bride as she watched her big sister put on her wedding gown, which was blue—blue being the traditional colour of purity. It was embroidered with deep-blue flowers, with a paler-blue panel set into the front of the bodice. Her slippers were of blue satin. She wore her hair loose, the honey-gold mane rippling down her spine to her waist.

'You are so beautiful. You look perfect,' her mother said, adjusting the circlet of orange blossoms that adorned the golden head of her eldest daughter. Returning Crusaders had brought back this Saracen tradition of weaving orange blossoms into a crown wreath. Each flower had a particular meaning. In her hands she carried a small bouquet of herbs for luck and fertility.

Stiff and unsmiling and with a strange sense of unreality, Jane descended the stairs. The mighty castle loomed upwards, overpowering in its intensity, and she, small and insignificant, stepped into the hall. She was numb to the world about her. Followed by her family, Jane fixed her gaze on her husband-to-be.

Tall and powerful he stood, garmented regally in black velvet and flawless white. She was reminded of Satan. Handsome. Ruthless—he could draw her soul from her body and never feel remorse. If she were brave, she would turn now and flee from the insanity of what she was about to do. This marriage had been forced on them both and she must never forget that he was marrying her for no other reason than to avoid scandal and for the children she would eventually give him.

When the conversation in the hall became subdued, Guy turned in the direction of the stairs, as though he felt her presence. For a moment he paused, mesmerised. A slow smile of admiration swept across his face as he watched his bride descend the stairs, cool and serene, like a high priestess descending the temple steps.

Reaching the last step, Jane paused and stared at her future husband like the prey entranced by the predator. She was momentarily transfixed by

the way his vivid blue eyes glowed in the light—
his stare stayed fixed on her intently.

Guy waited immovably. Those present held their
breaths. Their looks took on a palpable tension as
the bride looked at her groom as if she were about
to take to her heels and run.

Without thinking what she was doing, as if he
had wordlessly called her, Jane took a step towards him and then another. Belatedly realising
that he was forcing his young bride to come to
him, Guy met her halfway, looking down into
her eyes with unconcealed admiration, seeing the
strain on her face. He sensed that she still ago-
nised over her decision to wed him. The war of
emotion was transparent on her lovely face.

'You look exquisite,' he murmured, raising her
hand to his lips. 'Are you ready to become my
wife, Jane?'

Her gaze fixed on him. There was a splendid radiance about his dark male beauty today, his glowing skin clean-shaved, his black hair combed and
tamed neatly into place. Very well, she thought.
So she was marrying the man, and once she spoke
those vows she would never be free. After a long

moment she felt a softening inside her and she slowly yielded.

'Yes, I am ready.'

Stretching out a strong, brown hand, he offered it to her. Placing her hand in his, he escorted her to where the priest was waiting to perform the ceremony. She stood by his side and there was a moment when all the sounds in the hall fell into silence. It was as if there was only Guy and Jane alone in the whole world.

They slid to their knees and bowed their heads to pray for the blessings of God. Time stood still as they were swept into the marriage ceremony, which lasted almost an hour. It was a private plighting of promises, some of it in Latin, so half the vows were incomprehensible to Jane.

Then, finally, it was over and she rose on shaky limbs as her new husband drew to his full height. Arching a brow, he looked down at her, his blue eyes holding hers.

'I believe it is customary for the groom to kiss the bride,' he said.

'Yes,' she replied, her voice nervous and strained.

His fingers moved around the delicate bones

of her jaw and gripped it firmly so she could not move her face away while his other arm slid behind her back. He crushed her to him suddenly in a fierce, possessive embrace. Jane felt the eyes of everyone present on them, but Guy seemed not to mind. On the contrary, he seemed to welcome their stares. His arm was like a band of iron around her, pressing her tighter against him. His head lowered and his parted lips moved over hers in a passionate kiss.

His lips were searing, demanding. Jane considered the kiss too sensual for such public display. She felt helpless and aroused and angry with herself and him, especially when she heard the ribald cheers of some of the male guests resound around them.

At last his grip slackened and she could breathe. Her quivering mouth burned from his blistering lips. She turned and smiled tremulously as everyone came up to them to wish them well. Reverently Guy placed his hand on her arm and escorted her out of the castle into the inner bailey and through to the huge courtyard beyond.

A crowd of a thousand or so people who lived and worked in and around Cherriot Vale waited to catch sight of the earl and his countess. Guy's powerful voice rang out, carrying to the far reaches of the crowd as he introduced his wife, demanding that the same fealty they gave to him should be given to his wife. His stern gaze passed over the crowd and for one heartstopping moment there was silence. Then, to Guy's relief, the noise started as a slow rumble, getting louder until it was almost deafening and they greeted his bride with uninhibited, heartfelt enthusiasm, awed by a power too potent to resist.

Guy cynically put this down to the large quantities of ale and food he had ordered to be distributed among them rather than their acceptance of her as the Countess of Sinnington. Oblivious to this, tears of poignant gratitude were in Jane's eyes as he escorted her back into the castle.

The rest of the day was a blur to Jane. She sat beside her husband at the wedding breakfast, for it was now her place. Ale and wine flowed freely—some of the best to be had from France—although the bride and groom drank sparingly. Tables loaded with food were laid out with as many people packed inside the great hall as could be housed. The noise became a cacophony of voices and laughter and singers and jesters, punctuated only by the endless toasts.

Already anticipating the night, Guy played the doting bridegroom to the hilt, remaining at Jane's side throughout the day. Nearing the end he rose to his feet and, gathering the entire hall to silence with a look, he raised his goblet to toast to his bride. Everyone drank and cheered.

The time was fast approaching when Jane would have to take her leave. Not only her mind, but her whole body seemed churned with a mixture of feelings—she was full of wonderment that she was now the wife of the Earl of Sinnington and was mistress of Sinnington Castle. But above all these other feelings she was fearful of what lay ahead of her in this first night of marriage.

She knew exactly what to expect and her nerves were jangling. But what woman would not want to take the handsome Guy St Edmond to her bed? When she thought of all the times his words and actions had angered her, even then he had seemed to melt her very bones. Their first night as husband and wife together was going to produce some anxiety and she hoped Guy would do all in his power to make it as easy as possible for her.

She was relieved he had agreed to forgo the bedding ceremony, when, with coarse teasing and joking, the wedding party would escort the bride and groom to their chamber. In the presence of Jane's parents, the priest had blessed the bed earlier and Jane considered that was enough.

Her mother and Kate accompanied her to the bedchamber. First they unpinned her hair and brushed it out, before divesting her of her finery. When they finally left her alone wearing a diaphanous nightgown and tempted her with honey mead to calm her nerves, she thrust her arms into her robe and wrapped it around her as if donning armour for battle.

Her gaze travelled round the room, coming to rest on the great bed. Wrapping her arms around her waist, she tried to imagine what he would do to her. Her cheeks heated merely to ponder what the night might hold, for she had a feeling that when he came through that door, he was going to do all the delicious things to her that would make it impossible for her to resist.

Hearing a movement outside the door from

her cushioned seat in the window embrasure in the dimly lit chamber, she looked towards it and steadied herself against a frisson of awareness as the door opened and Guy strode in wearing a rich velvet robe.

He had expected her to be waiting for him in bed. The sight of her nearly took his breath away. Tapers cast their flickering radiance on the long, honey-gold hair that tumbled in soft, glorious disarray around her shoulders, the colour in stark contrast to her crimson robe, creating a vision of beauty beyond compare. His eyes swept over her in a lingering caress, evoking a blush that left her cheeks nearly as red as her robe.

He smiled at her as he closed the door behind him. Jane was so nervous she found it impossible to respond. Her heart beat faster as he crossed the room, gazing at her in open admiration. When he was close, she was suddenly struck by the way the light from the candles played along the rugged line of his iron jaw, softening all the harsh planes and angles of his face.

'I almost thought you would be in bed pretend-

186 The Devil Claims a Wife

ing to be asleep. Are you waiting for me?' he asked in a low, husky murmur.

'Where else would I be?' she murmured.

'I did wonder if you would have flown. I'm glad you didn't.'

She blushed at his flattering stare and lowered her head as he came to stand in front of her.

'I can't believe that after all that has transpired, you are really mine,' he said, taking her hand and raising her to her feet.

She lifted her head and gazed into his eyes. 'Soon, if we are fortunate, you will have what you really want—a child.' There was a trace of bitterness in her voice, but her husband's mind was so steeped in lust he failed to notice. 'You should be well pleased.'

Chapter Six

Guy lowered his head and his parted lips played upon hers as he gave reply. 'Aye, my love, and we shall begin tonight. I am the luckiest of men.'

Holding her stare, he glimpsed the apprehension and naked fear within her eyes before she managed to hide it. A betrayal now? he wondered. Surely not. 'This is our wedding night, Jane, but I will not force you.'

'You won't have to do that.' She saw relief enter his eyes and she realised how vulnerable he was.

Guy brushed her cheek with the backs of his fingers, then murmured wonderingly, 'You're trembling.' Suddenly a chuckle came from deep inside his chest. 'What is it, my love? Do you think me a beast about to rend you upon my bed? Ah, Jane, this time of love is not a time for taking, but a time of giving and for sharing.'

His eyes revelled in their freedom as they feasted hungrily on her beauty, seeking every charm once hidden from him. Jane felt devoured and it took an effort of her will to remain pliant beneath his probing eyes.

'It is my intent,' she murmured softly, 'to be your wife in every way, whatever your desire.'

Guy's long-starved passions flared high, smothering the doubts and leaving only a small suspicion to nibble at the edge of his consciousness. This, too, he discarded. This night, and all the nights to follow, was fully worth the risk.

Again he bent to place a soft kiss on her lips, then drew back and began to unfasten the ties of her robe. All the while he stared into her eyes in sensuous challenge, sharpened by a trace of insolence, as though he would prove to her now who was in charge. She stood still, keenly recalling the desperate longing that had kept her awake for so many nights.

Instinct deeper than reason told her not to fight him. She was not sure it was wise, in any case, to argue with him—she was intimidated by him and more aroused than she cared to admit. All she could think about were the things he would do to her and the pleasure she would feel. Even now her traitorous body grew warm as her flush spread to every part of her body.

The robe slithered to the floor. Guy then began work on her nightdress, unfastening the ties at her throat. There was a haste in him now to know and to touch every part of her, to acquaint himself with her body, to claim her as his own, to let his lips wander at will over her soft flesh. At last the offending garment fell open and, slipping off her shoulders, it fell unheeded to her feet.

'There,' he breathed, his slow, steady hands warm and gentle as he placed them on her shoulders and drew her into his embrace.

Jane forgot all. A whisper of a sigh escaped her as, with an eagerness born of the pleasures that were already creeping into her body, she raised herself on slim toes, reaching parted lips to meet his and sliding silken arms about his neck. She came to him with a fervour that astounded him, having no thought of holding back or refusing him. Locked in each other's embrace, they were caught up in the fierce tide of passion. Their lips blended with an impatient urgency, their kisses now savage and fierce, devouring with hungry impatience.

Releasing her, Guy threw off his robe. His strong muscular body, eternally masculine, proud, savage and determined, gleamed in the soft light of the candles. Seeing him thus, a tremor of alarmed admiration seared through Jane. In the glow of lamplight, his skin was like oiled bronze, the heavy muscles in his arms and shoulders and thighs taut. Completely naked he was splendid, she realised, magnificent. He bent and swept her up into his arms and his eyes met hers with an intensity that took her breath away. His gaze lowered and she was devoured as he boldly drank his fill of the vision of her creamy flesh.

Vaguely, Jane was aware of the tremor in his arms as he carried her to the enormous bed. Beneath the edge of the heavy drapes that bordered the high tester, he withdrew his arm, letting her legs slide down against him. The blue flame of his eyes flared bright. His mouth lowered to savour the sweet, heady nectar of her lips and his tongue touched hers in provocative play. Like a feather caught on an airy breeze he gently pushed her back so that she lay on the bed. He leaned over her and Jane shivered in ecstasy as his hands leisurely stroked downwards over the roundness of her breasts, the shock of his bold, manly flesh startling and awesome.

She looked up at him, unable to bear his attention, the sweet torture he so freely gave her. 'Is this it?' she whispered. 'Is this what marriage is all about?'

Guy smiled. 'Listen, my love, and mark my words well.' He drew her closer. 'This is it. The playing is over.'

His voice was low and husky in her ears and Jane had to dip deeply into her reservoir of will to dispel the slow numbing of her defences. The pressure of his touch was light, but to her it felt like a trap of steel. She was aware of his naked chest and the manly feel of his lean, muscular body pressed to hers, while he was made totally aware of her naked form. They stared at each other for a second of suspended time, which could as well have been an hour or more. Then slowly, almost haltingly, Guy lowered his mouth to hers.

The shock was abrupt for them both and the gentle touch of his lips turned to a heated, crushing demand. Passions flared and their needs grew, mounting on soaring wings. Passion had become raw hunger and desperate need—everything else was cindered beneath the white heat of their mutual desires. It happened quickly, coming upon them in a rush, the awakened fires, the hungering lusts, the bittersweet ache of passion so long restrained. Guy clasped the lithe form in his arms. The warmth and softness of her set his mind and body aflame.

It seemed to Jane as though they sought to unify their bodies into one single being—as though by kissing they gave to each other their life's breath. She knew she shouldn't want this, but she did. She knew that it was dangerous, but she wasn't afraid. Her world turned to giddy spirals. As if they had a will of their own, Jane's arms wound themselves about his neck. The pounding of her heart refused to slow and she reviewed the condition of her mind as if from a distance. If not held in check by her struggling will, her hands might have urged him back, but she clung to him as though to hold him even closer, his name moaning in her throat.

She was aware of his desires, knowing he wanted her to yield. Their bodies fitted together, breast to breast, thigh to thigh, mouths fused, moving, caressing, enfolding, their tongues touching. She waited for the screaming denial to come from some dark, unfeeling recess of her mind, this time determined to vanquish its intrusion. But she was met with only empty silence as if her conscience watched in amused approval.

When his lips left hers and he pressed fevered kisses along the ivory column of her throat and the gentle swell of her breasts, throwing back her head to allow him easy access, with closed eyes and breathing quickly, Jane murmured, 'Please stop. I don't think I can stand more of this.'

He chuckled low and deep. 'Yes, you can,' he said, his mouth going even lower. 'We have only just begun. You are more of a woman than I thought. I will teach you to provoke me, Jane. I will have you begging for mercy, you beautiful, irresistible girl.'

From that moment onwards, Jane stopped belonging to herself. As she found again the lips that had already intoxicated her once, she also recaptured the whirlwind of unknown sensations, whose memory had left a dim yearning deep in her flesh. Everything came alive within her.

Guy's knowledgeable fingers stroked and caressed the contours of her body, her shapely thighs, while his restless blood clamoured for a deeper fulfilment. There was a haste in him to know and touch every part of her, to claim her as his own. She held his head, wrapping her arms about it as again his mouth slid to her breast, taking the hardness of her rosy nipple in his mouth.

Glowing waves of pleasure spread like liquid fire through Jane's body as he gently sucked and teased. Her head thrashed from side to side and a breathless moan slipped from her as his lips continued to caress a pink, pliant crest. His tongue branded her with its fiery touch and her lithe form shook with the fervour that built within her. Raising his face to hers, Guy placed his mouth suddenly on hers, tasting with a hunger they both shared.

Jane closed her eyes. Within raged confusion and contradiction. With the promise of a fulfilment which nothing would hinder, her pleasure had risen to such heights that she was frightened by it. While only a moment before she had been ready to surrender, now she rebelled against seduction. She threw herself back, gasping, trying to escape from those hands whose every gesture brought to her new springs of rapture.

'Oh, please,' she gasped, 'do not do this. Please—you must stop…I never meant…'

'Nay, my love, we have come too far to deny ourselves now.'

He laughed without any sign of contrition and once more Jane succumbed to his superior strength. Her blood began to course more quickly through her veins. A rush of desire flashed deep within her and spread through her whole being. With breathless curiosity the surprising new sensations she was experiencing beneath his naked body and the thrusting of his manhood between her open thighs dissolved her will.

When he finally took her she let herself flow, unresisting, along the stream of voluptuousness. She did not cry out against the pain, for every particle of her body was furiously calling for domination by her master. Her green eyes opened wide, then waves of pleasure swept her from one summit to another in an ecstasy she had never known before. With her head thrown back over the edge of the bed, she heard the soft, plaintive moan and suddenly recognised her own voice.

With untiring patience he would bring her back to him, each time more yielding, warm and moaning, with fever-bright eyes. The sensual haze that descended on her made her wonder why she fought him. All she could comprehend was how gentle he was, how loving, and when he kissed her, there was nothing she could do but kiss him back. She struggled and surrendered in turn, but when the emotion she could not control had reached its peak, she felt utterly spent.

Then a finger touched her chin and raised it until she looked full into his soft, deep blue eyes. They were not smiling, but intense to such a degree that she was almost startled. He was easing her back on to the bed, using his strength, kneeling over her, and her skin glowed like a pearl.

She should not be letting him do this again, Jane told herself feverishly. She should not be allowing him to enslave her like this. But he was already rearing over her, his hands sliding up her thighs and curling over them. His tongue flicked against her and she arched up like a bow. She was surprised at her own abandon, for she came to him again, pressing to him, answering his every passion with her own, losing all awareness of herself as her senses mastered her entirely. Between them they had created a need for each other that was now consuming them, overwhelming them, blotting out everything around them. Quenching that raging thirst would take more than a few moments' desperate embrace. But it was now no longer a matter of choice. Desire had become necessity. She sighed as his lips found her breasts, his hand boldly stroking her thighs. He held her, his lips caressing her softly, stirring her until her mouth parted beneath the exquisite agony of it.

He did not rush to possess her as he had done before, but savoured each passing moment of pleasure, and in the waiting a budding ecstasy began to bloom and grow within Jane, a feeling which she could neither quench nor deny. His delay attacked her senses, the throbbing heat of him warmed her and she began to respond to his ardent kisses, the hot flame of heat enveloping her so that she was no longer herself, but his.

His hands were beneath her hips, lifting her to him. At last he slid into her, to the very core of her, sinking deeper and pulling away. There was something pagan that spoke to a part of her she had not known was there, and he took her to a place she had never known before as once again they tasted the full joy of their mutual union. Her moans were of pleasure, until the climax swept over them with a power they had thought unimaginable. Jane was his again and she revelled in the sweetness of bliss.

When at last their passion was spent and she was nestled beside his manly warmth, Jane's mind came together from the nether regions where it had fled what seemed like a long time ago. She wasn't sure what was happening to her, but the exquisite pleasure she had taken in their lovemaking was something she had not expected to find. It was a pleasure that was more than physical, but she felt there was a part of him she could not reach.

'You are mine now, Jane,' he murmured, gently kissing the top of her head, 'my wife in every sense, and from this moment on this is how it will be between us.'

His words stirred Jane back to awareness. Pulling away from him, Jane stared into his eyes, feeling his possession of her and her own willingness to be possessed.

My God, could she be falling in love with him?

she wondered, and then firmly dismissed the notion. No, she absolutely was not falling in love with him. For her there would always be the ideal. Not only must she love, but she must be loved equally in return. Anything less was unacceptable. Besides, she absolutely refused to fall in love with a man who regarded her as nothing more than a brood mare.

Guy opened his eyes when sunlight streamed across the bed. Jane was asleep beside him, curled up in a nest of covers, her hair a tangle of silken tresses about her head. His heart turned over at the sight of her. She was warm and soft, her face serene in slumber, her dark curling lashes sweeping her cheeks.

The aching memory of her response to him, the open generosity of her lovemaking, touched him deeply. He could succumb to the temptation of a beautiful woman as easily as the average man, but he had never experienced anything like what he was beginning to feel for his wife. He was uncomfortable with the feeling. Cynically, he tried to ignore the protective need she roused in him. It had been many years since a woman had touched that chord in him. The memory brought a return of bitterness he had thought long dead. It was an experience he had vowed never to repeat. Isabel's betrayal had been as though a part of him had been severed, and the only way to staunch the blood had been to make sure he never fell for a woman again. Which he had done, until Jane Lovet had come along. Just one night in her bed and gone was the reserve, the restraint he exercised over all aspects of his life.

Here he was, trapped by a guileless woman, all his self-esteem set aside. The longer he remained with her, her hold on him would grow stronger, and before he knew it he would have become enslaved and no longer be his own master. It was a situation he could not even begin to contemplate.

The arrival of the king's messenger summoning him to Westminster could not have come at a more appropriate time.

A smile drifted across Jane's face as she stood at the top of the stairs and surveyed the hall below. The servants had done their work and now there was no sign of the previous day's revelries. Several knights slouched on benches against the walls, most of them sleeping off the effects of too much liquor. Some slowly lifted their faces to her and with an effort managed to open their eyes, their expressions pained and strained. One or two managed a wincing smile.

Shaking her head in amusement, she descended the stairs and walked across the hall to the door.

Guy came in from the courtyard. Having left her slumbering not more than half an hour before, he was surprised to see her up and dressed. The contrast between her very proper appearance and her lusty performance of a short while ago fired his interest anew. Even he was a little shocked by his appetite for her. His speculative gaze riveted on her with rapt fascination.

'Good morning again, Jane. I trust you slept well?'

'Very well,' she replied in a voice that was an embarrassed whisper, but her eyes were bright and sparkling. 'I was just going to take a walk outside. As you see, everyone is suffering the after-effects of the wedding.'

Guy's glance at his fellow knights and the smug grin that accompanied it was without sympathy.

'They're paying the price of an orgy of drunkenness—unlike myself. I plead complete innocence.'

Jane shot him a reproving look. 'Had you not been otherwise engaged with your wife, my lord, I have no doubt you would have been as drunk as the rest of them and in dire need of a restorative.'

The look he gave her was positively wicked. 'There's only one kind of restorative I am interested in, Jane. I shall be more than happy for you to administer it to me at a later date. Come. Allow me to accompany you outside where you can bid your husband a safe journey.'

She stared at him for a speechless moment. 'What journey? Where can you possibly be rushing off to at a moment's notice?'

Avoiding her eyes, he strode out into the courtyard. 'I have a message from the king. I'm going away for a few days.'

'Going away? Where?' Jane demanded, having to run to keep up with him.

'To London. To the court. I am needed for urgent consultations.'

'London?' she gasped, trying to ignore the panic that was making her heart race. 'But—what about everything here? What about me?'

'What about you?'

'Well, you can't just go like this.'

'Why not?' he asked with iron politeness.

'Can I go with you?'

'No. You will remain here.'

The news hit her like a physical blow. Her cheeks flamed with indignation. 'You mean to abandon me the morning after our wedding? You really are leaving me here alone?'

'The castle is full of servants. You won't be alone.'

'But—you can't do that.'

'Yes, I can, Jane,' he told her firmly, his eyes hardening. 'You'll be perfectly all right. The servants will look after you and I'm sure you will find plenty to occupy your time.'

'Did you know you would be leaving last night?'

'No,' he replied, walking briskly to where Cedric was waiting with the horses. 'I have very little time. If you have something to say, please get it over with.'

Her back ramrod straight and her eyes jewel bright, she said, 'I—I thought—after last night, we—we…' She fluttered a hand, not knowing quite what to say. She went on. 'I—I see now I was wrong about your feelings. I—I will miss you.'

There was an odd, searching look in his eyes. 'Will you?'

She nodded. 'Though I cannot see why you have to go. We've been married less than a day and you will not be here when I need you most.'

Slowly, he turned and for a moment she saw his profile outlined, hard as a cameo, against the light coming from the sun behind. Then he was facing her again. Taking her face between his big hands, he kissed her lips. It was brief and without passion. And then he was hoisting himself up into the saddle. He looked down at her. 'I'll be gone a week, no more.' Then he was gone, leaving his wife staring after him.

'Of all the self-centred, heartless blackguards! He cannot even speak the truth,' she whispered. 'He will never return.'

Each day that passed was longer than the one before. She refused to go home. She shuddered to think how her father would react if he were to find out her husband had abandoned her the morning after their wedding. But why had he left her? What did it mean? And why should she care?

After three days, clear-headed and able to think and attack problems, she dispassionately confronted her position in its entirety, concentrating on the realities of her future. She had to depend on herself. For whatever reason Guy was gone to London—to partake of courtly pleasures?—she dispelled the hurt of his betrayal. For her there was work to be done.

The castle had been managed by the bailiff and run by old retainers since the demise of the old earl. Jane had been pleasantly surprised to discover how efficient the servants were. Before her marriage when she had visited the castle, some of them had shown her kindness, while others looked upon her as the girl from Cherriot and considered her no better than they were. It was a situation she had been determined to rectify as soon as she became mistress in her new home.

Under the watchful eye of the bailiff, she took the matter in hand from the start, refusing to allow him to interfere in a matter which she had to sort out herself if she was to gain their respect. After just one week in which she went out of her way to be courteous and polite, yet always firm in making her preferences for this and that known, she evinced a vivacious charm and caring thoughtfulness that evoked their reluctant fondness.

The servants, male and female, both inside and out, thought she was beautiful and her airy laughter and ever-ready humour infected them all. With her presence, it seemed the sun shone brighter and the day grew warmer. Their hearts were lightened and they attacked their chores with a zealous determination to please her. The great castle came alive and functioned as never before.

As the days became weeks and she became convinced that Guy had truly abandoned her, try though she might to calm her fears and push her doubts aside, it seemed an eternity had passed when he finally returned late one night.

She was crossing the empty hall to the stairs when the door opened. She whirled round, startled. His tall figure was outlined in the doorway. She paused and watched him stride halfway towards her and then he stopped.

'So, you came back,' she breathed, giving no

hint of her own soaring joy. 'I'm sorry. You gave me a frightful turn.'

'Since when have you been such a nervous type?'

'Since spending the last six weeks alone!'

'I'm back now.' His voice sounded strange, studiedly casual.

'I see that.'

'Are you glad to see me?'

'You could have written. You could have let me know when you were coming back.'

'I should have. I apologise.'

He looked at her intently, hiding his surprise. The last time he'd seen her she was pale and anguished at his leaving. Before him now stood another Jane, vibrant in health. Clad in a dark-green gown, her sunburst hair tumbled flowing over her shoulders and back. She straightened proudly to meet his gaze as he soaked up the sight of her, for which he was more thirsty than water by far.

'Why aren't you in bed?'

She came towards him from the shadows and the candlelight made her eyes sparkle. 'I thought you had left me. I thought I would never see you again. You abandoned me at a time when I needed you most. In the beginning people were—not kind.'

'But you survived.'

'It has been hard winning their trust.'

For a moment Guy gazed at her with some surprise. He had borne a heavy load of self-recrimination for the way he had left her. When the king's messenger had come the morning after his wedding, summoning him to court on an urgent matter—which, to his annoyance, he found to be nothing more than to inspect two of his majesty's newly arrived horses from France—he should have delayed his departure instead of haring off. And when he was at Westminster there were duties that made it impossible for him to leave. Yet what he had done was cruelly unjust.

He should have been conscious of her feelings on a matter that was sure to worry her. It was inevitable that she would meet with hostility from some—and how humiliating would that have been for her? With a twinge of pity and a good deal of self-condemnation for leaving her alone at a time when she had needed him, he admitted that though she was young, she had been very brave, and he shouldn't have left the hostility to her to chance.

He'd missed her since he had ridden off six weeks ago and been too stubborn to admit it.

'I shouldn't have left you alone. You had no way of knowing what it would be like living here. Nothing had prepared you. You had to face problems you had never encountered, with which you had no way of dealing, a fact I failed to understand.'

'Yes, well—as you said, I survived.'

'Are you glad to see me, Jane?'

'Of course I am,' she said quietly.

'You've a strange way of showing it.'

'I—I have a headache and I'm out of sorts and very tired. I'm sorry if I'm not as enthusiastic as you expected me to be. You—shouldn't have surprised me like that.'

He didn't reply, merely gave her a strange look she couldn't quite fathom. His deep-blue eyes were sober and seemed to be examining her as though looking for some change. It made her quite uncomfortable.

'I was just going to bed. Is there anything you want before I do?'

He shook his head. 'No. You go. I won't disturb you. We'll talk in the morning.'

'Thank you. Goodnight, Guy.'

She left him then, disturbed by that peculiar look he had given her. Something had changed between them. She could sense it. It was as though an invisible wall had sprung up between them.

Guy was remote during the days that followed. He was polite and considerate, and that was somehow much worse than harsh words or anger would have been. He spent most of his time out of doors either hunting, hawking or attending to matters on the estate. They did not share the same bed so they did not make love. The strain was almost unbearable, so when he suggested she join them in their hawking party she was happy to accept.

She rode with Cedric along a winding stretch of rutted road through the woods. The hood of her cloak fell away and her hair tumbled free of its simple ties, falling around her shoulders in shimmering waves.

Eventually the woods gave way to a clearing and fields beyond. A large party of Guy's men were milling around with their falcons, their horses restive. It was a beautiful day and glorious country for hawking. The gently rolling hills promised fast galloping, the meadows full of rabbits and the woods full of birds.

Seeing Guy, she rode towards him. Wearing a leather jerkin and hose, talking and joking with his men, he looked so relaxed atop his great, powerful horse, and he spoke to them with such lazy good humour that she could hardly believe he was the same relentless, predatory seducer who had stalked her and acquired her hand in marriage. It was as if he were two people, one she could like very much and one she feared and mistrusted— with excellent reason when she considered the reputation he had acquired as a ruthless soldier and his neglect of her after their wedding, for which she found hard to forgive.

Guy watched her approach astride her dark, dappled-grey mare, a look of unconcealed appreciation on his handsome face as he surveyed her jaunty bright-gold riding habit, the skirt spread out behind her and rippling over the mare's rump.

'How can you look so lovely so early?' he asked, the blue eyes probing hers, his lips sliding upwards at a corner. Leaning over, he took her gloved hand in his and lifted it to his mouth. 'Are you ready for your first lesson?'

Unable to contain her own smile, Jane cast a coy glance upwards. For the life of her she couldn't deny the way her senses seemed to soar to bracing heights in his presence. 'Absolutely—although I shall probably make a complete idiot of myself and do everything wrong.'

'No, you won't. I have every confidence in you—and John, my falconer, and myself, will explain everything as we go along.'

Her mare snickered and his stallion's ears shot forwards. Sliding from the saddle, he gestured to John who had a hooded merlin on his wrist, her tiny bells jingling as she fluttered a little. Guy helped Jane down and took the merlin from the falconer.

'I would like to present to you this merlin, Jane. Her name is Melody.'

'She's adorable—or she will be when the hood is removed.'

Handing her a glove, he asked her to slip it on. As soon as she did so, he secured the merlin's claws with the jesses on her glove. 'Once the hood is removed, do not blink or she might attack, and don't hold her too far away from you otherwise she will flap her wings as a sign to bring her closer. Do you understand?'

'Perfectly. I'm just wondering what I can do to stop myself blinking.'

'Don't worry. You'll soon get the hang of it.'

As the merlin moved she turned to her, this beautiful, powerful bird on her arm, with her hood fashioned from soft leather and a jaunty plume of blue-and-gold feathers. She was adorable and, with her soft hood and sweet-sounding bells, might have been a spoiled pet, but her claws, sharp beak and powerful wings were a reminder of her true character.

'I think she likes you,' Guy said, 'but then what bird in its right mind would not—to find itself perched on the arm of the beautiful Countess of Sinnington.'

His compliment spoken in soft, warm tones helped her relax. 'Countess or not, I doubt my arm is sufficiently strong enough to carry her whilst I'm riding.'

Guy took the falcon from her and handed it to the falconer. 'Don't worry. I'll hand her back to you when we are in the field. It's some way off, but no doubt you are familiar with the countryside.'

'I know it well. The woods are where, as a child, I climbed trees with my brother and searched for mushrooms, and the fields are where I picked wildflowers.'

'One day you and I will pick mushrooms together. They are a favourite of mine.'

She glanced at him with surprise. 'Forgive me, but I can't imagine you indulging in anything as mundane as picking mushrooms.'

He laughed. 'There are many things I do that would surprise you.'

Lifting her back into the saddle, together they followed the others and the tracking dogs out into the fields. Jane cast a sideways glance at Guy. One could tell a born rider simply by watching the way they sat their horse. Guy's mighty stallion was attracted by her pretty mare, but he controlled the animal effortlessly, without thought, with legs, body and hands, as fluidly and as softly as the horse himself moved.

Riding alongside a hedgerow, they were about to turn into a meadow when Jane heard a whimper. Looking at the hedge, she was surprised to see what looked like an animal with its hind leg caught in a snare. Pulling her horse to a halt, she slid from the saddle. Looking back to see why she'd halted, Guy went back and dismounted, seeing immediately what was wrong,

As he approached the animal he saw it was one of the pack of hounds. The dog leaped to its feet, blood streaming down its back leg as it struggled to be free. It was clearly distressed.

'Sit! Good dog.' Squatting down, he held out his hand for the dog to sniff whilst continuing to speak quietly. 'Be still. I'll not hurt you.'

Growling, the animal eyed him warily, but as he spoke, its growl subsided and he allowed him to examine the wounded leg.

'Will he be all right?' Jane asked, crouched by his side.

'The wire of the snare has cut into his flesh, but not deep to damage the tendon. But I'll have to work quickly to remove it in order to prevent the dog becoming crippled.'

Guy's long fingers worked at the wire, eventually managing to prise it apart. The dog rose to his feet, wagging his long tail and holding his injured leg off the ground. Guy ruffled his ears, his tall frame stooped as the animal licked his cheek.

'Oh, thank goodness!' Jane exclaimed. 'Your prompt action will have saved his leg.'

Guy straightened just as two of his men rode up to see what had happened.

'Have him taken back to the castle and his wound treated,' Guy ordered, giving the dog a final pat. 'He's a fine hound. He should be back hunting in no time at all.'

Remounting, Guy and Jane rode in the direction of the meadow in which they were to hawk.

'It has not escaped my notice that you rarely visit the village since our marriage, Jane,' he said, glancing at her. 'Why is that?'

'I admit that I find it difficult going back. As a child I knew everyone and was readily accepted for who I am, but since our marriage there has been a change in their attitude towards me. Oh, they are polite enough. They call me countess or milady, but there is a distinct reserve and, I suspect, a bit of resentment as well. I am no longer one of them, I am an outsider and am treated as such. I am rejected by my own class, and,' she said, meeting his gaze, 'I doubt very much that yours will ever accept me. You have done the unthinkable by marrying me. I may have won the servants over, but it is not enough. Not a single one of your friends has come to visit since we wed, nor have we been invited to any of their houses. It matters not a jot to me, but I am rather concerned for your sake.'

'Don't be. I'm sorry if there is resentment in the vale and can only hope that in the future things will change. I have certainly seen a change in the attitude of the servants here at the castle—which is down to you. I know our marriage has caused something of a furore among our noble neighbours and the king's court, who think themselves the select few of this world, but I'm not worried. As I said before, we shall win them over,' he assured her. 'As soon as they meet you they are sure to respond to your beauty and your charm. I intend for us to visit my mother. She will be holding one of her elaborate affairs which we will attend.'

'Her guests might not want to come if they know I am to be there.'

'They will all attend,' he promised, 'out of curiosity, if for no other reason, and they will find the new Countess of Sinnington enchanting and welcome you into the ranks with open arms.'

Jane had her doubts about that, but she wasn't going to argue.

Reaching the meadow, they dismounted once more. John handed Jane her merlin. Cedric was first to raise a hare and fly his hawk. The kill was swift and clean. Jane followed the falconer's careful instructions and removed Melody's hood. Her eyes were wild and cunning, and for a moment Jane could not breathe, as if the bird had ordered her immobile while she considered her. By some miracle Jane managed not to blink during the long examination. When the falconer called out that they were ready, she must have moved, for Melody flapped her wings irately, but calmed the moment she drew her closer.

Guy showed her how to loosen the jesses and she had hardly done so when Melody took off after a small bird. Jane gave little thought to the prey. What held her transfixed was Melody's graceful flight, her fierce attack, her return to her glove when she tapped it as Guy had shown her, dangling a gobbet of meat from her gloved fingers as a lure.

Laughing with pure joy, she looked at Guy. He nodded his approval, regarding her with a tender smile filled with admiration. Her heart swelled.

Listening to her laughter, filled with admiration, Guy looked at her astride her mare, with the merlin hooded on her arm, her mantle thrown back, her eyes alight and her cheeks glowing with youth and good health. 'You have done well, Jane. Already you look as though you are seasoned falconer. Were I a king and you a soldier, I would have knighted you right there on the field. Your father would be proud of your prowess.'

'My father would not be quite so enthusiastic,' she said without rancour as they rode to join the others. 'My brother's skill at hawking was the pride of my family—something that was denied me, being a girl, you understand. Instead of knighting me on the field, my father would chastise me for daring to interfere in what he considers to be a male sport.'

'And would you have liked to go hunting?'

'Oh, yes, but I couldn't.'

'Didn't your brother support you in your ambition?'

'Not really…' As if loyalty prevented her from

painting an unflattering image of her dead brother, she smiled brightly and said in a determinedly reassuring voice, 'He didn't know, of course, as brothers often don't know things about their younger sisters, and he was always too busy being a soldier to notice.'

'I'm sorry,' Guy said, his voice filled with gruff gentleness.

Jane stared at him across the short distance separating them, while a startling discovery slowly revealed itself to her. At that moment, the man who people called a ruthless, brutal barbarian appeared to be something quite different—he was, instead, a man who was capable of showing immense gentleness when taking care of an injured dog, and of feeling acute sympathy for a disappointed young girl—it was there in the soft lines of his face. Mesmerised, she rode beside him without awareness, seeing nothing but him and scenting the smell of his horse, the leather of his saddle and the smell of him, spices and sweat. She felt her smile turn up her lips and she looked into his face.

'I am beginning to think,' she murmured, her

eyes captured by his when he turned his head to her, 'that legend plays you false.'

'Why do you say that?'

'I think that all the things people say you've done—they aren't true.' Her lovely eyes searched his face as if she wanted to see into his soul. His face became shuttered.

'They're true,' Guy contradicted her shortly, as visions of countless bloody battles he'd fought paraded across his mind in all their lurid ugliness, complete with battlefields littered with corpses of his own men and those of his enemies. He had never discouraged his reputation as a brutal warrior. It was his way of deterring his enemies.

Jane knew nothing of his bleak memories and her soft heart rejected his self-proclaimed guilt. She knew only that for the first time she'd had an insight into the man standing before her who had just now shown sympathy at the silly young girl who'd told him she had wanted to hawk.

'I don't believe it,' she whispered.

'Believe it!' he warned. Part of the reason he wanted her was that she did not cast him in the role of bestial conqueror when he touched her, but he was equally unwilling to let her deceive herself by casting him in another role—that of her knight in shining armour. 'Most of it is true,' he said flatly.

Jane moved closer until they were knee to knee. Then she placed her hand upon his own and looked into his eyes. 'We will not speak of it now. See, Cedric beckons you. Come, there is more hunting to be done.'

He moved at that, his chin lifting, the cold passing from his eyes.

The hunting over, Cedric rode with Jane back to the castle.

Wrapped up in her thoughts of the day and the confusion Guy wrought on her mind, as they rode through the dappled gloom of the woods Jane was content to ride in silence. After a while she turned her head and looked at her big and brawny blond-haired escort. 'I understand you've been with Guy for many years, Cedric.'

He nodded. 'Ever since he became a soldier.'

'Then you will know him better than anyone.'

He grinned at her. 'I like to think so, but then, I don't think anyone knows what goes on inside that head of his.'

'Will you tell me about him?'

'That depends what you want to know.'

'Most of what I know of him is mainly hearsay. I don't know what is true and what is false. By the time I was ten he was already a legend in Cherriot. It was said he never lost so much as a skirmish. People said he was a ruthless, brutal warrior who gave no quarter to his prisoners. They also said he was the spawn of Satan.'

Cedric rolled his eyes and his laughter was a rumble that came from deep within his barrel chest. 'Spawn of Satan! Aye, there is that about him. But his reputation is much a matter of gossip and wishful dreaming. He acquired his reputation by being a tough soldier, skilled in warfare and brave on the field.'

'That I can believe.'

'Not every man would care to be accused by those who know no better of the wholesale slaughter of men. This is what they whisper of the earl, even though in other ways he is held up as the type itself of a nobleman. Sadly it is harder to kill a whisper than a shouted defamation. Besides, in the minds of the ordinary soldier, to whom their leader is the ruler of their lives in battle and the dispenser of all fates, he would be held account-able for all that happens on the field—evil and good alike, from resounding victory to defeat.'

'So, would you say his reputation has been ex-aggerated out of all proportion?'

'It would be good to declare that the tales you've heard are a lie. But it is not quite that. It's a lie that he slaughtered prisoners with indiscriminate bru-tality. On the whole he did not decide their fate. They were taken before their king's ministers and their fate decided there. In that Sinnington was fair and just, purposeful and never cruel—but he is gentle with women,' he said, casting her a side-ways glance, his lips stretched wide with teasing amusement.

'And you are unswervingly loyal to speak so highly of him, Cedric—but then, were you the enemy you would have a different tale to tell.'

'Aye, that I would.'

'Clearly Guy must be a great leader to inspire dedication from so many men.'

'I told you. We've been together a long time.'

'He's fortunate to have you.'

'It is my service.'

'I think it's more than that.' It was clear to Jane that Cedric was valued for his devotion.

Guy chose that moment to join them. He was staring ahead of him, his gaze fixed intently on a small party of horsemen riding towards them. Suddenly his body became taut and alert.

'Guy? What is it? Is something wrong?' Jane asked, peering anxiously in the direction of his gaze, but seeing nothing untoward.

'I believe,' he said coldly, 'that we are about to be confronted by Aniston.'

Chapter Seven

Something cold gripped Jane's stomach. 'Richard? Oh well, I suppose we had to meet some time. I pray there is no trouble. Please don't let him provoke you, Guy.'

'The only thing that galls me is the wound to my pride if I have to step aside.'

She shot him an irate glance. 'You cared little for *his* pride when I was promised to him. How do you think that made *him* feel—and his parents? I know they are suffering very badly over it and I do not wish to inflict on them any further distress. For my sake, I beg you to set aside your pride for a moment and don't allow him to provoke you. It will be all right. He—he will ride on by.'

'If you believe that, then you are a fool, Jane,' Guy growled without taking his eyes off the oncoming riders, 'and if he tries anything, then he is an even greater fool.'

'If we meet peaceably, then I will happily be a fool,' she replied tartly. 'But I ask you not to harm him. Please give me your word that you won't.'

Meeting her eyes, he nodded. 'I give it,' he said reassuringly. 'I will not harm him.'

'Thank you.'

Having seen Sinnington and Jane from a distance, on the point of leaving Cherriot Vale with his companions to join John Neville in the north, Richard rode towards them with the arrogance and self-assurance of a man oblivious to anyone but himself.

Pulling his horse to a halt in a cloud of dust, his full lips were stretched in a lewd smile, but the eyes that rested on Jane's face were hard as stone. 'Permit me,' he said, lightly mocking, with a slight inclination of his head, 'to pay my respects to the Countess of Sinnington.' His eyes flicked insolently to the darkly glowering earl holding his horse in check beside her, but he did not accord him the deference of his rank, which only served to increase Guy's wrath.

Jane read the mockery on the faces of Richard and his companions. For a moment she studied this man, whom she had once thought she would marry, as dispassionately as if he had been a stranger. It was the first time that she had set eyes on him since she had told him she would not marry him. So many things had changed. Then, she had been someone to be sacrificed, a helpless victim in the hands of this heartless and unscrupulous man. Today she had Guy for strength and protection.

'You may.' Considering the turmoil within her, her voice was curiously calm. Her proud, disdainful eyes met and held Richard's without flinching. She was discovering, agreeably, that now that she was face to face with him, in fact, the vague terrors which had haunted her ever since their last encounter had melted away.

'Or perhaps you have no wish to speak to me,' Richard went on, 'that as a humble soldier I am an embarrassment to be brushed away like you would an annoying fly. Although it is not so long ago when you were quite devoted to me, as I recall.'

Guy had heard enough. 'That will do,' he said sharply. 'You are amazingly impertinent, Aniston.

Have your forgotten the circumstances of our last encounter—when you had the audacity to forcibly try to take what a lady should only give to her husband on their wedding night?'

Richard shrugged contemptuously, but his eyes shifted to avoid the earl's hard gaze. 'If she had not been such a naïve fool, that's all it would have been. It was she who turned it into high tragedy.'

'I think you will recall that it had more to do with my arrival than my wife's objections,' Guy stated coldly.

Richard's companions held back, their horses shifting restlessly. The atmosphere was suddenly filled with tension and hostility.

'Interference, I would say,' Richard grumbled.

'My wife's conscience may trouble her on the odd occasion about refusing your suit, Aniston, and believe you might put it behind you with no ill feeling, but my own nature is less trusting—and for good reason, as well you know, since you appear to make a practice of deflowering innocent maids. Now if you would stand aside, we will be on our way.'

Richard laughed, its mirthless sound like a dagger chipping into ice. 'I see you cherish some prejudice against me, sir,' he said, feeling unaccustomedly brave now he had taken on a new role in life. He shrugged. 'For the life of me I cannot think why—unless a mutual acquaintance has been feeding you with lies and put it into your head that I am some kind of blackguard.'

'What I think is neither here nor there,' Guy said stiffly. 'However, I have seen nothing in your behaviour to cause me to change my mind.'

'As you so rightly say, sir,' Richard agreed easily, 'that is neither here nor there.'

'You said you are a soldier, Richard,' Jane said. 'What did you mean by that? I—thought you were to go to Italy.'

He gave her a sneering look. 'Unlike my father and brother I am not a cloth merchant and never will be. Along with my companions here, I am to take up arms. The Lancastrian cause may have been badly wounded at Towton, but there are still pockets of fierce resistance in the north-east. I am on my way to join John Neville. Another battle is highly likely.'

'Best thing for you,' Guy remarked. 'Better by far that your aggression is channelled into fighting rather than ravishing maids. The mutual acquaintance you spoke of is deceased, as well you know, but before that he had a score to settle with you, a heavy score, one he had every intention of making you pay in full.'

'Then I thank God that he is dead, rendering his threat harmless.'

Guy's eyes, as hard as flint, narrowed dangerously. 'Have a care what you say, Aniston. Lord Lambert has two sons with Neville. They have long memories and never forget a slight.'

Feeling the full impact of the earl's underlying threat and unwilling and unable to challenge it since it would bring to the surface an issue best left buried, seething with incandescent rage that the earl had thought to taunt him with it now, Richard blanched and looked back at his companions. 'Come. Let us ride on.'

Jane glanced at Guy curiously, disturbed by his words. Not for the first time she thought there was something in Richard's past that Guy knew about, something dark, that remained hidden from her and had something to do with the time Richard had spent as a squire in Lord Lambert's household. However, since she was now another man's wife, it had nothing to do with her any more. But his decision to take up soldiering again went a long way to explaining Richard's arrogant, cocksure manner and the excitement she saw in his eyes. For Richard to be offered the chance to distinguish himself in battle, to become a knight, was worth much more to him than all the gold in London.

Jane looked from Richard's accusing face to Guy's granite one. Thinking to put an end to this unpleasant encounter by riding on, she urged her horse sideways to pass Richard's, turning her head away as she did so. She was two lengths of a horse away when a shout from Richard's companions made her blood freeze.

'You bastard! You've killed him!'

The sound of Jane's thundering heart drowned everything out as she turned back and stared. Richard was slumped in the saddle, blood seeping through the fabric of his jerkin. A scream rose up in her throat and she pressed her knuckles against her mouth, trying to stop it. Even then she felt as if she was going to vomit. Richard's companions quickly closed ranks to aid him. With a cry she moaned his name brokenly, looking desperately at her husband.

Her eyes became riveted on the bloody dagger in his hand, a gleaming blade with a handle carved in the shape of a ram's head.

'Jane…' His voice sounded strange, as if it came from a long way off.

She froze, before turning her attention to the injured man. Before she could get to him one of his friends shoved her away, his eyes blazing with fury.

'Leave him—*my lady*,' he hissed, his address intentionally insulting. 'We'll take care of him. Have you and your murdering husband not done enough harm to him already?'

'You saw my husband do this?' she asked in small voice.

'Aye—drew his dagger, he did, on a defenceless man. He didn't stand a chance.'

One of the men lunged at Guy, but Cedric managed to restrain him.

Jane held back and watched as the men rode away, supporting Richard in the saddle, who looked as if he wouldn't make it to his home.

Guy nudged his horse close to hers. 'Jane…'

Her eyes were drawn again to the blade that he still held before lifting to his face. Forcing herself to take long, steadying breaths, she finally brought herself under control. All the doubts, the warnings, the hints, crystallised in her mind, focusing on the proof of the dagger he held, and an icy cold stole through her, numbing her to everything, even the pain. Guy had been her lover—she had lain in the arms of the man who could do this.

She glared at him, her eyes alive with pain blazing out of a face that was white with rage. '*You* did that!' she hissed. '*You*! By God, Guy, for what reason? If Richard dies from your hand, you will have *murdered* him. I'll *never* forgive you. *Ever*!'

With his eyes riveted on hers, he calmly wiped the dagger on his breeches and slipped it into the top of his leather boot. 'Listen to me, Jane—'

'Listen to you?' she flared, wild with grief and pain. 'I shall never listen to you again! You promised me you would not harm him and like a fool I believed you. You *are* a devil—an animal. Everything they say about you is true! You are a—a barbarian.'

Guy's rapier gaze stabbed into Jane's furious wide eyes, imprisoning them. 'Be quiet and listen to me,' he ordered harshly, grabbing her wrist as she was about to ride on. The eyes she turned on him were sparkling with hatred and glazed with tears she refused to shed.

'Listen to you! I'll never listen to you again,' she cried, her chest heaving.

She glowered at him stonily and her readiness to judge him guilty without giving him a chance to defend himself enraged Guy yet more.

'Don't tell me you didn't do it because I'll call you a liar. Fortunately for civilisation, I do not share your pleasure for butchery,' she flared furiously, then gasped in alarmed surprise as his arm coiled around her like a striking snake, squeezing the breath from her as he hauled her awkwardly against his chest.

'Don't *ever*,' he said, enunciating in an awful voice, 'use that tone or those words to me again!'

'Why?' she cried, struggling to free herself from his grip before her horse threw her. 'Do you challenge the accuracy of my words?'

'I challenge,' Guy improvised coldly, his mouth close to her ear, 'your accusation of butchery.'

'I'd no idea you were so sensitive on the subject,' she mocked. 'I was under the impression you enjoyed shedding the blood of your enemies—as you did my brother's. I was beginning to think you could not have perpetrated such an ignoble deed, but now I have seen at first-hand what you are capable of I am not so sure. I shall never believe anything you say again.'

'*That* is your prerogative,' Guy bit out, releasing her wrist and shoving her from him.

'And I mean it,' she hissed contemptuously, thrusting her face close to his. 'You gave me your word that you would not harm him. He was going away and you had to—to—do that. Have you not thought of the distress his parents will feel?'

'No,' he bit out from between his teeth. 'I can't say that I have.'

'That does not surprise me,' she snapped, her eyes shooting sparks of ire. Digging her heels into her horse's flanks, like a dervish she whirled her horse and galloped off.

Guy let her go and, when she was no longer in sight, he turned to Cedric. 'You saw what happened?'

Cedric nodded. 'It happened quickly, but he drew his dagger.'

'Aye.' He sighed. 'But how to convince my wife?'

'I'll speak to her, tell her what I saw.'

'No,' Guy said quickly. Cedric saw his shoulders

stiffen and he could almost feel the effort he was exerting to keep his rage under control. 'Don't do that. She called me a butcher and a liar. Truth and honour are an important part of the way I live my life. Jane has to learn to trust me. I must restrain my temper in order to prove myself innocent of the crimes she's set against me. Go after Aniston, Cedric, and bring me news.'

Exhausted and trembling so violently she could hardly stand, Jane managed to make it back to the castle and to her quarters and close the door. All manner of doubts and fears crept in. Much as she shrank from the idea of her gallant, handsome husband killing any man—especially her beloved brother—in cold blood, she could not dismiss what she had seen with her own eyes. He had been holding the bloody knife and had in all probability killed Richard. How could she thrust those facts from her mind? Dark, impenetrable gloom settled in with a vengeance.

Her face contorted with wrenching emotions as cascading tears flowed unheeded. Guy was her husband. He had transported her into a world of luxury and had taught her the joy of marital bliss and fulfilment as a woman. Yet, at the moment, she felt as if she really didn't know him at all.

'Please go away, Guy,' she choked, dragging herself out of the chair when he came to her room and opened the door.

His brows snapped together in an ominous frown. 'Jane?' he asked, reaching for her.

'Don't touch me,' she cried.

Her maid's voice came from the doorway. 'Is aught amiss, my lady?' she asked, glaring bravely at Guy.

'Get out of here and close that damned door behind you,' Guy snapped furiously.

'Leave it open,' Jane said nervously and the brave girl did exactly as she bade.

In four long strides Guy was at the door, slamming it closed with a force that sent it crashing into its frame, and Jane began to vibrate with terror. When he turned around and started towards her Jane tried to back away, but she tripped on a rug and had to remain where she was.

Guy saw the fear in her eyes and stopped short only a foot away from her. His hand lifted and she winced. Meeting her gaze through the wealth of tears brimming in her eyes, he made every attempt to speak calmly. 'Jane, I realise you've had a terrible shock, but there's no reason for you to be afraid of me.'

It was his voice that made her want to weep at his feet, that beautiful baritone voice—and his face—that face she adored. His face looked strained, his mouth drawn in a grim line, his eyes strangely shadowed by an emotion she had never seen in them before. She stared at him as if he were a stranger, and only a short while ago… She looked away, afraid now to meet those beautiful blue eyes silently pleading for her to listen and to believe in him, for they had the strength to rend her very soul.

'Would you please get out of here? I need time to sort this matter out in my mind and for the shock to ease. Perhaps I can think more clearly after I'm allowed some time to myself.'

Guy raised his hand to make another appeal, but when her eyes became riveted on the extremity, he glance at it and realised his fingers were covered with sticky gore. Slowly he lowered his arm and heaved a despondent sigh. Talking to his wife at this point seemed futile. Turning on his heel, he walked away, retreating to the hall and leaving her to consider his innocence or guilt.

* * *

Guy had apologised, but Jane could tell that he wasn't sorry. Although on the face of things she appeared to accept his apology, her trust in him had been shaken and her demeanour towards him had cooled. The hurt could not instantly be forgotten. She felt like a fool for having given so much of herself, holding nothing back—she had thought he had been doing the same, but to her shock, it had turned out that he had not.

He did not see her as an equal the way she had believed he did, but more like a possession, a receptacle to bear his children and nothing more. Even though she had known this before she married him, it made her sick to realise this was the extent of her role in his life.

Brooding on it and stewing in the hurt left her bruised inside. But truly, he had never offered her a logical explanation of *why* he hated Richard so much or fully explained the manner of her brother's death at Towton.

After two weeks, Guy thought lovemaking could help heal the breach, that passion might thaw her, but when he went to her, she wouldn't let him touch her. She didn't fight him or accuse him, she merely turned her face away and told him to leave her alone. He could tell she wasn't just denying him to punish him—this was no game. It seemed the bruise he had dealt to her trust had inhibited her ability to respond to him.

They ate their meals together and conversed with the calm politeness of strangers, but she kept herself from him. Everyone in the castle was conscious of the rift between them and tried to cover it with forced joviality. Guy became angry with her, confronting her with the matter, accusing her of coldness, thinking that the heat of anger might succeed where bedding her had failed. But feeling low and depressed and past quarrelling, she turned from him.

In frustration Guy wondered what the hell he was supposed to do. Damn it, Aniston had recovered from his wound weeks ago and ridden north to fulfil his ambition. His wife's displeasure with him preoccupied his thoughts when he most needed to focus. He wanted Jane back, his happy and loving, smiling companion, and to recapture the magic they had tasted together on their wedding night. The memory of that blissful time darkened his mood progressively, for it brought to mind the difference a moment's passing could make in a man's life.

He knew he had to extend every privilege a man could bestow upon his wife during this time of uncertainty. It would be madness for him to try to force her into some kind of acceptance of what he had done by bringing her to heel with husbandly dominance. Coercion of that nature definitely ran contrary to his principles. Yet, in giving her time to reaffirm her trust in him, he could foresee himself having to endure a lengthy abstinence.

Finally, when their polite co-existence became too much for him, and in sore need of something that would take his mind off the cold, dark emptiness that had settled into his vitals, he ordered the horses and litters to be made ready. They were leaving to visit his mother. Perhaps some time spent away from Cherriot Vale would help them resolve their differences.

Rosemead was as beautiful as its name. Down river from London, it was a large stone-built manor house, beside the shimmering waters of the Thames teeming with river traffic of wherries, beautifully painted private barges and wine-laden galleys from France. The sparkle of the evening sunshine gleaming on the smooth surface of the river dazzled Jane.

With apprehension she entered the house, awed by its splendour. With a line of servants following in their wake, Guy escorted her down a corridor lined with beautiful hangings and lit by silver torches, then stepped into the expanse of the great hall. They went behind a screen into a light and airy solar chamber. The thick walls were whitewashed and decorated with painted flowers and hung with rich wool tapestries.

Guy's mother, the Dowager Lady Cecilia Courcy, was sitting in a large upholstered chair swathed in impressive folds of pale-blue silk encrusted with jewels. A sapphire necklace adorned her throat and she wore a horned headdress on her head, her hair captured in a thick net on each side of her face. She looked very grand, like a queen. Her face was smooth and pink and smiling, her eyes as sharp as a hawk's. They were also blue, very blue and penetrating—just like her son's.

'Ah, here you are at last,' Lady Cecilia said, reaching out her hand, heavy with large-stoned rings. Her voice was low-pitched and strong. 'Guy, how lovely to see you.' Her face shone with adoration as she looked up at her handsome son. Bending his tall frame, he lightly kissed her proffered cheek 'What kept you?'

'My wedding—which would have been all the better had you been there.'

'It was my dearest wish, but you understand why I was absent. Yet you are here now. It's so good of you to come so soon after your marriage. I was hoping I would be able to meet your young bride.' Her eyes went past him to the young woman standing a few steps behind him, a look of apprehension on her young face. 'And you must be Jane. Welcome to Rosemead,' she said with a gracious smile.

Jane dipped a curtsy. 'I am happy to meet you at last, Lady Cecilia.'

'Come here, my dear, and let me look at you. I've been so looking forward to meeting you. You are very lovely,' she observed, studying the creamy visage. 'I can understand what has driven Guy in such a fever to wed you. I am delighted to have you in the family and hope we shall be the best of

friends. I suppose Guy has been completely ne-
glectful of telling you anything about me.'

'Guy?' Jane glanced at her husband with wide
uncertainty. 'It would seem there is much he has
failed to tell me.'

'You must forgive him, my dear,' Lady Cecilia
begged with a chuckle. 'His manner must have
been much afflicted by his enchantment with you.
Forgive me for not rising. I am sure that one of the
things Guy has told you about me is that I am not
as agile as I used to be—a horse threw me when
I was trying to coax it over a rather large hedge.'
She chuckled softly. 'I can't say that I blame it. I
would have refused to jump the wretched hedge.'

'I'm sorry,' Jane said quietly. 'It must be hard
not being able to do something you enjoy.'

'It is.' She sighed deeply, her eyes suddenly sad
with regret. 'I miss it more than I can say—but—
there we are. What is done is done. Do you ride,
Jane?'

'Yes, I do.'

'And she's recently begun hawking,' Guy remarked. 'Pretty good at it too.'

Lady Cecilia graced Jane with a breathtaking
smile that lit up her eyes, dispelling her earlier

sadness. 'Then you must ride out with Guy in the morning when he joins the hunt. An early morning ride will lift your spirits after the long journey. I like a woman who enjoys country sports, Jane. Would that I could join you, but...' she shrugged '...alas. A chamber has been prepared for you. Tomorrow we have guests descending on us, so accommodation is somewhat limited just now. However, I'm sure you'll be comfortable enough cosied up together.'

Jane refrained from looking at her husband, but she could imagine his smug smile.

She had seen nothing so fine as their bedchamber. It was large and sumptuously furnished, with a great carved bed and cushions in reds and gold, stuffed with down, and scattered in chairs and along the window seat for their ease and comfort. The large window offered plenty of light, inviting one to sit and gaze out at the river and fields. A great wooden bath stood in one corner, by the hearth, and an intricately carved screen was nearby, ready to shield the bather from draughts.

Looking at the bed, in some chagrin she glanced at her husband and found him peering at her closely, as if trying to discern her thoughts. The handsome face was stoic as the cool blue eyes flicked over her.

Jane sought to swallow the lump that had risen in her throat. When she had left Cherriot Vale two days ago, she was confused by what had happened, but now, when she entered their bed-chamber, with nowhere to shield herself from her husband, her fears were far more complicated.

Guy sensed her apprehension. 'Don't worry, Jane. You'll be safe enough,' he remarked drily.

'But where will you sleep?'

'With my wife,' he stated coldly. 'I have no intention of spending the night in a chair and leaving you the bed. You'll have to contend with my presence or sleep in the chair yourself.'

'You're not being very chivalrous,' she complained mutedly, her face downcast.

Guy snorted in disgust. 'I don't suppose the fact that I let you dismiss me from your bed after I stopped Aniston killing me would be considered gallant,' he retorted. 'But know this. I'm not of a mind to let it happen again. That much I've decided. We'll at least share a bed, if nothing else.'

'Would you force me—?'

'Good God, woman, no,' he barked. 'But neither am I going to let you throw me out of our bed or flee to another room. As long as you live under my roof—or be it my mother's for the time being—from this moment on you'll share my bed.'

'How easily you forget the conditions that drew us apart,' she retorted heatedly.

'Aye—you never stop reminding me and, sensitive to your feelings, I allow it. But I am no puppet, Jane, waiting for you to pull the strings for me to dance at your bidding. Be damned! I'll not be at any woman's beck and call. You either conform to this marriage or we will have no marriage at all.'

An icy hardness came into those luminous blue orbs, making Jane draw back. Perhaps, she thought wildly, this was what Richard had seen just before Guy had stabbed him, a coldness so intense she was sure it could slice through rock.

'So what is it to be?' he demanded. 'Do you object to sharing a bed with your husband?'

Jane's jaw sagged another notch as she realised that she had been goaded into foolishly tweaking his temper. Indeed, she had cause to think that this man, from whom since their marriage she had seen gentleness and consideration, was definitely not the sort to antagonise. He had a mind and will of his own and kowtowed to no one.

'Not at all, providing you keep to your own side of the bed.'

'You can count on it. We will give the servants no reason to gossip. I have no intention of letting my mother know there is anything amiss with our marriage. But first I intend to take a bath. I have two days' dust on my person and I'm in no mind to bed down in it.' He settled a pointed stare upon her. 'Any objections, madam?'

She shook her head and turned away. 'I doubt I shall be unduly shocked by the sight.'

'Perhaps you might be if you stared hard enough,' Guy quipped drily. 'I still consider myself a newly married man.'

'Don't worry. I won't look if it bothers you.'

'It doesn't bother me, Jane. Aroused would better describe the way I'd feel.'

'Even when you're angry?'

'Even then. I doubt I'll ever be angry enough to ignore your presence. You need only glance my way for me to rise to the occasion.'

Jane flushed scarlet at the implication. 'Pull the screen round. That's what it's for.'

'You know I have trouble reaching my back. Will you not—?'

'No,' she was quick to reply. She could not bring herself to be that familiar with him. Her carefully erected defences would be sure to crumble. 'I'll sit on the window seat until you're done,' she said quietly, seeing no other choice.

'You will stay? Are you no longer afraid of me?'

She turned away, not daring to meet his gaze. 'I'm still cautious.'

'Aye, damn it, I know you are.' The disappointment in his tone reluctantly drew a weak smile from her, but he had already turned away.

Nothing more was said because at that moment two male servants arrived with jugs of steaming hot water. When they went out, leaving linen towels before the hearth, Guy began removing his clothes, pleasurably contemplating his dire need for a long hot soak.

Jane turned her head sideways to look at him before looking quickly away. Every night she would lie awake, fighting the urge to go to him and ask him to somehow ease the ache in her heart. How foolish it was to ask the person who had caused the pain to heal it.

She looked at him once more. Then she forgot about the ache in her heart altogether. He was silhouetted against the firelight with his back turned for the most to her. He had removed his upper garments and was in the process of tugging off his breeches. She felt her cheeks becoming inflamed with her own temerity as she eyed him surreptitiously. The sight was certainly more revealing than any she had seen in a long time, for the dancing flames vividly defined everything that was manly about him.

Tossing his breeches over a chair, he turned and faced her. 'Have you acquired a fetish for my baser parts, Jane?' he teased on seeing where her gaze was directed. 'Although considering the explicit conversations we were involved in while making love on our wedding night, you did not display any timidity about discussing such intimate matters.'

'That was then,' she retorted, averting her gaze, wishing he hadn't said that. It aroused many disconcerting memories of how he would instruct her in what pleased him, or where she was most sensitive to stimuli.

Guy smiled smugly when her gaze went chasing off out of the window. With casual disregard to his nakedness and oblivious to her gaze when her eyes were drawn to him once more, he stepped into the bath.

Even now, after what he'd done, the sight of his strong body made Jane's heart cry out for him.

Seeing her chance to make herself ready for bed, she scooted across the room and dragged the screen round the bath. Never had she scrambled out of her clothes and into her nightdress so fast in her life. By the time Guy had bathed and dried himself, she was seated on a bench, brushing out her flowing hair.

Securing the drying cloth around his loins and rubbing his hair with another, Guy paused when he saw her seated before the mirror. The gown she wore was like a soft white veil over her body, more alluring and revealing than bare flesh. It was tied with soft ribbons at the waist on each side, but from the waist up and down it was slit with nothing else to hold it together. As a result the sides of her breasts were exposed and one of her slender legs was partially bare to his gaze. He was ever wont to admire her long, sleek limbs and, with husbandly appreciation, hovered near with all the dedication of a lusting *roué*.

The hardest thing Jane had ever had to do was to sit calmly before him and let him look at her as he was doing now.

'You're very beautiful, Jane,' he said hoarsely, taking a step towards her. His eyes were like flames of fire, scorching her. Then he checked himself and his face hardened. 'Go to bed. It's been a long day and tomorrow will seem even longer. Unless, of course, you've finally decided to end this charade. Would it assuage your fears now that we're alone if you could find something in what I might have to say to which you could give credence?'

Jane shook her head. 'I only know what I saw and that you were at the core of that bloody scene. I—'

Guy flung up a hand to forestall her. 'Spare me your repetitive declarations, my dear.' His tone was snide. 'I know what you saw. I was there— remember?'

'I really had no wish to alienate myself from

you, but when I'm repeatedly haunted by the grizzly impression of you holding that knife in your hand, I have trouble sorting things out in my mind. I don't want to believe you are guilty of trying to kill Richard—or Andrew for that matter.'

The bloody scene flashed before her mind's eye, making her recoil in shuddering revulsion. The gallant knight whom she had once supposed was her husband now seemed in these passing days far less real and more of a figment of some girlish fantasy. He had been too handsome, too noble and far too admirable to have been realistic. Yet, in spite of what had happened, her heart cried out in protest, assuring her that she was wrong, that he was all those things and more, and that she was an utter fool for doubting him.

Guy's expression was bitter. 'When you've sorted it out, Jane, tell me. As far as I'm concerned I've been condemned as a villain by the very one who should believe in me.'

Jane looked away. For the life of her she couldn't manage to swallow the thickness that had risen in her throat. She blinked away the sudden tears that blurred her vision and after a moment gained some semblance of composure.

Guy released a pensive sigh. 'I am a warrior, Jane. On the field of battle it's a matter of kill or be killed. But when I am off the battlefield, that's where it ends. I cannot bear being looked upon as a would-be murderer in my own home and by the very one who should trust me.'

'I don't mean to seem disloyal—only…' Unable to go on, she bit her lip and looked away.

Snorting in disgust, he threw the wet linen into a chair. 'Then get into bed.'

Jane didn't need telling twice. She got into bed with haste and drew the covers under her chin, watching him warily. 'You will keep to your side of the bed?'

A muscle twitched in Guy's cheek and Jane knew that slight movement meant she had roused his anger. He glared down at her, his blue eyes fierce and frigid. 'I'm not going to rape you. Now go to sleep. I won't bother you unless you invite my attentions.'

Irritated with his wife, Guy climbed into the opposite side of the bed.

Jane turned her back to him. It wasn't long before the weariness of the past two days claimed her and she knew nothing more.

Guy lay awake, listening to the house quietening for the night. Jane's sleep was troubled and he was aware of every whimper or whispered word she uttered in her dreams. It was as if she was locked in the same nightmarish torment that had sent her fleeing in panic from him in the woods on that fateful day.

A feeling of dread swept over him. It truly seemed his wife had cast him as the villain in this dark, gruesome travesty. Yet, for the life of him, he could think of no way to assuage her fears and convince her of his innocence and that he had only attacked Aniston in self-defence. Tormented as she was, she would never return to his arms until he had rid her of the demons that haunted her and proven himself blameless in her sight.

The newly risen sun glimmered through the branches of the trees on the horizon, with its rosy glow tingeing the sky. There was evidence of frantic rushing about as servants prepared for the guests to arrive. The courtyard, where a large complement of people had gathered in merry mood, eager for a day's sport, was a hive of colourful activity. Serfs scurried about in anxious haste with heavily laden trenchers to set before the hunters. A pack of hunting hounds were creating a cacophony of yelps and whines as they sought to lick up whatever scraps of meat had fallen from overflowing trenchers.

Some of the hunters who took the hunt seriously and were confident of their own abilities were quietly inspecting their arrows and spears, honing them to a sharper point, while several well-dressed noblemen on impressive mounts were setting off for a morning's hawking instead, their hooded peregrines, calmed in their enforced darkness, gripping their sleeves.

The atmosphere was relaxed as people mounted their horses, all champing at their bits, eager to be off. Attired in dark-blue velvet and feeling strangely light-hearted, Jane glanced about her. Her breath caught in her throat when she saw Guy. He had left their chamber while she was still asleep so they had not yet had a chance to speak. But Jane's spirits were high and she was looking forward to riding out.

Her husband's broad shoulders and clear-cut profile were etched against the green fields and forests beyond the courtyard. He was just finishing tightening the girths on his hunter, a big, strong beast which the king had given him from the royal stables as a token of his friendship.

At that moment he turned and caught Jane's appraising eye. She saw his face quicken and felt her heart give a sudden leap. If only everything could be normal between them and that wretched business with Richard had never happened.

Leaving his mount, he strode over to her, stopping in front of her, his eyes on her face, his expression serious and at the same time enquiring.

'Good morning, Jane. You slept well?' he said in a quiet voice.

'Yes—thank you,' she replied, having already regretted insisting that he kept to his side of the bed.

The heat of his gaze travelled the full length of her in a slow, appreciative perusal, before making a leisurely inspection of her face upturned to his. 'You look wonderful this morning. I've been thinking of you,' he murmured for her ears alone, his eyes, watching the movement of her lips, far more eloquent than his speech.

'I can't think why,' she replied, feeling the blood rush to her face, remembering their harsh words of the previous night and finding it difficult to appear calm and unconcerned for the state of their marriage. 'Am I late?'

'No, although I was beginning to wonder if you might have had second thoughts.'

'Not at all. I'm looking forward to the ride, although I'm not familiar with the countryside.'

'Don't worry. You'll be perfectly safe.'

'You—must have risen early.'

'I'm an old campaigner. Once the sun has risen I find it difficult to sleep. Besides,' he retorted pointedly, 'the lady who occupied my bed had declared quite categorically that my presence wasn't welcome.' He looked around him and, before Jane could think of a reply, said, 'I believe the hunt's about to start. Are you ready?'

'Yes, but unfortunately I don't have a horse.'

'I've selected a mount for you. Come and see.'

Moving with the supple grace of an animal, Guy took her elbow and propelled her to where a groom was holding a beautiful grey, its coat so bright in colour that she was almost like silver in the sunshine, with ears that flicked one way and another.

Everyone's attention was drawn to Jane in the

company of their host—the lady's husband, they came to realise. Some strained to hear what they were saying, others were openly admiring, others resentful. Jane did her best to ignore the unwelcome attention, for it made her uneasy, but it was difficult not to and she was certain that if their attitude towards her did not change, it would become intolerable as time went on.

Guy took the reins from the groom. Sensing her distress, he murmured, 'Do not be discomfited. Things will change when they get to know you. Come. Let me introduce you to Joy. Joy is to be your mount for today.'

Jane ran her hand over Joy's glossy flank before stepping to the front to take in the dark, liquid eyes, the beautiful face and the silvery mane. 'What a sweet name. Does Joy have any peculiarities that I should know about before I risk life and limb?'

Guy lifted one eyebrow lazily. 'She's as docile as a lamb.'

'Not too docile, I hope. Although I should hate to make a spectacle of myself by being tossed over her head. Now that really would give everyone something to talk about.'

'Nonsense. You are an accomplished horse-woman so I don't think there will be any danger of that.'

Keeping her eyes lowered, Jane pulled on her gloves, aware of Guy standing close behind her, so close she could feel the warmth of his body. Instead of holding out his hands for her foot to hoist her up on to the horse, he placed them about her waist, steady and firm, lifting her with ease into the saddle, making her acutely aware of his strength and complete masculinity.

Hooking her leg firmly round the pommel, she arranged her skirts so they fell down either side, hiding her leather riding boots. She watched Guy as he stepped on the mounting block and swung himself up into the saddle with perfect ease. Taking the reins as Joy moved restlessly, Jane controlled the horse effortlessly, but her apprehension was apparent.

Guy grinned. 'Don't look so worried. The truth is, there is nothing to compare with riding a high-spirited, courageous horse in the hunt. Hunting is one of man's oldest activities, from when they would hunt for food. I think it brings out all the primitive instincts in the hunter. It's the thrill of it, the exhilaration of the chase ending in the final capture and subjugation of its prey.'

Jane stared at him, her face turning scarlet. 'I have a distinct feeling you are not speaking of the fox or the deer at all, but of me,' she quipped, aware and hopelessly appalled that she was unable to work up any indignation. As so often had happened in the past, she felt completely out of control of her life when they were together. It was like being swept along into the heart of a hurricane. She trembled slightly. After all, she was flesh and blood and not immune to her husband's sexual magnetism.

Guy looked deeply into her eyes, knowing she had interpreted his words in the way they had been intended. He smiled without contrition, for he was well satisfied that he had been able to reduce her to confusion. Suddenly things didn't look as bleak as they had last night. He was even more determined to expend all his patience in breaking down the barricades she had erected to keep him out.

Chapter Eight

The huntsman blew his horn and with everyone bristling with excitement, armed with crossbows and swords, they rode out of the courtyard and into the open countryside. Following the hounds, the hunters poured over the land with a fluidity reminiscent of a river in full flow, sending up clods of earth and grass in their wake. Jane joined those following the hunt while having decided to take no active part.

The exhilaration of speed and the rush of the morning air brought a glow of colour to her cheeks. The sun shone and the trees cast long shadows over the land drenched and sparkling with early morning dew.

Jane spotted Guy out in front, riding well in a class of his own, at one with his horse, leaping with absolute confidence over hedges and ditches.

The hounds soon took a scent and a majestic stag went crashing into the forest. Horses and hounds plunged in after him. Jane's horse reared with excitement at the sound of the horn, but she held it back, having no wish to be in on the kill of such a beautiful animal.

Having killed the prey, hunters began to emerge from the forest with their spoils. After their exertions of the chase, happy and subdued, they began to drift back to Rosemead. Jane saw Guy sitting his horse on the edge of the forest. As if he sensed her watching him, he turned in the saddle and met her gaze. He rode towards her, reining in his horse when he reached her side. Bareheaded, his dark hair was ruffled by his exertions. Jane was filled with the impulse to run her fingers through the tousled curls.

'I think it is time to head back,' he said. 'A couple of deer and a wild boar make for a successful hunt. Come, we'll ride back together. I know how anxious you are to look your best for the entertainment later. The hunt took longer than anticipated so, with time of the essence, I know of a shorter way through the woods.'

Jane sent a wary glance his way and caught him staring point blank at her mouth, the drift of his thoughts perfectly plain on his handsome face. Despite the increase in her heart rate, a crisp, cool smile was briefly bestowed on him. 'I would like to say that I would rather take my chances alone— I believe I would be safer—but since we are both heading in the same direction it would be churlish of me to refuse.'

'I agree, it would. You will be quite safe with me, I assure you.'

Jane looked at him askance. 'As to that I am not convinced. You have a habit of taking advantage of me when I'm at my most vulnerable.'

His eyes twinkled wickedly. 'A husband's prerogative, surely! I would like to take advantage of you right here and now, my love, but I shall abstain until I am assured of a genuine welcome.'

Jane gave him a shy smile before averting her eyes. 'That would be advisable,' she commented in husky tones, wondering how long she would be able to hold out against him, how long it would be before she gave up the battle she had been waging in her lonely bed, for the fires he had lit had been difficult to quench. After tasting passion's appeasement to the fullest extent, she was now fully conscious of what she was yearning for.

He gazed at her soft lips as he led her down a path through the woods that would take them directly back to Rosemead. 'There is no way I shall allow this situation to continue indefinitely, Jane. It is foolish when you know how I ache for you.'

'Ache?' she quipped in mock rebuke, a reluctant smile twitching at the corners of her lips. 'A hungry greed is how I would describe it.'

Her remark made him laugh out loud. 'I won't argue against the truth. You ride well, Jane,' he remarked admiringly after a moment of riding in silence, 'as I have observed on more than one occasion. May I ask who was your instructor? Some handsome suitor, perhaps?'

Jane's lashes lowered as she gave him a sidelong glance. 'In the main, my brother.'

Guy tried not to react. To do so at this present time would open old wounds which were best left closed until her trust in him had been built up completely. 'Ah, then he taught you well.'

'Andrew was a superb horseman—none better,' she said, swallowing down the lump that clogged her throat at the memory of her handsome brother. 'H-have you heard anything about Richard?' she asked bravely, knowing that the mention of his name was sure to anger Guy, but the issue that had torn them apart could not be avoided indefinitely. She observed Guy's mouth tighten ominously.

'Having recovered from his wound, he went north. He was with John Neville when they routed the Lancastrians at Hexham in May.'

'Where is he now?'

Guy turned his head and looked at her. 'It matters to you that much, does it, Jane?'

'I cannot forget that we were to be married. Nor can I overlook what happened between the two of you.'

Guy fixed his stony gaze on the path ahead. 'He is still in the north. After the battle most of the rebel leaders were executed. Only a few pockets of resistance and castles remain in Lancastrian hands. It is expected they will fall very soon. You should know that for his courage and daring, it is rumoured that Aniston will be knighted.'

Jane was surprised to hear this. Richard's elevation brought her no joy. 'I see. If this is true, then he will finally achieve his heart's desire.' After a moment she turned and looked at him. 'Will you explain something to me?'

He glanced at her, noting her grave expression. 'If I can.'

'Richard was known to you, wasn't he, before you returned to Cherriot Vale?' He nodded, his expression stern. 'And did your dislike of him stem from the time he spent as Lord Lambert's squire?'

'The circumstances at the time did not endear him to me.'

'What happened? I recall you telling me that Lord Lambert had a daughter who drowned.'

'She was the only daughter of Lord and Lady Lambert—their youngest child. They—and her two brothers—adored her. The coroner's jury found her death was caused by drowning, the verdict accidental death. Her body was found in the lake—the circumstances of which were regarded as suspicious by her family.'

'For what reason?'

'There was evidence that she had received a heavy blow to her head and Lucy never went to the lake. She had a fear of water, which was why it was so strange to find her there. Her death caused a scandal at the time. Despite the inquest's outcome, Richard Aniston was widely suspected to have orchestrated her death—a view shared by her family—hence his dismissal.'

'But why? If Richard was responsible for what happened, for what reason would he kill her?'

'Apparently she was with child. One of Aniston's companions let slip that Aniston was enamoured of her, and she of him, and that they met in secret. But nothing is certain.'

'And do *you* think Richard might have murdered her—that he is capable of committing a crime as atrocious as murder?' A sickening knot clenched in her stomach that this might be so.

'It's not unlikely—which was one of the reasons I was so concerned when I discovered the two of you were about to become betrothed. Not only did I want to protect you from him, but from the first moment I saw you, I wanted you.' His voice had gone low and deep, almost hoarse. 'I've never made any secret of that.' His blue eyes were now darker than ever, the colour seemingly taken from the most tempestuous water of the Thames.

Elevating her chin, Jane fixed her gaze on a spot in the distance. 'As much as you want a child?'

'That isn't the same and you know it,' he ground out.

Jane looked him. 'Is it, Guy? Is it really?' Finding it hard to remain unmoved by what she saw in his eyes, she said, 'Why didn't you tell me—or at least make my father aware that Lord Lambert suspected that Richard was in some way connected to his daughter's death?'

'I did—when I called about the rumours Aniston had started about us.'

'He never said anything to me.'

'I doubt he wanted to worry you.'

'Probably not.'

'If Lord Lambert and his sons had any proof of Aniston dallying with Lucy, he would have been beaten to a pulp, his ambition of becoming a knight that he craved a forgotten dream.'

'Which happened anyway, when he rode north to join Neville and by some miracle distinguished himself. Poor Lucy.'

'Lord Lambert burned to find Aniston and wring the truth out of him about what he did to her, but he did not *know*—he only suspected. He was a quiet, upright man, respected—noble. He could not go hurling wild accusations with nothing to back them up. Such rash behaviour on his part would generate a whirlwind of gossip and scandal both in Wiltshire and at court, which was one thing he would not tolerate.'

'If someone indeed ended Lucy's life, then she deserves justice.'

'True, but Aniston is not going to confess and, without evidence, it's hardly likely to happen.'

'No, I don't suppose it is,' Jane murmured.

Lucy's story affected Jane deeply. If Richard really had murdered her, she realised she'd had a lucky escape, which made her think of Guy and the accusations she had heaped on him. Through all her past debates over his guilt or innocence, she asked herself if a man who had been so caring and tender with her on their wedding night could try to murder a man in front of her eyes in cold blood.

The question flared without warning in her mind, as if to accuse her for her irrational condemnation of her husband. If indeed Guy was capable of such a monstrous act and some dark demon truly lurked behind that gallant facade,

then wouldn't he be tormented by the wickedness lurking deep within him? Wouldn't she have
glimpsed some evidence of those malevolent char-
acteristics in him in some brief, carelessly unguarded moment?

Aware of her preoccupation, Guy looked at her.
'Knowing this, does it change anything between
us, Jane?'

She thought about his question. A wavering sigh
escaped her lips. 'It doesn't change what you did.
And, as you said, there is no evidence to say Richard did murder Lucy. But I do have difficulty ra-
tionalising a man of your integrity being capable
of such a despicable act as to murder a man in
cold blood.'

'Does this mean that you're suffering some
doubts about my guilt?'

His blunt question brought tears to her eyes.
Diffidently she met his searching gaze. 'I haven't
been able to come to any definite conclusions
about what happened that day, if that's what you
mean. At times, it seems utterly foolish to even
suspect that you could have done such a thing,
but then I have a recurring nightmare in which

your appearance changes and the demon you've become makes me afraid.'

Guy certainly had been disturbed as he had lain beside her last night and listened to her tormented whimpering. 'But you're still not certain,' he said in a matter-of-fact way. 'And then there's my reputation, which doesn't make it any easier for you. Don't believe everything you hear, Jane, or, for that matter, only bits of what you see.' Rather than stir up past hurts, after a few moments of silence, he said, 'Are you looking forward to the entertainment later?'

'Yes, although I'm also apprehensive.'

'I should tell you that the king and queen are expected to attend. The visit will be short. It is expected that they will leave after the meal.'

'So I understand,' Jane replied. 'Lady Cecilia told me when I was leaving the house earlier.' The imminent arrival of the royal guests had put her in a state of excitement. 'I'm looking forward to seeing them.'

'And they are looking forward to meeting you, Jane.'

'Then I must make sure I look my elegant best.

I am grateful to you for taking the shortest route back, which will give me more time.'

'Nonsense. As always you will look ravishing.'

They were almost at Rosemead and she looked straight ahead, as if fascinated by the large gathering of courtiers in the courtyard. She wished she could look him in the eyes, but knew she would be unable to control her heated emotions.

Midday saw barges transporting and shedding guests and the courtyard was filled with litters and neighing horses, resounding shouts and garrulous voices. It seemed that the whole city of London had come to Rosemead that day. There were people everywhere, courtiers more beautiful than Jane could have imagined. She was terrified and equally suffused with a frivolous joy. She squirmed in delight, longing to be an accepted part of it.

Bathed and dressed in a gown of forest-green with russet trim, exhausted after the hunt—which was most unusual, for she always managed to keep up with the best of them—she would have liked to rest, but the royal barge had been sighted on the river and the arrival of the king and queen was imminent. Jane saw herself in the mirror like a strange idol made entirely of precious fabrics. She was shocked to her soul by the wanton richness of her gown, which was just one of many she had acquired since her elevation to the noble ranks. Guy came and stood beside her.

'You are very beautiful, Jane. You are sure to draw attention to yourself. After everything that has happened, it is my dearest wish that you are able to put it behind you and look to the future.'

Smoothing her skirts with her hands, she glanced at him. 'Do not worry about me. The life I thought of as bleak has surely taken a turn for the better.'

As she stepped from the darkness of the corridor into the glittering hall with her husband, his tall figure clad in scarlet-and-black velvet studded with precious gems, she roused an answering flash of envy in the eyes of every woman present, and of their male escorts too. And yet there was something remote and detached in the attitude of this dazzling creature newly descended in their midst. She looked like a beautiful, gilded statue and no man watching her as she moved forwards slowly to the soft rustle of her forest-green skirts could have said whether his admiration was given most to the perfection of her eyes, or the tender, irresistible curve of her smiling lips.

Jane's attention was drawn to the sumptuously attired ladies and gentlemen in courtly dress, flashing with costly jewels. She trembled with apprehension. Her sudden painful awareness of the gulf between her status and that of this elite gathering added a terrible weight to her body. She was both nervous and excited about meeting the royal couple, her anticipation not without apprehension. There was an air of excitement in the Great Hall, with vassals going about their business with a spring of expectancy in their step, and lords and ladies preening themselves. Lady Cecilia had gone to a great deal of trouble and expense.

Protected by the royal guard, King Edward and Queen Elizabeth arrived with an entourage of servants and lords and ladies of the court. The Earl of Sinnington and Lady Cecilia welcomed them to Rosemead.

'Oh, look at them,' a lady next to Jane whispered in awe as the glittering royal couple paused for a leisurely perusal of the assembled company before advancing into the hall.

Everyone in the hall appeared riveted by the couple and, indeed, they were a breathtaking sight to behold. With lithe, liquid movements the queen walked beside the handsome young king. Jane was fascinated by the way she glided as if her feet merely skimmed the floor. Elegant of manner and with a beauty that shone when she smiled, the queen was resplendent in a pale-blue gown trimmed with gold and decorated with pearls. Everyone stepped aside to allow them to pass.

Jane looked close at this tall and slender woman with the red-gold hair. She had been a widow with two sons when she had married the king in secret in the spring. Her husband, Sir John Grey, who had been killed at the second battle of St Albans, had fought against the king. With high hopes of King Edward marrying one of the great princesses in Europe, the marriage had caused a fury at the time.

Moving to stand beside Jane, Guy's appreciative gaze travelled downwards over her green-clad body with a confident, possessive smile. 'You look, as always, stunning, my love.'

She gave him a warning look in response to his impudent endearment. But she was given no time to reproach him for at that moment the king appeared in front of them.

'Ah, Sinnington! How was the hunt? Productive, I hope.'

'It went well, your Grace,' Guy replied, at ease with the monarch. 'You missed a treat. Two fine stags and a boar.'

'I would have ridden with you but for affairs of state.' He directed his gaze at Jane standing several paces behind. 'And who is this, pray?'

Guy took Jane's hand and drew her forward. 'This fair lady is my wife Jane, the Countess of Sinnington.'

'I thought as much.'

'How?'

'A lucky guess,' the king countered smoothly.

King Edward was well loved by his people. Blond haired and over six feet tall, his amused eyes were fixed on Jane's face, as if he knew a secret and couldn't wait to divulge it. 'Sinnington has spoken of you often, Lady St Edmond. I am happy to meet you at last. You are as lovely as he professed.'

On trembling legs Jane sank into a graceful curtsy. She could feel her cheeks burning, but she could not look away from him. 'You are very kind, your Grace, but I fear my husband has a tendency to exaggerate.'

The king chuckled low. 'Your wife is clearly a woman of delicate sensibilities, Sinnington.'

'Do not be fooled, sire. She has the heart of a warrior when crossed.'

'Then she is a woman after my own heart,' the queen murmured, peering at Jane closely. 'I am happy to meet you at last, Lady St Edmond. I have heard a good deal about you and I am interested to hear more. Come and sit with me when the meal is over. We will speak then.'

'Yes, your Grace,' Jane managed to say as she bowed, though she was dumbstruck and more than a little bewildered. What could she, Jane Lovet, possibly have to talk about to a queen?

When it was time to be seated for the banquet, with places for at least a hundred people, Lady Cecilia was helped to her seat at the garland-bedecked high table, Jane was seated beside Guy on her left, the king and queen in the centre of the table on her right. Jane could feel her husband's presence with every fibre of her being and increasing comforting warmth suffused her. He was powerfully masculine, more attractive than any man present. His commanding presence was awesome, drawing the eye of everyone present. He was dashing, charming, handsome, a man any woman could easily be enamoured with.

Guests were served goblets of wine or tankards of ale, depending on their individual choices. A quartet of musicians played as an incalculable number of dishes was served: various meats, candied fruits, sweetmeats and oysters, and wines of all types from the darkest red to the clearest gold. The feast was extravagant, beyond anything Jane had yet seen. From then on she listened to the conversation going on around her with only one ear. The banquet swept past in a relaxed and congenial atmosphere.

Guy's warrior instincts were stirred by the depths of his passion for his young wife. His desire to possess her and recapture what they'd had after their marriage was now stronger than ever. The battle to win back this woman might well turn out to be the fiercest of his life, but win her he would, no matter the cost.

* * *

Afterwards when Jane was summoned to speak to the queen, she found her courteous and pleasant. They spoke of the court and her children, the fashions and Jane's background—the kind of things women talk about when they are relaxing together—but all the while she was acutely aware that Guy wasn't far away. As soon as she had taken her place beside the queen, his stare had homed in on her and his blue eyes seemed to gleam.

'Sinnington has spoken of you, and although your association with Lady Cecilia is of short duration, she speaks highly of you,' Elizabeth said, raising the issue for this interview at last. 'She agrees with Sinnington that I would benefit by having you in my household.'

Jane stared at her, somewhat bemused. 'Your household, your Grace?'

'As a lady of the chamber. I have several ladies who assist me in dressing and all manner of things. I am sure you would settle in very well.'

'But—your Grace, I am a merchant's daughter,' Jane stammered, the suggestion that she live at Court an unappealing prospect. 'Apart from visiting London with my father on occasion, I have never left Cherriot. I—I am deeply honoured by your offer—indeed, I could never have imagined such an honour—but I am completely ignorant of courtly ways and lack the experience you require.'

'I see nothing wrong with nobles and merchants mixing together. It is, after all, important that we have a deeper understanding of each other.' She rose and held out her hand, smiling softly. 'I shall be delighted to welcome you at Westminster, Lady St Edmond. I am certain we shall both benefit from this arrangement.'

Jane dropped a curtsy and backed away, though through her anguish and fear another, stronger emotion was making it difficult for her to breathe—anger about all the planning, the secret arrangements made by Guy behind her back.

'Well?' Lady Cecilia asked, almost bursting with anticipation. 'What did you talk about?'

'The queen has summoned me to the royal court—to be a servant to her Grace. I really don't know what to say—and my parents! They will be astonished.'

'You must write to them. This is a great honour, Jane, and your parents will see it that way.

Just think about it. You will live at the Palace of Westminster. You will be close to the king and queen. It is a wonderful thing.'

'But why was I not warned so that I might be prepared for this? Guy should have discussed it with me at the very least.'

As the festivities progressed and she smiled and pretended to enjoy the festivities, with a feeling that she was being manipulated by her husband, anger and resentment simmered in her breast. She watched him seated at the high table. He was among a group of men, talking, drinking and laughing with the king. When a servant approached with a warm bowl to wash their hands, Guy's easy assumption of his domineering role in her life did more than put her in a high temper. She was tempted to march up to him and pour the bowl of water over his arrogant head.

There were jugglers, acrobats and dancing dwarfs to entertain them and jolly music. Guy sat back in his seat, idly conversing with his fellow knights. His smile and words were all for them, but the hot glint in his eyes searched for and found Jane. They dwelt on her as she bent her head to listen to what Lady Cecilia was saying. He became distracted by the curve of her mouth, the soft swell of her pouting bottom lip and the curve of the upper one. He wanted to press his mouth to hers, to follow its shape with the tip of his tongue—as he had the last time he'd kissed her.

Heat burned in his blood. His groin hardened. He couldn't have stood up, despite the covering of his tunic, or everyone would have noticed his predicament. He clenched his jaw. This was madness! Why did he torment himself like this? He drank deep of his goblet, trying to cast the sensations away. His moody glance about the hall at the merrymaking courtiers told him there were plenty of other beautiful women he could have. What was it about Jane—a woman who was less than confident of his integrity—that made him blind to all others?

He gulped more wine. As he lowered the goblet he realised Jane was looking at him. Though she was seated on another table, he could see those beautiful green eyes were anything but friendly. Having seen the queen speaking to her, he had a good idea why—that she was not as enamoured of moving to Westminster Palace and her new position as waiting woman to the queen as he thought she would be. Her eyes continued to burn into him. He raised his goblet to her and wondered how long it would take to turn her angry mood into panting desire.

There were times when he wished he had never laid eyes on her, for he could not put the thought of her out of his mind. Yet he did not want to. She sat there in her forest-green gown, the colour a perfect match for her eyes, and he knew in his heart that to put her from his mind was as impossible as stopping breathing. He wanted her badly. He wanted her as many times as he could have her, and there was a recklessness in his thoughts that was completely alien to his cautious nature.

He watched her being led by the hand by her partner into a quickly forming circle as couples young and old merged together. The steps were simple enough to follow as she began to demonstrate her talents and abilities in time with the music, doing a sprightly jig or a tapping of a toe and heel as she moved around in a never-ending wheel of cavorting dancers, her smiling face evidence of the pleasure she was savouring.

Cursing softly, he summoned a hovering vassal for more wine and adjusted his tunic. This was ridiculous! He was behaving like a lovesick knave with his thoughts centred between his legs.

The hour was late when their majesties left. Those who had been inclined to think the banquet would be a solemn occasion were delighted that it changed into a very lively affair, obviously the sort the king and queen preferred.

Jane had smilingly accepted every invitation to dance, but throughout the festivities she had felt Guy watching her with a great deal of absorption. Still furious with him, she felt a great relief that he had not asked her to dance. To refuse outright would publicly dishonour him and herself, but her fierce pride ached to do precisely that. However, when he suddenly presented himself in front of her and made a courtly bow, inviting her to join him in a country dance, she found herself reaching out and taking his hand.

For several moments he swept her around the perimeter of the floor in ever-widening circles, leaving her to interweave with the other dancers and then coming back to her, relishing the music and her presence in silence. Then Jane peered up at him, her smile for the benefit of others.

'This is rather bold of you, Guy, coming out into the midst of everyone to stake your claim on me. Did you want me for something in particular?' she asked, hoping he would mention her new appointment to the queen, only to find he had other things on his mind.

Arching a brow, he grinned down at her. 'Only to dance with my wife. I'd hardly call that bold, merely...' he lifted his head and swept a thoughtful glance at the other dancers who were eyeing them curiously, then nodded decisively '...sensible.'

From beneath a fringe of silky black lashes, Jane shot him a glance that was somewhere between dubious and amused. Such a look made Guy smile in secret contentment. The idea of keeping his wife a bit uncertain as to how *sensible* he intended to be regarding his husbandly prerogatives was certainly not objectionable to him. All the same, he felt a nagging uncertainty when he saw her tilt her head back and meet his gaze with a determination of her own.

'Jane, my love, I'm not overly jealous when I

see other gentlemen dancing with my wife, but I look forward to the time when we can be alone.' He went on to make soft, sensual suggestions in her ear until Jane flushed scarlet like a new bride. His proposals proved provocative, especially to Guy, who became increasingly dedicated to the idea of enjoying some marital intimacy later.

Jane's breath caught in her throat at his softly spoken words. A moment later it escaped in a fluttering sigh as she gazed up at him. 'You say the sweetest things, Guy, but now is not the time and I feel discomfited by the proximity of others. Later—when we have more privacy, there are things I will say to you—though I must warn you that you will find them far from sweet.'

It was much later when Guy let himself into the bedchamber after carousing with fellow knights long after Jane had gone to bed. He was renowned for being able to hold his drink, but tonight his head was spinning in an alcohol-fuelled haze. Casting a heavy-lidded gaze across the room, he observed the top of his wife's head above the covers. Supposedly she was fast asleep.

Trying to make as little noise as possible, he

stripped down to his black hose and shirt. He was about to remove them when she stirred and sat bolt upright, blinking sleep from her eyes, giving no hint of how she had tossed and turned on coming to bed, too exhausted and tense to sleep until ten minutes earlier when, tired of waiting for her errant husband to come to bed, sleep had finally claimed her.

'Jane!' His first word came with some surprise, but he quickly recovered and smiled lopsidedly, his fascinated gaze moving over her. Her shining hair tumbled over her shoulders in a gloriously untidy mass of honey-gold curls, framing a face of heartbreaking beauty. 'Your pardon, my love. I did not mean to disturb you.' Ruefully his eyes did a downward sweep of his clothes. 'As you see, I am preparing myself for bed.'

He stood quite still as she flung back the covers and swung her legs over the edge of the bed. In the dim light his eyes gazed into hers. Pride and courage showed in every feature of her face, from her high cheekbones and stubborn little nose to her small chin. And yet her mouth was vulnerable and soft—as soft as the breasts that swelled beneath the bodice of her nightdress, practically begging for his touch. But it was her mouth he wanted to taste first...'You look angry, my love. Is anything amiss?'

Jane glowered at him, irate at having her sleep disturbed. 'Amiss? You might say that.'

'Alas.' He sighed as if forlorn. Stepping close to her, he brushed a lock of hair from her face, bending near as he did so, fanning her face with his wine-laden breath which made her wrinkle her nose and turn away her face. 'I am to be tortured more, then. The merest sight of you is enough to bring me pain.'

'Control your lust,' she bridled, brushing away his hand and moving away from him. 'And I will not be pawed.'

'Perhaps a small libation, then,' he suggested in a cajoling voice. 'Some wine. Perhaps it will— settle your nerves.'

'My nerves!' The words were lashed out. 'It is your nerve that must be reckoned with. Of that, my lord, you have no short supply—and you have drunk enough wine to float a barge on the river. Where have you been? I have things to say to you that cannot wait until morning.'

'You abuse me, Jane.' He shrugged. 'I simply know my wants and seek them out.'

Guy longed to put his arms about her, to enfold her against his chest and kiss her. But any tender feelings vanished when she began to stride about his chamber like a warrior queen going into battle. Her hair, freed from the conical headdress she had worn earlier, flowed down her back in a golden mass. Her eyes snapped in a green blaze, the golden specks in them clearly visible. Guy thought he had never seen such a glorious creature in his life.

When he attempted to interrupt her in her pacing, she shook off his restraining hand with such violence he fell back, and as her anger mounted his took shape. He wanted this woman more than any other on earth—and all she wanted to do was talk. He knew what about—that after she had vented her spleen about his securing her a position as a lady to the queen she would throw in some more about his attack on Aniston—but in his opinion, it could wait until later. The arrogance, the pride, the stubborn belief that he was right, which had been bred in him from boyhood, for a man needed these traits in battle, erupted to the surface of his mind.

He leaned his hips against the edge of a table, his arms crossed and from beneath hooded lids he watched her stride up and down, kicking aside her robe at each turn as though she did not know what she was to say or even where to begin. He waited patiently. He didn't attempt to touch her. He was more surprised by her attitude and even more by her explosive temper. She positively crackled and he was sure if he looked close he would see the sparks.

She stopped her pacing and turned at last, standing with her hands on her hips, her breathing deep and uneven.

'Aren't you at least going to ask me why I am so angry?'

'I was hoping you would cease your pacing and stand still long enough to tell me,' he said, the fumes of liquor clearing from his mind. He continued to lean against the table, his face as blank as hers, but in his eyes was a snap of something that said he was not as calm as he appeared.

Jane tossed back her head and he was alarmed to see not only the rage she had managed to subdue somewhat, but what looked like a mixture of contempt and anguish.

'You really do have an inflated opinion of yourself, don't you, Guy? How dare you speak of me loosely to the queen? How dare you order my life in this way?'

'What?' Guy unfolded his arms and his long, lean, handsome body rose to its full height. 'May I ask what the queen has to do with this…this temper you are in?' he asked unwisely.

'Temper? Temper, is it?' she flared. 'Has it not occurred to you what you are doing? You know perfectly well that the queen has requested my presence at court.' She laughed bitterly. 'After all, it was you who put the idea into her head, although being the simpleton I am, it did not occur to me at first. But now I do know.' A muscle began to tick on the side of his jaw, but Jane wasn't finished and she was too infuriated to care that he looked murderous. 'How could you do that—without discussing a matter as serious as this with me?'

'Am I to understand by your anger that you have objections to being one of the queen's waiting ladies?'

She stared at him incredulously before throwing her arms into the air in frustration and resuming her pacing. 'I do not believe this. Of course I have objections! Is there no limit to your interference in my life?'

'Interference? Is that how you see it? I am your husband, madam, and I have every right to do what I consider best for you.'

'Best for you, you mean. You should have told me what you intended so that I could have prepared myself, instead of manipulating me.'

'Prepared yourself? Look at you now. Jane, you would have resisted this had I told you.'

'So, my lord, you resorted to trickery. To do something so underhand is what I have come to expect of you.'

'For God's sake, Jane, what will it take?'

She whirled round, her eyes flashing fire. 'You think I have a price? A diamond necklace? A bigger castle? Is that how you measure everything between us?'

Guy just stared at her. 'Well, well,' he said at length. 'It seems I've found me a little spitfire.' He leaned forwards so his face was on a level with hers, looking deep into her eyes. 'Are you so afraid of me, Jane?'

Lowering her eyes, she shook her head, trying to dispel the sudden image that sprung to mind— of the awful violent fury her father had heaped on Andrew when he had learned of his support for the Lancastrians. As a witness to the scene and countless other before, she had kept her face void of expression during their exchange, but she had not forgotten.

'Of course not,' she said in answer to Guy's question, for no matter what wrongs he had perpetrated as a warrior, she knew deep inside that he would never hurt her.

'I know you're not,' he countered softly. 'That's one of the reasons I wanted you for my wife.'

She smiled thinly. 'Aye, my lord, but I believe your desire for an heir was at the forefront of your mind.'

Drawing himself upright, he combed agitated fingers through his thick hair. 'I do not deny that. To have an heir to carry on after I am gone is important to me. But I care about you, Jane. You know how I feel about you. Dear God, I've told you often enough. I want to look after you—see you come to no harm. And don't look at me like that. God's teeth, you look at me as though I'd offered you some insult.'

'Which was precisely what you did when you suggested this latest mad scheme to the queen. Every time you come near me you do damage. Every time you try to repair what you have done you make it worse. Did it not enter that stubborn head of yours that I might not want to go to court? If tonight's display of resentment is a sample of what I shall be forced to endure at Whitehall, then I do not want to be a part of it.'

'It won't always be so.' Guy turned furiously away from her, leaning the palms of both hands flat on the top of the table. He was a man who was accustomed to having his own way in most things and, just recently, on making Jane his wife, he had become even more sure that his way was the right, the *only* way of doing things.

'Stop this, Jane. Why do you fight me so?'

'You know why,' she cried. 'I cannot help myself.'

'Jane,' he said, trying to control his impatience. How he wished that day he had stabbed Aniston had never happened. 'We have been over this.

Nothing can change what has happened, so let it be. I am sincere, I beg you to believe that.'

Jane was stirred despite her anger by the truth of his words. He was right—nothing could change what had happened. He stood still, but it seemed to her that his broad shoulders drooped, as if under the force of some strong feeling.

'My God, you are not very complimentary to me—or to yourself,' he said. 'Can you not see that I am not your enemy? I want nothing more than for us to live in harmony.'

'And how can we do that with me at court and you at Cherriot Vale?'

'If it will calm your fears, I will tell you that we will not be apart. I have been summoned to court—to arrange a tourney at Windsor. So that we would not be parted, I suggested to the queen that you become one of her ladies. Was that so very wrong of me?'

Jane whirled away, touched to know that he had been thinking of her after all. 'That's the trouble,' she answered on a less aggressive note. 'Your meddling has cost me dear. When I decided to cast Richard out of my life, I did so because I wanted to make my own decisions, to be my own woman. Perhaps then I would be allowed to get on with my life—to be my own mistress. I now realise that it was an impossible dream. It is not possible for a married woman to exist without the interference of her husband, who believes he has the power to control her and to order her at his will—that she must know her place, to be a servile nonentity for the rest of her life.'

Savagely Guy turned to face her. 'Did you actually believe you forfeited the right to make decisions when you married me? Is that what you thought?'

Jane paled visibly. She drew herself up straight. 'What else was I to think?'

'The last thing I want to do is control you. You are like a free spirit, a woman who blossoms under her own will. May God help me if I attempt to take that away from you.'

Jane was touched by his declaration, but apart from a softening in her eyes her expression was unchanged. She did not intend letting him off the hook altogether. 'Very well. I will go to court and be whatever the queen wants me to be—and you. You are my husband and no matter what you say, you *own* me. I am the one without the right to hold myself from you. For you, it seems a wife requires the same qualities as needed when choosing a charger.'

Astonished, Guy stared at her. 'You think that because you had a beautiful face and spirit you would suit my purposes admirably? As a bedmate, perhaps a brood mare for my children? Good God, woman, I did not marry you for that.'

Even as he spoke his mind and senses were drawn to how she looked—the fine creamy smoothness of her skin, the firelight playing on her hair that hung gloriously down her back, picking out the gold lights. He noted how her dark eyebrows swept upwards and the dark green of her eyes blazed at him from across the room. Like a doe poised to run from him, she watched him as he closed the distance between them. When he was close she whirled about and headed for the bed, only to find him right behind her. His tone ominous, he said,

'Don't walk away from me, Jane.'

'Why not?' She flared, nearly sizzling with indignation. 'I've said all I have to say for one night.'

'But I haven't,' he murmured, pressing himself close to her back. A throbbing pressure grew in his loins. He had played out his hand with patience, but now it was waning before the tumult of his passions. His concern for her timidity dwindled apace with his growing need. Drawing aside the sweet-scented tresses from her face, he placed his mouth close to the ear of the virgin-minded temptress. He would see that she understood the full weight of what she had started.

'I have plenty to say, but it can wait. You ought to be nicer to me, Jane. A position with the queen is an enviable one, even if you don't deem it so."

Furious, she spun round. Her clothes hid nothing from him and she saw the hard flint of passion strike sparks in the deep-blue eyes as they moved over her. Her full, ripe breasts swelled against the fabric that moulded itself to her and to the delicate peaks which thrust forwards impudently and lured him with their eagerness to be out. Guy's breath caught in his throat. He was already familiar with the delectable body concealed beneath her nightdress. She was what every man dreamed of, a vision of incomparable beauty. His eyes revelled in their freedom as they feasted hungrily on her body, seeking out every charm hidden from him.

Jane felt devoured and it took an effort of her will to remain pliant beneath his probing eyes. 'Don't you dare touch me,' she hissed. 'I do not intend for you to molest me. If that is what you want, then I am sure there are women you can buy cheap down by the river, my lord, but I'm not for sale.'

He laughed in derision. 'It is not a matter of cost, Jane. More a matter of need—and you suit my need better than any woman I know.'

His taunt was too much! When she raised her arms to push him away, it seemed to Guy that she meant to vent her rage in a more physical manner. He caught her slim waist and snatched her to him to prevent her from striking him.

Jane's breath left her in a sudden gasp. 'Release me. You press yourself beyond the bounds of decency.'

'Aye, Jane, that I do. But listen, my love, and mark my words well.' He drew her closer. 'The playing is over.'

His voice was low and husky in her ears, and Jane had to dip deeply into her reservoir of will to dispel the slow numbing of her defences. Suddenly nervous of him, she glanced about the room, unable to bear his attention he so freely gave her. The pressure of his touch was light, but to her it felt like a trap of steel. She began to seriously doubt her wisdom in confronting him tonight. She should have stayed asleep and waited until morning.

She was aware of his naked chest beneath the white shirt and the manly feel of his lean, muscular body pressed to hers, while he was made totally conscious of her meagrely clad form. Her eyes lifted slowly to regard his face and her body quivered as she remembered his lips upon her breasts, his hands upon her naked flesh.

Why do I hold myself back? she asked herself suddenly. This was what she'd wanted and yearned for. Must her pride tear them apart?

They stared at each other for a second of suspended time, which could as well have been an hour or more. Then slowly, almost haltingly, Guy lowered his mouth to hers.

It seemed like an eternity since he had last tasted her lips. The lengthy separation certainly wasn't because he didn't want her. On the contrary, he had often found himself pacing the floor as he tried to remind himself of his goals and bolster his will against an almost overwhelming need to have her back within his embrace. From the very first, it had been his plan to keep his distance for extended periods of time, in so doing allowing her to come to an awareness of his innocence and of what her true feelings were towards him, yet knowing all the while that he was playing a dangerous game of chance wherein he could lose her for ever. By dint of will, he had held to his resolve, but the lengthy wait had made him unwilling to accept the situation.

And so he kissed her with all the passion he had been holding in check since she had turned her back on him. Only he knew the agony he had suffered during their separation. His mouth moved on hers with tender fierceness and, when she began kissing him back, his kiss became more insistent. He parted her lips with his tongue, urging her to respond. Jane trembled at the intimacy of his touch, but instead of pulling away, as Guy expected her to do, she fitted her body tightly against his rigid arousal, as lost in the passionate kiss as he was. She curled her tongue into his consuming mouth, sliding it around and under his in a slow, sensual dance, tasting the essence of the wine he had consumed earlier.

When her nightdress got in the way of his questing hands, she pulled it up, whisked it over her head and, with an outward sweep of her arm, tossed it away.

'That's much better,' her husband muttered against her throat after thrusting her back on to the soft covers. He divested himself of his clothes and, from the edge of the bed where he stood tall and naked, slowly perused the curving form now illuminated by the whimsical radiance of the candles. It was just like considering a lavish feast— he didn't know exactly where to begin.

Bending a knee upon the edge of the mattress, he leaned across the bed until he lay braced on an elbow beside his wife, who was watching him from beneath her lowered lashes, her breathing quickening the closer he came. For a long moment, he made no effort to touch her, only admire her features and softly parted lips, but the temptation to do more than just look proved stronger than his power to resist. As lightly as the brush of a feather, his mouth caressed hers with fleeting kissing, parting her gently curving lips until they began to respond.

Her fingers threaded through the hair at his nape as his lips traced downwards and he heard her gasp in delight as his open mouth found a nipple. Hungrily he devoured the soft peak, tasting its sweet nectar, teasing, evoking small, quickening tremors that seemed to shake her whole body. She arched her back to receive the best of his attention, which he gave eagerly and continued on with fervent dedication until she was all but writhing beneath his delicious assault.

'Don't ask me to stop, Jane, for I fear I cannot,' he murmured, raising his head momentarily. 'I've wanted you for so long, hungered for you. I couldn't wait a moment longer.'

'Please don't stop,' she whispered emphatically, as she abandoned her now-vulnerable softness against him. 'I want you…'

Guy sucked the words from her lips, his mouth eagerly taking hers as their bodies strained together. She moaned softly under the exploring, practised hands and clung to him as she gave herself wholly to his passion. She thought she was still dreaming until her thighs were gently urged apart and the exploration deepened. Her heart soared with joyful relief as gentle fingers moved with tantalising slowness over her softly swelling flesh, eliciting within her womanly being a quickening excitement. She felt his manhood questing against her, finding its place and entering deep within her. She gasped at the sensations she was experiencing, sliding her arms about his neck and pressing her soft breasts in the mat of hair that covered his chest, pulling his head down to hers. Her kiss was full and inviting, without reserve. He held her close and began to move, gently at first, but the violence of their passion consumed them both and they forgot themselves in its mounting storm. They gloried in it as they were dissolved in a mutual fire which faded slowly.

Chapter Nine

The candle flame flickered in the gentle breeze that stirred the curtains at the windows and bounced eerie shadows across the walls and ceiling. Jane lay back against the pillows, wrapped in Guy's arms, their legs entwined. Her face burned where his lips had caressed her tender flesh. Her mind dwelt on how he looked, his long, lean body stretched out on the huge bed, and when he had reached for her again, it was impossible to hide the sudden naked desire that shone in her eyes. She had felt her body heating up, her heart rate quickened once more.

Saturated in this renewed passion, she knew she could not pretend, because she wanted to remember everything that they did together. She *wanted* to think about it, linger on it, close her eyes and squirm with pleasure at the thought of those hot, blissful moments they had made love. She wanted to dwell on each and every glorious detail.

Feeling strangely disembodied, as if she floated on a cloud, her eyes flickered open and a contented smile shaped her lips as Guy lightly traced his finger down her thigh.

On a sigh she tilted her head to look at him, looking deep into his eyes. It was strange, but even now she still felt that there was an inherent part of him she could not reach, that there was a part of him he was holding from her—as if his heart was elsewhere.

'What a lot of time we've wasted,' she murmured, thrusting the intrusive thoughts away, hoping that whatever was holding him back would resolve itself in time.

He half-smiled as his finger left her thigh and found her breast, lightly running it around the pink peak thrusting forwards impudently. 'You hated me, remember.'

'No, I didn't. I just know your actions frightened me more than I could stand.'

'I admit I was at my most cruel that day. But it happened and I cannot retract what I did, much as I would like to. I should not have allowed you to alienate me, but I thought after what happened you couldn't bear my touch, that you would fight me if I tried to have you. Strange, how our minds played against us. We should have followed our instincts.' He pressed his lips against her white throat. 'We'd have found each other much sooner.'

Jane warmed to his words and knew as long as she had breath in her body she would thrill to his touch. She could summon no resistance when he caressed her. Her very soul seemed to be his and her body responded more to his will than her own. But until the issue of Richard and what had happened that day could be resolved in her mind, could she say she was his without reservation?

Until she was summoned to court, Jane was to stay at Rosemead. With its privilege and luxury, she imagined that most people would dream of being at court, but as the daughter of a lowly cloth merchant, she had thought such privileges beyond her. Her parents were delighted with her sudden elevation to a lady of the royal household, and since her father's business had suffered in the past and showed improvement since her marriage to the illustrious Earl of Sinnington, she began to understand how much more he might gain by her royal connections.

Wanting his wife to look at her best for her new appointment, Guy purchased an assortment of her father's finest fabrics to be made into gowns. With the help of two of Lady Cecilia's most accomplished maids, Jane began to sew. To make sure that she was prepared for her new life, for there was so much she had to learn about life at court, while they worked her mother-in-law talked about what would be expected of her, the routine and social functions she would have to attend, and how much her life would change.

Jane wanted so much to learn of this world she was about to enter, but the more she learned the more overwhelmed she became and realised she was woefully inadequate and unprepared for court life. When she was finally summoned to the queen at the Palace of Westminster, Lady Cecilia kissed her and wished her every happiness, despite her servitude, and told her that she must be guided by others.

Jane rode away from Rosemead with an armed escort provided by the queen. Guy would have accompanied her, but he had left for Windsor a week earlier to begin preparing for the forthcoming tourney. The day was cold and she shivered as they travelled along the Strand towards Charing Cross, and on to the sprawling Palace of Westminster, which housed the king's court and government.

Already the life ahead of her had taken on a whole new meaning. She was filled with anxiety as she was about to enter a life that was completely alien to her. There was another matter that concerned her, something she had kept to herself since coming to Rosemead. She had reason to believe she was with child, a child conceived on their wedding night. She would tell Guy when next they met, and she knew how happy this would make him. But without him by her side as she rode to Westminster Palace, never had she felt so alone.

The palace was a busy, bustling place. Jane was overawed by its sheer size and opulence. Men-at-arms, servants and heads of state were everywhere, and she wondered if she would ever find her way around the bewildering maze of corridors and chambers.

She shared a room high up in the palace with

a young lady by the name of Ann Rowland. An attractive, pleasant girl, she was the daughter of an earl. On seeing Jane's nervousness among the queen's other ladies—despite being a countess, some of them considered her an inferior commoner who did not know her place—she took her hand and smiled.

'Don't look so worried. You'll be all right. I'll take care of you,' Ann assured her, and Jane's nerves calmed on hearing the soothing sincerity of her tone. 'You will find it a little bewildering at first, meeting so many people whom you do not know, but you will soon get used to it.'

Jane was overwhelmed by the strangeness of the court and confused by its many rituals. Her life took on an established pattern as she became caught up in her many duties, which were not as arduous or as challenging as she had expected. With some of the other ladies, as well as general duties such as walking with the queen, serving her refreshments and accompanying her to the chapel, she was one of several ladies responsible for preparing the queen's clothes and jewels for her many activities, mending and cleaning and embroidering gowns as required.

There was plenty of time for recreation, when they would recite poetry and sing along to the lute played by the Queen's favourite musician, and even though the weather was turning colder there were trips upon the river and rides into the country. Jane kept a modest demeanour at all times, and as the days passed, the acceptance she had prayed for happened gradually.

As the Countess of Sinnington she wore only the finest clothes—velvet and silk and gold thread, ermine, sables and jewels which Guy had presented her with. When not in attendance on the queen, she was forever surrounded by adoring swains. Taking advantage of the absence of the formidable Earl of Sinnington, they all vied for her company—dashing young knights young girls' fantasies were made of. But there was something in their eyes Jane did not trust—their smooth, cocksure smiles made her uneasy. But she laughingly accepted their attentions, seeing no harm in partaking of a little innocent revelry.

The queen and her ladies were returning to the palace after spending the afternoon sailing on the river. It had been a fine, colourful procession, making its way to the tower and back to the palace, each barge containing the queen's favourite ladies and lords. When it was time to disembark at the palace stairs, all were tired, but in good spirits as they walked through the gardens to the river entrance.

As usual there was great activity in the palace yard, with horses being made ready. Jane's gaze settled on a broad-shouldered man tending a great black destrier with flowing mane and tail. The man was bareheaded and there was no mistaking that shock of fair hair. It could only belong to Cedric, her husband's loyal squire.

With a supreme effort, Jane stood still, but the hand that held her cloak beneath her chin trembled. If Cedric was here, then Guy must be here also.

'Jane!'

The voice was behind her. She turned slowly. There could be no mistake. It was Guy, his tall, powerfully built figure shrouded in a wine-coloured cloak lined with sable. Why had he not sent her a note informing her that he was to return to Westminster? She looked up at the familiar, almost too-perfect features, set in an expression of sombre calm. Her face was flushed, her eyes bright with her welcome. A ready smile curved her lips, which faded on seeing his grave expression and how his lips were pressed together. She imagined that he was a stranger, someone she had never met before, someone who had never held her in his warm embrace.

'My lord,' she murmured.

Considering the turmoil within her, her voice was curiously calm, her green eyes seeming to swim in some luminous light. Ever since he had left her at Rosemead she had not allowed herself to dwell too long on those nights they had spent together, but now that he was here she started and could not stop. She felt again the almost-pain as her breasts had been crushed against his unyielding chest and the warmth of his breath against her cheek—once more she remembered the urgency in his deep-blue gaze as he lowered his lips to hers. She remembered his endearments spoken during the passionate moments of their lovemaking, and the awful, stabbing ache that grew and grew in her throat was evidence of how much she had missed him.

'How fortunate that we should encounter each other here, Jane. It's good to see you again.'

Taking her arm, he drew her aside as the other ladies proceeded to the royal apartments. His gaze had riveted on her the instant she crossed the yard and the sight of her had the devastating impact of a boulder crashing into his chest. Never had she looked so radiantly beautiful or so serene. The three weeks they had been apart, he had missed her more than he thought possible. Every muscle in his body had tightened, straining to endure the torture of her nearness. But it was a torture he welcomed, an agony he didn't want to be spared.

In the beginning he had always been the sort of man who, when he made a decision, seldom changed his mind. He devised plans entirely by his usual mode of thought: logical, precise, effective. But so much had changed, his whole life had changed since he had made Jane his wife, and now the old way of thinking didn't make sense any more. He had not anticipated the effect she would have on him. But despite the nights they had spent in each other's arms at Rosemead, it pained him to think that she still could not bring herself to trust him entirely.

When he looked at her he gave no hint of his thoughts. His face was harsh in the gathering dusk, his eyes expressionless. 'I hope you are in good health, Jane.'

'Yes—yes,' she replied awkwardly. 'But you have taken me by surprise. I—I—did not expect to see you here.' She searched his face for those telltale signs that he had missed her, but saw no evidence of it. 'But what has brought you to Westminster?'

One of the reasons that had driven Guy back to London were the rumours that his young wife was enjoying an extraordinary popularity among the gentlemen of the court and that she had no end of admirers. His imagination had run riot, an array of fleeting emotions engulfing him. The spurs of jealousy were sharp and pricked him to a painful depth. Jane was no sophisticated courtier, too innocent to know what was really in those scoundrels' minds who trailed after her day and night—namely, bedding her the minute his back was turned.

His reply was brusque. 'I've come to see you. We need to talk.'

Her heart was pounding. 'Now?'

He nodded. Taking her elbow, he escorted her swiftly inside the palace, along a corridor and into a small panelled room overlooking the river.

'We'll not be disturbed in here.' Closing the door behind them, Guy waited for her to be seated in one of two chairs in front of a small desk. He perched his hip on the edge of it, crossed his arms over his chest and, with one well-defined eyebrow jutted sharply upwards he studied her, his leg so close to her own leg that the fabric of his breeches touched hers. His face was hard and implacable.

Jane stared at him, her mind in a complete turmoil as she tried to combat her mounting alarm. 'Guy? What is it? Is there something wrong?'

With eyes as hard as blue flint, Guy stared down at her beautiful, bewildered face. 'You might say that. It concerns your behaviour. Rumours have reached me that, when you are not waiting on the queen, your time is spent surrounded by admirers. Apparently not only do they wait on your every whim, but you encourage their attentions.'

Jane gasped, appalled by what he was implying. 'But that is quite ridiculous.'

'Is it? At Windsor I have listened as my fellow knights have regaled me about courtly matters, and on more occasions than I am comfortable with, your name has been mentioned. If they are to be believed, it would seem the fact that you are the Countess of Sinnington enables you to do as you please without impunity.' Guy's companions would have been dumbfounded to know that, as he languidly listened, he was seething inside. 'Apparently the entire male population at court seem to be on intimate terms of friendship with my wife.'

Jane stared at him, resisting the urge to laugh, unwilling to antagonise him—she had forgotten in these past quiet days that his eyes could look like that. 'Dear me! Is that all? And this is what brings you back to Westminster?'

'What have you to say for yourself,' he demanded coldly, displeased that she could treat the matter so lightly.

Her attitude was quick to change. 'What you mean is how do I defend myself,' she replied equally as coldly, anger, full-bodied and fortifying, bringing her to her feet. 'Never in my wildest dreams did I expect you would have the gall to criticise *my* behaviour. Next to the life you have led, I am as innocent as a babe. Of all the loathsome, hypocritical, arrogant...' she burst out furiously, and then with a superhuman effort she took control of her rampaging ire. Lifting her chin, she looked straight into his enigmatic eyes.

'Very well! I am guilty—guilty of every grossly exaggerated, meaningless, harmless, innocuous incident I am accused of. But I have done nothing to be ashamed of or to make you ashamed of me. You *cannot* believe the rumours you have heard. If so, it is unworthy of you and insulting to me. Am I to believe that this outrageous slur gives proof that you care for me, or are you merely concerned that I might bring dishonour to your name?'

Guy gazed at the tempestuous beauty standing before him, her eyes flashing like angry jewels, her breasts rising and falling with suppressed fury, and his anger gave way to a reluctant admiration for her honesty. 'I will not be cuckolded, Jane.'

The insinuation stung her. She was also hurt at the mere suggestion that she would ever be unfaithful. 'How dare you think that of me? I would never do that.'

'You might feel that way now, but a few more days alone at court would be plenty of time for a beautiful young woman to begin to feel neglected and look elsewhere for company.'

Her jaw clenched, her hurt expression hardened to one of angry defiance. 'That is not true. You cannot believe that of me. If you have married me and cannot trust me, then all our life is a mockery.'

His lips curved in a cynical sneer. 'Trust? That's a fine word coming from you.'

Jane had the grace to look contrite, for despite the times they had spent in loving, her trust in him had been shaken that day he had drawn his dagger on Richard.

Her bitter voice spoke to Guy's heart, but yet he was deafened by the shock he had felt when the rumour had reached him. 'If you do not welcome their attention, then why do you encourage it?'

She stared at him with scornful green eyes. 'That is unfair. I do not. I never have. Can I be blamed for overzealous males who give me no moment of respite? If you don't want other men to look at me then perhaps you should take me back to your castle and lock me in your deepest dungeon out of sight.'

'Don't be ridiculous,' Guy said, rising to his full

height. 'This has gone on long enough. It doesn't have to be like this. Jane, I am trying—just in case you haven't noticed.'

'It would be difficult not to,' she quipped. 'I have enough jewels to adorn the necks of every lady at court. I doubt even the queen has anything comparable. But I do thank you for such fine gifts.'

The expression on his face was so hard that her smile faded and she drew back. 'Thank me? Why? Do you forget that you are the wife of the Earl of Sinnington? In this capacity, you must be the most exquisitely adorned woman at court. Do not consider yourself obliged to thank me.'

Offended, she raised her chin a notch. 'Then I take it back. But I had hoped they were personal gifts given by a husband to his wife, not family heirlooms to be handed on as tradition dictates.'

He glowered at her. 'I'm beginning to think you must enjoy baiting me—you do it better than anyone I know.'

'I do not bait you. I have never played games with your affections.'

Raking his fingers through his hair in frustration, Guy walked over to a flagon of mulled wine resting near the fire and poured some into a goblet. Turning, he studied her in silence. After a moment he said in a quiet, almost-apologetic tone that startled Jane, 'No, you haven't.' When she remained silent, watching him with wary suspicion, he said with an irritated sigh, 'Whatever has happened between us in the past that has upset you I apologise for, and if I have wronged you… nothing can change that, but I never meant to hurt you. There must be harmony between us if we are to make our marriage work.'

'How do you propose we do that when there has been so much distrust between us?'

He shot her a hard look. 'The distrust was on your side, not mine,' he was quick to remind her. 'I need you—we need each other.'

Paling significantly, she pulled back with a frightened look, thinking of her unborn child, the child that remained her secret. 'Would you leave me, Guy?'

Her words brought him up sharp. When he thought of life without her, he found himself faced by an abyss so vast, so terrifying, he would literally close his eyes and turn away. He could not imagine a world without her. He could think of no other. 'No,' he said, placing the goblet down. 'I would not do that.'

He gazed down at her. He had seen the loss of innocence, the disillusionment in her eyes over the months he had known her, eyes that had once been candied and trusting and soft when she had looked at him. 'I barely know you now, Jane,' he murmured. 'I'm not sure you know yourself. You're changing—and I liked the way you were when I first met you in that woodland glade. You were not like anybody I'd ever met. You were utterly unique.'

His words tugged at her heart. 'I am still the same. I am not changing.'

He caught her face between his hands. 'Yes, you are,' he said urgently.

'But, Guy—'

'But nothing. Stop punishing me! Can't you just once give me the benefit of the doubt?' he retorted fiercely, trying to justify himself, although he didn't know why he should have to. 'You cast me in the role of villain—but I am no villain. I don't deserve this—nor do I have the time to wait out another of your grudges. What more can I do?'

Feeling very close to tears, which seemed to

happen often of late, she shook her head. 'I don't know,' she cried. 'I wish I could tell you. Truly I do.'

'Then I will tell you. You are mine, Jane, and what I have I intend to keep. No one will have you but me. I am your husband and I will have my due. Only I shall taste your body's joys. And when I snap my fingers you will come.'

'And as an obedient wife I shall obey you,' she replied coolly. 'Is there anything else you wish to say to me? The queen will have need of me.'

'No. I have not yet done,' he replied, remembering the other reason that had brought him back to Westminster. His voice took on a note of urgency and he moved closer to her, his eyes intense as they held hers. 'Jane, you should not stay here. No, don't speak,' he said when he saw she was about to interrupt. 'I know what I am saying.'

'You want me to leave the court? May I ask why when you were so insistent that I come here—and where would you have me go?' In spite of herself, Jane found her eyes captured and held by Guy's blue ones. She stood and faced him, like a sparrow mesmerised by a bird of prey, riveted by that sparkling gaze, not daring to move. It seemed to her that if she uttered a word something rare and precious would be broken. In the end it was Guy who sighed and spoke.

'I want you to go back to Cherriot—to the castle. I have reason to believe that it is not safe for you here.'

Jane felt a sudden coldness creeping over her. 'For what reason do you believe I am in danger?'

Drawn by the depths of the green eyes looking into his and by the freshness of the lips slightly parted to reveal moist, shining teeth, Guy had to master a passion that was in danger of getting out of control.

'Because Aniston is here—at Westminster. His company has been disbanded and returned to London. I believe he will seek you out, which is why I think you would be safer at Cherriot.'

Jane paled. 'Richard? He—he's here?' She glanced about the room, as if she expected him to materialise at any moment.

Guy nodded. 'Yes. I would advise you not to be alone. He bears a grudge because of what happened between us.'

'Is it me he means to harm—or you?'

'There's no telling what he will do. Elevated by

his imminent knighthood, he believes nothing is too great or impossible to be overcome.'

'I see. Thank you for telling me, but I have no intention of running away from Richard,' she said, stiff with pride and anger. 'I will not give him the satisfaction. Besides, I am protected by the queen.'

The warm light went out of Guy's eyes. 'Have you understood nothing?' he said grimly. 'The queen will not be able to protect you when you are alone in your bed, Jane.'

'I do not sleep alone. I share a room with another of the queen's ladies.'

He nodded. 'Ann Rowland, who is about to go on temporary leave. She is to visit her family in Kent.'

'How do you know that?' Jane asked, her voice quick with indignation.

'Because I have made it my business. Jane, you do realise that I could order you to go home to Cherriot.'

'Order me, my lord? You would *order* me?'

Meeting the coldness in her eyes, he sighed. He was all too well aware that for him to issue an order to his wife would only serve to alienate her further. Persuasion was the best ploy to get her to do his bidding. 'I have your best interests at heart, Jane. Believe that. Will you do as I ask and return to Cherriot?'

'With Ann about to visit her family, I doubt the queen will give me leave to do so.'

'She would if she realised you are in grave danger here.'

'Then if I am, it is all your fault,' she flared, turning from him.

'What is?'

'Everything?' she replied irrationally, tears of frustration brimming in her eyes. 'Had you not attacked Richard, he would not be seeking vengeance.'

'Jane.' On hearing her name spoken softly, she paused and slowly turned to face him. 'Come here.'

His hand shot out and grasped her wrist as she made a move to leave him. Jane tugged furiously at her imprisoned wrist, but Guy's lean fingers were hard and unyielding. Realising that she could not free herself without an undignified struggle, she let her arm go slack and stood still, but her ire was undiminished. How could he send her away when she wanted so much to be close to him?

'You are not leaving until I have said what I have to say,' he said, moved by her moist eyes. 'I am shortly to return to Windsor. As lady-in-waiting to the queen it is important that no scandal is attached to either of us. Do you understand what I am saying?'

Abruptly Jane stepped away from him, once more struggling to suppress a look of disappointment. But, she thought bitterly, what else had she expected him to say? That he wanted her safe because she actually meant something to him? That he loved her? No. His main concern was for his good name.

She nodded stiffly. 'I understand. Do you know where Richard is now?'

Guy released her and she snatched her hand away and stood rubbing it, her breath coming unevenly.

'He is ill, but not in the accepted sense of the word.'

'What do you mean?'

'I mean,' said Guy with brutal clarity, 'that the libertine and drunkard that he is, he is suffering the after-effects of a debauch and was incapable of standing upright when I left him at a local ale house.'

'So you have seen him?'

'Briefly.'

Jane stood quite still, her eyes wide and frightened, and once again Guy was conscious of that bewildering pain in his heart. He said harshly, 'Now that you know the truth, perhaps you can understand why it is that I want you to return to Cherriot as soon as possible.'

She shook her head. 'No. I will not run away. I came to court to be a handmaiden to the queen and this is where I shall remain.'

'For God's sake, Jane, have the sense to look things in the face—and do not stupidly refuse to do what is right.'

Guy saw her flinch as though he had struck her, then he turned and with long purposeful strides left her, his cloak flying behind him like the sails of a ship.

That night Jane retired to her chamber and slept immediately. It was past the hour of midnight when she came fully awake in an instant and lay staring blankly in the dark, hearing Ann's steady breathing. Then she realised what had awakened her. It was her meeting with Guy and knowing he was close.

She hadn't told him that she was carrying his child. Having known the heat of his body close beside her, his warm lips parting hers, his arms holding her tightly and the thrust of his maleness between her thighs, afraid he would insist on sending her away if she told him, hating the thought of them being apart, she would nurse her secret a while longer.

Dizzy with the remembrance of what they had shared, her confusion came from the haunting sense of pleasure that now overwhelmed her. What spell had this man, her husband, cast upon her that she should want him so fiercely? She had never felt so much a woman as when she lay on his bed. 'But he is but a man,' she whispered in the dark, 'with no special gift above other men.' So why, she thought in her confusion, must he be the one to rouse her above other men?

When sleep came again it was not the peaceful slumber of before.

A measure of disquiet existed between Jane and Guy following their meeting, and a day of dubious calm passed. Her defiance had set him on edge and her refusal to return to Sinnington Castle made matters difficult for him. The only way he could make sure no harm came to her was for him to keep an eye on her himself.

Accompanying the king when he visited the queen in her apartments, Guy saw Jane seated behind a large embroidery frame by the window. Her green eyes with their long shadowing lashes were looking across the room. In one quick glance he saw the long creamy neck exposed and the soft flesh in the cleft of her breasts, which were outlined by the tight blue bodice of her gown. Since coming to court she seemed even more voluptuous, sensuous and provocative, glowing with colour like an exotic bird. Little wonder, he thought angrily, the gentlemen of the court couldn't keep their eyes off her.

He drew a long, harsh breath, trying to bring his temper under control. When he finally managed to do that, it occurred to him that he was condemning Jane and deciding her future on the basis of common gossip—and she had put up a good defence.

He was tempted to install her in his own chamber, but it was small and lacking in female comforts—a man's room, where his companions came without invite. But he would often dwell on the nights they had spent together at Rosemead. He could still feel that warm, rounded slenderness in his arms and the way in which, for a long moment, she had melted against him and become so much a part of him that her every nerve and pulse and breath and heartbeat had been as though it were his own.

The memory was so intense that it was like experiencing it all over again. She was loving, sensual and warm. She was also imperious, spirited and rebellious, and she had learned to be tough—but she was not cold, not cruel, not heartless.

The day was warm and sunny following two days of constant rain. Taking the opportunity for some recreation in the fresh air, the queen and her retinue of ladies were walking in the grounds of the palace. They were a happy, chattering group, the queen dazzling in full magnificence of jewels and ermine and smelling of jasmine.

As Jane glanced down a flight of stone steps into a yard bustling with activity, her attention was drawn to a small company of men. There were five in all, but Jane felt no inclination to move her gaze past the man lounging closest to the steps. His gaze was fixed on her.

It was Richard.

On seeing her he shoved himself away from the wall and sauntered towards the steps. He stood looking up at her, making no attempt to approach her. A hollow sickness inside her could not be appeased. His eyes devoured her with greed and she would have run from him, but she did not want to cause a scene. His eyes were bloodshot, his face bloated. He'd been drinking. He stood with his arms folded across his barrel chest, watching her with a hard, sombre expression. Nothing in his face indicated the path of his thoughts, yet Jane felt the weight of his unrelenting gaze as surely as if it were a hand upon her shoulder.

Wanting to put as much distance as possible between herself and Richard, she turned her back on him and walked on to join the queen's ladies.

That same evening when the queen had retired and had no further use of her, Jane left the royal apartment with the intention of retiring. The cor-

ridor which led to the stairs to her room was filled
with shadows. Sconces were lit and the small windows were open to let in the cool night air. As
Jane reached the long flight of stone steps, like a
wily serpent Richard stepped out of the shadows
in front of her.

'Richard!'

He lurched towards her, slurring his words. 'Did
I frighten you, Countess?'

'No—you—you took me by surprise.' He was
drunk—so drunk that he could barely stand. 'Why
are you here? What do you want?'

'To speak to you. It is what old friends do.'

Taking her hand, he held it in a hard grasp with
fingers that were feverishly hot and unsteady.
Lifting it suddenly to his fleshy lips, he planted
a wet, alcoholic kiss on it.

It was not a light gesture of gallantry, but a kiss
as greedily passionate as the kisses he had forced
on her once before. The memory repulsed her.
She tried to drag her hand away, but he held it
hard, kissing it again and again, moving his hot,
slack mouth against its cool softness. And when
he lifted his head at last and looked at her, his
eyes were as hot and avid as his mouth had been.

He stared at her for a long moment, breathing hard and unevenly, a dark flush on his cheeks and his eyes bright with a feverish excitement that was as inexplicable to Jane as it was terrifying. Her body shrank and turned cold with a primitive fear and hazy comprehension that the passion she had aroused in him was beyond her control.

She had been disgusted and shocked and furiously angry when he had kissed her before, but she had not been afraid. It had not occurred to her to be, for it had happened in broad daylight and Guy had come to her rescue. But she was afraid now. She was so frightened that for an appalling moment she thought she was going to be physically sick from the fear that cramped her stomach.

A sound of voices and an occasional laugh came from somewhere among the labyrinth of corridors. Irritated, Richard at last released her hand and stepped away. Taking her chance to escape, Jane turned and stumbled up the steps. On reaching her room she closed the door and threw her weight against it, terrified that he might follow her. A candle had been lit and a wan glow of moonlight streaming in through the window allowed her to see the room. Her heart was racing and her teeth chattered as though with cold, and when at last she fumbled for the bolt her shaking hands could not find it. Then she remembered that she had noticed it missing on her arrival, but, having Ann to share the chamber with her and being under no threat, had seen no reason to fasten the door.

Frozen with terror, she stared at the door, wondering what to do on hearing someone—Richard, stumbling up the stairs. His intentions had a terrifying effect on her. This was no longer some nebulous evil that she had to deal with, but a concrete thing. Panic rose within her once more and she tried to fight it down. There was nowhere to run.

Suddenly the heavy door slammed back on its hinges and Richard staggered in. The candle gutted and its disturbed flame sent shadows dancing across the room. The russet bed-hangings seemed to flutter and points of candlelight flickered in the diamond panes of the window. He stared at her standing on the opposite side of her bed. As if he were already savouring a luscious sweetmeat, his tongue flicked slowly over his fleshy lips. Jane was shocked by the glittering, pleasure-seeking lasciviousness she saw in his eyes. She watched as he lurched round the bed towards her, weaving a little in his walk, blocking her escape. With her back to the wall, she could go no further.

Then, quite suddenly, the numbness left her and gave place to sheer panic and horror. This man— this gross, repulsive, drunken man—was going to force himself on her and ravish her. That day in the woods she had first seen the evidence of the suppressed beast within Richard. Now it had re-emerged and showed no sign of any willingness to withdraw into its hiding place inside Richard's savage heart. She bit into her bottom lip, afraid she wouldn't be able to survive this.

'Go away, Richard. You have no right to be here.'

'Want to go to bed, do you? That's right. You go to bed. I won't keep you waiting.' He laughed uproariously, which turned to a drunken chuckle of approval. 'Don't pretend to be shy—not when you've lain with Sinnington. But after tonight you'll know what it's like to lie with a real man, my pretty. Aye, when I'm done, be assured, I'll teach you to spurn me. No woman get's the better of me, Jane.'

'Not even Lucy Lambert?' Jane flung at him.

He stiffened and his eyes widened. And then he opened his mouth wide and laughed loud, yet it was a sound without mirth. 'Aye—Lucy—delectable little Lucy Lambert.' He wagged a warning finger at Jane. 'You've been listening to Sinnington. How else would you know about Lucy?'

'It was rumoured that you had an affair with her. Did you kill her, Richard?'

His expression hardened and he shook his head, as if to clear it of Lucy's image. 'The stupid wench got with child,' he grumbled. 'Her father and those damned brothers of hers would have run me through had they found out.'

'So you did kill her—to silence her, was that it?'

'She became hysterical when I told her nothing could come of it. She clung to me and I pushed her away, knocking her down. When she didn't get up I saw she was dead…'

'So you put her in the lake and made it look as if she had taken her own life.' Jane saw the truth in his eyes and shuddered. 'That was a despicable and cowardly thing to do. You disgust me, Richard. What you did was beneath contempt—just like the malicious rumour you started, telling everyone that you called off our betrothal because

I had given myself to Guy. And Guy? You drew your dagger on him that day in the woods, didn't you? He reacted in self-defence and yet you tried to put the onus on him.'

Richard's eyes flared and his teeth were bared as he hissed, 'Aye—for his arrogance he deserved to die.'

Jane stared at him. So Richard *had* tried to kill Guy, not the other way round, and Guy had defended himself the only way he could. He hadn't lied about that. The pain of betrayal began to hammer in her mind. The thought of what she must have put him through chastened her. Her heart contracted with the shame of it. She'd had her chance to prove her loyalty and failed him. It broke her heart to see it now, but she knew the charge was true.

'You're despicable, Richard. Guy was simply defending himself when he attacked you. Go away at once before someone comes. I never want to see you again. I share this room with another— she will be arriving at any minute.'

'Ah, but the Lady Ann is away visiting her family, so we won't be disturbed. By God, you're a beauty, Jane. Sinnington's a lucky man to have you.' The thick voice held a note of awe. He reached out an unsteady hand and lifted a long tress of her unbound hair.

Quite suddenly the numbness left her and gave way to sheer panic. She struck his hand in fury and terror. 'Don't touch me! Don't dare to touch me!' Her voice was hoarse with fear and loathing.

Swaying, Richard looked down at her and his red-rimmed eyes lit with hunger. He gave a drunken chuckle of approval. 'Gad, but you're ravishing!'

He lunged for her. His clutching hands were on her hair and they gripped it and jerked it brutally, pulling her to him with frightening strength. His eyes seemed to burn into hers and his breathing deepened until he panted over her like a hungry dog over a bone.

Jane screamed and strained against him, pushing at his chest, but he was strong and only laughed at her pitiful struggles. He crushed her to him, forcing her to arch away in disgust, and covered her neck with loathsome kisses. They fell on to the bed. Panic was soon joined by wild instinct as she struggled to free herself, but Richard's sweaty weight and the swathing folds of her own skirt were against her. The looming possibility that she would soon find herself a victim of his lust caused her to fight with every measure of resolve she could muster. She would not surrender her body to this disgusting lecher. She clawed at his face and tried to turn her own aside, but he dug his fingers into her jaw, causing her to cry out in pain.

'Quiet, you little fool,' he ordered, his over-bright eyes terrifying. 'If you know what's good for you, you'll lay back and—'

His words were lost as the door was flung open and a feral growl rent the air, and, as quickly as she had been flung on to the bed, Jane was freed. Befuddled, she lifted her head and found herself staring into a pair of all-too-familiar blue eyes. His strong hands gripped her upper arms and lifted her up.

'You vile dog, Sinnington!' Richard snarled thickly. He was wheezing heavily, having exerted himself well beyond the limits when he was full of drink, and in the gloom his sweaty, reddened face seemed far more bloated than usual. He balled his fist threateningly and shoved it in front of Guy.

'You've intruded too often in my affairs—but this time you've gone too far.'

Guy easily knocked his fist away with the back of his forearm. There was a dangerous edge of scorn in his laugh. 'Get out, Aniston. My wife has made it plain that she doesn't want you here. You'll find yourself dead if you lay one finger on her.' His eyes raked him with contempt. 'You're drunk—which comes as no surprise after spending the day guzzling copious tankards of ale. Go and find a woman more suited to your—sordid inclinations, and leave my wife alone.'

The taunt caused Richard's bulging eyes to flare, vividly attesting to his mounting rage.

Jane stood at a loss, despairing of this confrontation ending well. For now, at least, Richard was distracted from her, but unless he left, the danger wasn't over.

Having expected something like this happening and having kept a watchful eye on Aniston for days, it had been no accident Guy had been close by to hear Jane's cries. Vulnerable and innocent, he could not let Aniston hurt her. He could not let his wife be degraded and hurt by a monster. Taking the initiative, he took Richard's arm and forced him to the door. Opening it, he shoved him into the corridor, following him out. Having followed Guy, Cedric appeared at the top of the stairs.

A foul, guttural oath issued forth as Richard lunged towards his adversary with fingers curled into claws. Come what may, he intended to tighten them around Sinnington's throat. 'You filthy beggar,' he roared. 'I'll teach you to take what should have been mine.'

A second before Richard reached his antagonist, Guy stepped deftly aside. A sharp, gasp was promptly snatched from Richard's throat as he saw stretched out below him the steep flight of stone steps. Desperately he thrust out his hands for the iron rail and strove to untangle his feet, but to no avail. A moment later he was teetering on the brink, experiencing stark terror. His arms flailed in a desperate attempt to halt his forward momentum, but he was unable to gather his equilibrium no matter how he strove to stop himself from falling.

Guy rushed forwards to grab at his tunic, but in an expanse of time that spanned the chasm between life and death, an eternity flashed before Richard's mind's eye. Unable to find anything to hold on to, of a sudden, his rotund body was plummeting head over heels in an awkward descent of the stairs, during the course of which muffled grunts escaped his throat. Then his head slammed into the wall. Though his stumbling descent continued unchecked, no further sound issued from his throat.

Chapter Ten

From where they stood, Guy and Jane and Cedric looked down to where Richard's body lay at a grotesque angle.

'Stay here,' Guy said to Jane, without turning to look at her.

'Please be careful,' she whispered shakily, shocked by what had just happened. She was afraid Richard might be stunned and have a dagger concealed in his belt, waiting for Guy to draw near. 'He will surely kill you if he can.'

Wary of deception, Guy went down the stairs and paused on the step above Richard's body. A pool of blood was spreading around his head and his neck was set at an unnatural angle. He was obviously dead, but to make sure Guy stepped over the body and dropped down on one knee. With two of his fingers he felt for a pulse in his neck. There was none.

Guy went back to Jane. As white as a ghost, she was visibly shocked.

'Is—is he dead?' she whispered.

'Very much so. Come.' He looked at Cedric. 'See that the guards remove the body will you, Cedric? I'll explain what happened to those who will question his death later.'

Placing an arm about her shaking shoulders, Guy drew Jane inside her chamber and closed the door. Clutching a trembling hand over her mouth, she sank bonelessly on to the bed. Not only was she shaking to the very core of her being, but her heart was pounding so hard she thought it would burst. She couldn't breathe, much less think.

'What am I to do?' she asked in a desperate whisper. 'How can I explain this? What can I say happened? Everyone will think I am to blame— how can they not when he's lying dead at the bottom of the stairs to my chamber?'

Seeing her in such distress tore at Guy's heart, but not so much that he had not assessed the situation fully.

'You will do nothing,' he replied firmly. 'You

will have no need to explain anything to anyone. I will do that.'

She stared up at him. 'But everyone will think we killed him.'

'There was no one to witness what transpired but you, me and Cedric. We know the truth. Richard fell.'

'But what if they don't believe us?' demanded Jane, deeply distraught, her voice hoarse to keep it steady. She hugged herself tightly, blinking through a blur or tears.

Sitting beside her, Guy reached out for her clasped hands and held them in his own. The flame of the candle wavered, illuminating her face. The pain in her eyes made his heart ache. 'Don't think. Listen to me. We will stay here together until morning. You will be safe with me.'

'But—Richard is dead…'

He squeezed her hands. 'Trust me, Jane, everything will be all right.' He saw the way she bit her trembling lower lip and went on, 'Considering the amount of liquor Aniston consumed and the state he was in when he left his companions, everyone will see that his own drunkenness led to his death. It will be nothing more than that. You are innocent of any wrongdoing—as I am, Jane.'

'If I have done no wrong, then why am I so consumed with guilt?'

'It will pass. When he was falling, I reached out to save him, but I couldn't. Do you understand what I'm saying? It was an accident.'

Jane nodded. His words made sense, but she was nearly frantic with fear. 'I was so afraid…'

'You had good reason to be. Aniston was a despicable monster. He meant you nothing but ill.'

Jane looked at him and considered him for the first time since he had come to her chamber. 'You already knew that. I know now that he tried to kill you that day in the woods—he—he told me—and I was so ready to blame you. I'm so sorry, Guy. Please forgive me.'

He drew her into his arms. 'Hush, my love, there is nothing to forgive. Aniston spoke the truth. When he drew his dagger, I swear *he* was going to kill *me*, Jane. My reaction was instinctive. Had there been time to think—or had there been distance between us…'

'You are a soldier, trained to protect yourself and others. Instinct made you reach for your dagger—and I'm glad you did, otherwise Richard might have deprived me of my husband. I should have believed in your innocence. I was so con-fused—swept out of my depth and into a helpless maelstrom of emotions that I was unable to under-stand or control. I was haunted by the possibility that you weren't as noble and honourable as you seemed—when all the time... Richard also told me the truth about how Lucy Lambert died. You were right. It was no accident. He confessed to killing her, Guy. Her father was right to suspect him of her murder.'

Guy stared at her, his eyes wide. 'Lucy? You spoke of Lucy?'

'I—I was stalling for time—I thought of all manner of things to stop him hurting me.'

'And he admitted murdering her?'

'He—he said that when she told him she was with child, he—he pushed her and she fell. He said the fall killed her when she knocked her head. He put her body in the lake to allay suspicion.'

'It was the despicable act of a coward. He de-served to die. I'll inform Lucy's brothers of what happened. What Aniston told you was what they suspected all along.'

'What I don't understand is what you were doing

Helen Dickson 351

here. How did you know Richard would come to my chamber?'

'I suspected he would try something like this. I've been watching him. I was proved right.'

'You will stay with me?'

Seeing the vulnerability in her eyes and knowing how difficult it would be for her to get through the rest of the night, Guy gathered her to him. 'All night.'

The official verdict of Richard's death was accidental with no blame attached to anyone. On his arrival in London, renowned for being a braggart and a drunkard, he had let it be known that before Jane's marriage to the Earl of Sinnington, she had been on the brink of becoming betrothed to him. When the guards had removed his body from the bottom of the stairs leading to the countess's room, it was assumed that after consuming large amounts of liquor, he had tried making his way to her chamber. In doing so he had tumbled down the stairs, hitting his head and breaking his neck.

Everyone was in agreement that she'd had a lucky escape.

This was not a lie or a flight of fancy, but the truth of what had actually happened.

Guy also wrote to Lord Lambert, informing him of Richard's confession, finally proving Richard was guilty of killing Lucy.

With Richard no longer a threat, as soon as Guy had seen Jane settled into her routine, he left to prepare for the lists. Jane found it so frustrating, this tendency of his to go tearing back to Windsor. How she wished the tourney would come and go quickly so they could get on with their lives together. She missed him desperately—her lover, her husband, her friend—and yearned for his loving to make her whole again.

Misery, loneliness and despair roiled inside her. After the days of abstinence, she knew she wanted him again. Alone in her bed she shifted and turned, running her hand down her body in restless need. Indeed, she wanted nothing more than to let him do to her every wanton thing he'd done to her before.

Recalling his anger over the rumours that had brought him hurrying back to Westminster, his accusation of casting him in the role of villain wrenched her heart. Guy was no villain. Though she had never accused him of being, in the past she had called him a devil, and she should have known better than to accuse him of such. In the next few seconds her emotions veered from hysterical panic to shaking rationality.

She faced facts. She wanted to be with this man, so badly that she was shaken by it. She loved him with all her heart and soul—loved him because he was strong and scrupulous and passionate. Her bitterness and resentment caused by his attack on Richard, which had bruised her and she had allowed to fester, had been like a huge stumbling block. If only she'd had the courage to climb over it and look into her heart, she would have seen the truth of her love. At this realisation it was as though chains fell away from her and with them the resentment and bitterness that had possessed her ever since that day.

Guy had known what Richard was like, what her life would have been like married to him, and he had cared for her enough to save her from that terrible fate. Now she knew that in the silent background, Guy had always been there for her. He had taken her to Rosemead and then to the court—always there, understanding her, ready to help. He had never let her down—not even on that dreadful night when Richard had died. He had been there, calming her, taking charge. It had been Guy's strong arms that had held her, whose broad chest had pillowed her head, Guy who had completely understood her and the situation because he saw the unobstructed truth.

No man would do those things for a woman unless he loved her. Ever since she had met him, she had unknowingly existed in the protective circle of his love. Why hadn't she realised that he loved her? For no man would do what he had done for her unless he did.

What a fool she had been. Guy was her life. He had told her he wanted the girl he had met in the woodland glade back.

Oh, Guy. If you did but know it she is still here, still the same.

She had to go to him, to tell him what was in her heart. They couldn't leave it like this. She wanted to tell him how much she loved him. To say that she was sorry. But she must wait until the lists.

* * *

Three barges set off from the Palace of Westminster to travel up river to Windsor Castle, where the tournament was to be held. The prospect elicited great excitement among the courtly ladies and gentlemen. The king's heralds had ridden far and wide, inviting courageous knights to participate. There would be knightly games—jousts and tilting and a final tourney for all contenders.

The autumn weather was cold but dry. Seated in the back of the barge listening to the swish of the river and the dip and pull of the oars in the current, Jane was relieved when they arrived at Windsor. The common people flocked to see the royal procession. The castle was a majestic pile towering over meadows and the town, stretching along the big hill on which it was built.

Some of the knights had arrived with their squires and some with their ladies some days ago, and were encamped below the walls in an assortment of multi-coloured tents. The light from the many fires glinted on armour and polished shields, turning them to shining gold. There was a festive feel about the crowds that gathered, with mummers and beggars, goodwives and children and whores in colourful array. The smell of meat roasting over charcoal fires permeated the air and vats of ale were being drunk.

The royal party passed through the Castle Gate into the Lower Ward of the castle. With a patchwork of half-timbered buildings, it lacked the uniformity of the Upper Ward of the castle, which housed the royal apartments. But, with a diversity of buildings around it, the dazzling, magnificent St George's Chapel, the final resting place of monarchs and knights of England past, dominated the Lower Ward.

With the gusty wind blowing her cape around her like a tourniquet, Jane drew it tightly about her. With the interest to look around, she saw the castle was like a bustling town within the massive walls. Her gaze searched the faces for one in particular—she was disappointed Guy had not come to greet her, nor did he come to her that night.

It was not until the following morning when she was walking to the field where the tournament was being held that she saw him with a group of knights drinking a last stirrup cup of spiced malmsey.

On seeing Jane, Guy froze. The sight of her beauty dazzled his eyes. The colours of her gown were brilliant—a skirt of bright-green and an underskirt of rich turquoise, the skirts flaring from the high gold belt tied on her ribcage. Her high conical headdress sprouted a veil of tissue of gold from the peak that drifted down her back, and when she spread her arms, the big triangular sleeves were trimmed with beautiful embroidery in gold thread. She wore scarlet leather slippers on her feet.

Placing his cup down, without so much as a glance at his companions, he excused himself.

Jane watched him come towards her. Their eyes met and held for what seemed like an eternity, and she could feel the slow pounding of her heart as he seemed to stare into her very soul. She had once vowed never to open herself up to the pain of falling in love with him. Now she knew she had no choice in the matter. She understood her emotions more clearly now, though she couldn't exactly say when her love had started to bloom, but it came upon her with a solid certainty that she had loved Guy for a long time without realising it.

Suddenly she felt a flash of contrition. *He needs*

me, she thought—*and I need him very badly,* and she knew it was time to set her hurt feelings aside.

Sensing a change in her and a look in her eyes that gave him reason to hope, taking her hand Guy drew her behind a tent so they could not be observed.

'I'm glad you are here,' he said, forcing his intense gaze on her. 'I wanted to speak to you before the tourney begins.' He took in her attire, a smile tempting his lips. 'You are beautiful. Every knight who rides on to the field will request your favour.'

Feeling strangely nervous, she returned his smile. His blue eyes were hot as they took in the length of her body. 'Then they will be disappointed. My favour is reserved for my husband.' When they had parted some days ago, it had left her feeling abandoned and in despair. Now there was an energy and excitement moving through her. It took her a moment before she could compose herself enough to say, 'Guy, I—I want to say I'm sorry.'

He looked down at her and felt a lump in his throat at her earnest gaze. He took her hands in his own as he gazed at her. 'For what reason are you sorry?'

'For calling you a villain and a devil and so much more.'

'Sweetheart, when I think what I put you through, I'm the one who should apologise.' He sighed. 'Was I insane to make you my wife, Jane?'

Sick with failure, Jane dug her nails into the flesh of her palms and shook her head in denial. 'It never had a chance to work because I wouldn't let it. Will you forgive me for being so blind, so stupid—and proud?'

'My darling...' he chuckled softly '...you have added spice to my life that I would have found with no one else. How can I be angry with you for anything? I can only count myself fortunate that you share my life and will continue to do so until we are old and grey.'

'It is my intention and my most heartfelt wish. You can't possibly imagine how much I've missed you of late. I don't think there's been a night during our separation when I haven't cried myself to sleep, worrying about everything that has happened.'

'Hush, my love. We have been through all this. It is over.'

'Nevertheless, I am ashamed of what I must have put you through. I should have listened to your explanation instead of shutting my ears.'

'And I should have been more patient with you. You had a terrible shock.'

'That's all over now.' Jane's green eyes were shining with surrender and her voice shook. 'I am yours, Guy, willingly.'

Guy frowned, suspecting there was something she was holding back. His eyes met hers and he quietly asked, 'Why, Jane? Why are you doing this? Tell me.'

Jane knew Guy was going to require an unconditional surrender from her. She knew what he was demanding of her now. Through joy and tears and relief constricting her breath, she found her voice and softly said, 'Because I love you, Guy. Very much—more than life itself.'

Taking her hands, he dragged her into his embrace with stunning force. 'God help you if you don't mean it!' he warned fiercely. 'Because I swear to you, my darling, that I'll never let you go.'

Shamelessly yearning for his loving, Jane whispered, 'Do you mean that? Because there were times—even when you made love to me—when I knew that I didn't possess you completely. It made me wonder if there was a woman in the past who might have hurt you very badly.'

His features tightened. 'Aren't you going to ask me who she was or what terrible deed she committed? Women always want to know everything.'

'If you want to tell me, you will. You've done and seen so much in your life, and your reticence to give yourself to me completely prompted me to draw a conclusion. I didn't mean to pry.'

'You're not.' There was an edge of bitterness to his tone. 'There was a woman—some years ago. Some of the women of the court at that time were reputedly the most beautiful and the most callous and ambitious in Europe.'

'And the woman you fell in love with, was she beautiful and callous and ambitious?'

'Isabel was all of that and treacherous into the bargain. She thrived on duplicity and deception.'

The harshness of his voice told Jane that whatever had befallen him at that time had left scars.

What treachery could so have hardened his heart? 'What did she do that was so terrible?'

'I adored her. I respected her innocence and proposed marriage—only to discover that she was no innocent. She was three months gone with child—her lover a man who had abandoned her for another. Like the callow youth I was, I would still have married her, but he came back and she made it clear that she wanted him in her bed, not me.'

He paused to stare vacantly into space for several moments. Despising the woman who had hurt him so badly, Jane reached out to put a hand on his arm and he looked down at it, covering it with his own before continuing.

'To cut a long story short, I walked away and vowed that my emotions would never again be engaged by a woman—until I laid eyes on you that day in the woodland glade.'

'Guy, I had no idea. I understand your cynicism, but it changes nothing between us.'

'You are right,' he said quietly, caressing her face with his eyes. 'You are not Isabel.'

'Then hold what we have in your memory and let us share this time we both hold dear.'

'We have a lifetime to be together. But were I

to spend every moment with you it would never be long enough. I love you, Jane. No man has the right to feel such joy.'

'And I love you. I shall be very happy to prove I do mean it as soon as it is convenient. And—there is something else I should tell you,' she added almost shyly.

'Oh?'

'I am with child, Guy. We are going to have a baby.'

His eyes, not always so expressive, opened wide and seemed to melt with love for her. He reached out for her, then seemed uncertain.

Jane laughed. 'You can touch me. I will not break. In truth, I need you to hold me.' He did, gathering her into his arms. 'Are you happy?' she asked softly, resting her cheek against his chest.

'Overjoyed,' he murmured. 'I cannot tell you what this means to me. How long have you known.'

'About two months.'

'Two months!' He held her away from him, his expression one of severe reproach. 'Good God, woman! Had I know this when Aniston came to London I would have dragged you back to Cherriot.'

'Which is precisely why I didn't tell you. I couldn't bear the thought of being apart from you. Windsor was bad enough, but Cherriot would have been miserable on my own. I know how much you want children...'

He captured her face between his hands and stared fiercely into her eyes. 'Not just any children, Jane. You are more to me than that. I want *your* children.'

Jane's eyes swam with tears. 'Thank you. You don't know how much it means to me to hear you say that.' She saw his eyes darken with passion as he bent his head to her and she reached up on her toes to place her lips on his to begin convincing him. She kissed him with all the love and yearning in her soul, her heart giving a wild leap when he returned her kiss.

It was Guy who broke the kiss and, placing his hands on her upper arms, held her from him, finding it a strain to keep his hands from her, to resist the pleasure of caressing the cherished curves and hollows of the slender, voluptuous body that haunted his dreams.

'You will prove it to me later. I will be in dire need of some female companionship.'

'You will not be disappointed.'

He cupped her warm cheek with his palm and looked deep into her eyes, as if everything he ever needed or wanted to know was to be found in her gentle eyes. For a moment he did not trust himself to speak around the swelling in his throat. 'I have never been disappointed with your response to me so far,' he said softly. 'I love you too, Jane. Very much.'

Jane tried to smile at him, but Guy saw the tears glistening in her eyes. Cradling her face between both his hands, he gazed at her misty green eyes, at the tears suspended between her thick lashes. 'Why the tears, my love?'

'Because until now, I was certain you would never say that to me,' she whispered brokenly.

'Do you think I would have gone to so much trouble to make you my wife if I did not love you? I have loved you honourably as a knight and as passionately as a man might love a woman.'

Jane felt as if she had become as golden warm as she could be. She could feel herself smiling, glowing, at these words. At once she knew that he was telling the truth—that he loved her, that he had always loved her. No matter what he had done, he had done to protect her, to keep her safe. And she was in love with him.

'I think I have loved you from the first moment I saw you that day in the forest,' he murmured. 'You cast your spell on me even then—indeed, I think I already loved you when you called me a conniving, black-hearted scoundrel.'

Her eyes twinkled and she smiled. 'I meant it then.'

'Have you changed your mind?'

'You're none of those things. I know that now. Are you happy, my lord?'

He laughed and kissed her swiftly and then enfolded her in his arms once more. 'Happy?' Aye, my love, you've made me that.'

'Then go and get ready for the tournament before the king comes looking for his errant knight.'

When the knights had sworn fealty to the king, the tournament was preceded by jousting matches. The colourful, exciting pageant was a venue for knights to practise various forms of combat to the delight of the crowds. It kept the knights in excellent condition for the role they needed to play in warfare—skill with weapons and supreme strength and fitness were necessary to knights.

Across a sea of banners of every colour and description, Jane was completely lost in the excitement of it all. Her heart did a somersault as she watched a tall knight she recognised as her husband ride on to the field with his opponent. He was magnificent in full tournament regalia. Mounted on his powerful warhorse decked out with a silver bridle with red-and-gold tassels, and silks and velvets that displayed his coat of arms, his brightly polished full armour gleamed like silver. Bare headed, his dark hair shone in the sun's rays and his face was so incredibly handsome that just looking at it made Jane's heart cry out for him.

Guy saw Jane poised, provocative and glowing with colour the minute he rode on to the field. She sat with the queen and her sumptuously garbed chattering ladies in the royal enclosure beneath a gold canopy.

Each knight approached their respective lady for a favour. Jane felt a pleasant warmth as Guy rode towards her. All the special feelings she held in her heart for this man were revealed as though it were something that was impossible to hide. They looked at each other, their eyes locked.

Guy halted his mount just below where she sat and held out his lance. He looked directly at her and smiled lazily.

'Jane,' he said, bowing his dark head, 'will you honour your husband by allowing him to wear your colours?'

Jane's heart swelled with pride. He looked devilishly handsome, his dark hair tousled and a roguish gleam in his vivid blue eyes, which gazed only at her. She turned scarlet at being singled out so publicly, knowing all eyes were focused on her.

'Come, Jane,' he urged. 'A token is all I ask. That fetching scarf around your neck will do nicely,' he suggested.

Entering into the spirit of things, laughing happily, Jane removed the scarf. Standing up, she felt so fragile as she pressed the flimsy material to her satiny lips and fastened it to his lance.

The gesture held so much promise, it melted Guy. He gazed at her, half-forgetting where he was, what day it was, all of life's tiresome practicalities. But when she flashed her saucy smile as though amused by his wistful stare, he snapped out of it and spurred his steed on.

Jane held her breath and watched as he tucked her favour into a joint in his helmet, where it waved jauntily when he moved his head. The sun glanced off his armour and sent blinding flashes off his wheeling lance. His regal physique was inspiring. She sat motionless, awed by the sheer magnificence of the man, and by the beauty of his deadly skill. Riveted, she watched him deliver blows of massive power with his lance, swift, precise and ruthless, as he successfully unseated his opponent.

It was mid-afternoon when the noise of the crowd of peasants, servants and villeins was drowned out as the guards raised their trumpets and blew an ear-splitting blast on their clarions, a sign for the general tournament mêlée to begin. Preceded by heralds, sixty opposing knights thundered on to the field. The sun bounced off their armour and lances, and Jane squinted her eyes as tabards and shields emblazoned with coats of arms passed below her. The marshals had rapped out the rules, which was a sign for the combat to begin.

Jane had not witnessed a tournament before and appreciated each point of ceremony and honour. When combat was underway, she realised that it took great skill and good horsemanship to avoid being thrown by a blow from the opponent's lance or sword. With interest and unconsciously holding her breath, she watched as some of the knights were unhorsed, more losing their helmets, and two opponents thundered towards each other at breakneck speed, lances poised and aimed at the opposing shields.

'Oh goodness!' she gasped, hardly able to watch as the field became a mass of threshing, whinnying horses, shields and broken lances. 'They'll kill each other.'

Ann laughed at her ignorance understandingly. 'No, they won't. The mêlée is but a mock battle—the lances are culled and the swords blunted by lead foils—but there is always danger that one of them might be injured when he's knocked off his horse. But see, your husband is still mounted.'

And so he was, to Jane's relief. Mounted on his huge steed, cool headed, lean and powerful after all his chivalrous training and one of the most accomplished knights at court, he went on to unseat two more knights. Jane held her breath when he wheeled his horse at the end of the field and rode towards another opponent. All of a sudden Jane's excitement fled and fear rushed in. Anxious that it might be Guy's turn to be knocked from his horse, she sprang to her feet.

Through his visor slit, his eyes half-blinded with sweat, Guy saw his opponent bearing down on him, when to his left his attention was caught by a flash of turquoise. Momentarily distracted, he did something he had never done before—he took his eye off the target. His opponent's lance glanced off the shield and with a resounding thud lodged in the joint of the iron roundel which protected his shoulder. The crash of wood on metal was deafening and sparks flew from his armour. Guy grimaced as a tide of pain washed over him. Much as he struggled to resist the assault, he was prised from the saddled and lost his grip on consciousness before he hit the ground.

A gasp went up from the crowd followed by an eerie silence and then thundering applause for the winning knight, for it was a coup indeed to topple the king's favourite.

Already on her feet, Jane stared at the scene below her, seeing Guy's opponent raise his visor and grin triumphantly at the royal enclosure before an opposing knight raised his sword and knocked him to the ground. But Jane could only stare at Guy's inert body, her pulse beginning to race like a maddened thing. Why didn't he get to his feet? Why didn't he move? *Please God, don't let him be trampled under the hooves of those massive, dancing beasts.* For one anxious, fear-filled moment she waited for him to rise, but he lay motionless. Cedric ran on to the field with an attendant and she watched as they picked him up and carried him off to one of the tents.

'He must be hurt. I must go to him,' she said when Ann anxiously turned to her.

'Yes—yes, but I think you will find he is merely stunned.'

'Oh, Ann, I hope so.'

Sanity returned out of dire necessity. Turning to the steps, she hurried down them as her trembling hands lifted her skirts, then flew blindly to where they had taken her husband, sweeping into the tent without pausing. Cedric was bending over Guy, who lay on a bed. His helmet had been removed and Cedric was in the process of doing the same to his armour. He looked up when Jane came rushing in. Oblivious to those around her, she only had eyes for Guy. She stifled a gasp when she was close enough to see his face. His skin was moist and dark shadows smudged his eyes. There was a calmness to his features she was not used to seeing.

Panic threatened, but she steeled herself against it, knowing it would do him no good if she broke beneath the lashing fear that assailed her. 'Is he badly injured?' she asked Cedric.

With the confidence born of being at Guy St Edmond's right hand since he began to fight, Cedric glanced at her. 'He suffered worse at Towton. He'll live,' he told her. 'He's got nothing more serious than a broken arm and a knock on the head and—when he comes to—a savage blow to his pride. It's a first for him to be unseated in a mêlée by a knight inferior to him in strength and experience.'

Jane was so relieved to know Guy's injury wasn't serious that the tears she had valiantly held back flowed freely. 'His pride is the least of my worry, Cedric, but a broken arm will take time to heal and will require the kind of patience that will drive Guy to frustration.' She glanced at Cedric. 'Guy was wounded at Towton?'

He nodded. 'Broke a leg when he was knocked from his horse. It was a long time before he was back on his feet.'

'And were you there?'

'Throughout the battle. The worst I've seen.'

'We heard that the Lancastrians suffered very badly. You know my brother was killed at Towton—when he was taken prisoner.'

He nodded. 'Before the fighting started, both sides issued orders that there was to be no quarter. It wasn't given. On the rout from the battlefield, your brother was just one of thousands heading north across the Wharfe. Guy recognised him and saw him try to cross. He was hit by an archer and dragged down by the current and drowned. There was nothing he could do—nothing anyone could do for those wretched souls.'

Jane stared at him in disbelief. 'But—I thought Andrew was taken prisoner...that he was executed.'

Cedric shook his head. 'No. It was as I told you. He was killed trying to escape.'

'And Guy knew this?' He nodded. 'Then why didn't he tell me?'

Cedric looked up at her. 'I suppose he had his reasons.'

'Oh, see,' she said on seeing Guy's eyelids flutter. 'I think he stirs.'

With the return of consciousness came the pain in his upper arm. Cool fingers were against his neck, and a strange wetness fell on his face. He thought he heard his name called from afar. Slowly he opened his eyes. The noise from outside the tent told him the mêlée was still underway. Cedric was busy removing the armour from his legs. Turning his head, in a bright halo of light from the sun shining through the opening in the tent, he saw Jane hovering over him.

She saw him open his eyes and her own blurred with tears and so much tenderness in their depths that her lips broke into a joyous smile. 'Welcome back, my lord. You had us all worried for a time.'

She drew back a lock of hair on his forehead. Guy sighed. Her fingers were gentle, her smile that of an angel. 'Jane? Is it really you, or has my dream befuddled my sight?' His fingers closed lightly around her wrist and brought it against his lips. Kissing her soft skin, he murmured, 'No maiden of my dreams could taste as sweet. Kiss me,' he commanded. 'I would know if this is a dream or more heady stuff.'

His eyes grew lambent, sending Jane's senses reeling. She bent low to press her trembling mouth against his, clinging with a leisurely sweetness that held still the very moments of time. 'I thought I'd lost you,' she whispered when she lifted her lips from his. The choice of whether or not to dare to love him had nearly been taken out of her hands.

He laid his good arm about her nape and kissed her again. She smiled against his lips. 'What?' he asked.

'Your kiss speaks much more of passion than of pain.'

'What pain is that, my love?'

'You have a broken arm.'

He winced. 'Is that what it is?' Then he smiled, cupping her cheek. 'It's not worth bothering about. It will heal given time.'

'And it needs strapping,' Cedric's voice boomed

out. Having removed the last of his armour, he reaching for the bindings to secure Guy's arm.

Jane smiled at him. 'I will leave my husband in your capable hands, Cedric.' She kissed Guy one more time and, with her lips on his, whispered, 'I will come to you later.'

The hour was late when Jane at last left her duties and sought Guy out in his chamber. To her shock she found him in bed and sleeping the deep sleep of the exhausted, his injured arm bound close to his chest.

With a smile of a doting, adoring wife, after blowing out the candles and leaving only the fire in the hearth, she removed her clothes and crawled into bed. He rolled on to his side. He was as naked as she and, drawing the quilts over them both, she curled against him, her thighs against his, her arm around his waist, and soon felt into a deep and peaceful sleep.

Guy woke before dawn to a luxurious warmth, then he realised he was not alone. His wife's curving form was against his side. Opening his eyes, he found her head pillowed on his shoulder, her long hair spread over the pillows, her dark eyes blinking open.

'Jane? I'm sorry I was not awake to welcome you, my love, but Cedric gave me some draught for the pain and it damned well knocked me out.'

'Shush,' she murmured softly, leaning over him, her mouth taking his. 'You're awake now, although we must take your injury into consideration if I am to do as I said and prove my love.'

Her hands explored his chest and Guy groaned and with his good arm gathered her against him.

'I want you, Jane,' he murmured between deep kisses.

'And I you,' She put her hands on either side of his handsome face. 'More than you will ever realise.'

He grinned and rolled to press her into the mattress, grimacing when the movement jolted his arm. But not to be deterred, his free hand wandered boldly, his purpose clear and arousing. He kissed every part of her as if relearning her body, setting her limbs atremble, and when he came to take her, she gasped at the very rightness of his possession. It was a merging, a blending, a coming together, wonder turning to rapture, bodies straining, two beings wrapped in the pure bliss of their union, giving all to the other and in return finding everything and more.

'Come, Jane,' murmured a deep, playful voice, beguiling her to wake. 'My lady's breakfast is served.'

Reality pirouetted into Jane's dreams. The morning light shone, filtering through her eye-lashes.

The husky whisper came again. 'There's freshly cooked slices of ham—and warm bread.'

Jane's stomach growled to the lovely aroma of ham. By the soft, gold, rosy light of morning, she opened her eyes to find the terror of the king's fighting force was watching her with a tender, slightly doting smile on his ruggedly handsome face.

'Only if you will join me.'

Chuckling softly, he gathered her against him, his good arm draped around her bare shoulders. 'Not yet, my sweet,' he said between kisses. 'Lay back. I'm starved for you.'

'And I for you, my love—my husband,' she whispered, the word delicious on her tongue. She smiled into his eyes. 'You cannot know how good it feels to freely admit it.'

'You cannot know how good it is to hear it. Nearly as good, in fact, as...' His hands wandered boldly, his purpose clear. When she laughed and playfully rolled away from him, he grasped her wrist and drew her back into his embrace. 'Trust me.'

'I do,' she whispered.

He let out a grateful sigh. 'At last. It does my heart good to hear you say it. Thank you.'

'It's my pleasure.' She brushed a lock of his dark hair from his brow, her hand straying in a lingering caress. 'Why did you not tell me what really happened to Andrew at Towton, Guy? Why did you let me think you gave the order for his execution?'

'Who told you?'

'Cedric. I asked him. After the battle, when news reached us of Andrew's death, we were told he was just one of multiple prisoners put to death by you. Cedric told me a different story, that Andrew was killed by an archer while attempting to cross the River Wharfe—that you saw him.'

Guy sighed and lay back. 'I did, but I was

wounded. I'd also been issued with the unenviable task of rounding up prisoners. I'm not proud of what I did that day, Jane, but Towton was like hell on earth. It was intense and fearful, the noise like nothing you've ever heard—so many bodies.'

'Why didn't you tell me? Why did you let me go on believing ill off you?'

'Because had he not been shot by that archer, I might very well have issued the order for his execution. There would not have been a thing I could have done about it.'

Jane rested her head on his chest and sighed. 'Then if he had to die, I'm glad it was the arrow that killed him.' Tilting her head back, she looked at him lovingly. 'I do love you, Guy. You are the centre of my life—although soon I shall have another to dote on,' she said, resting her hand on her abdomen. 'But for the time being I belong entirely to you. I trust in you and believe in you with all my heart. Don't ever think of going away from me, because if you do I swear I shall go with you and stick to you like your shadow.'

Guy hadn't imagined he could have fallen any more deeply in love with her than he already was, but her artless pledge positively enslaved him.

'Just being with you feeds my soul,' he declared. 'I wish we were back at Cherriot. There I would have you all to myself and not have to share you with the queen and courtiers.'

'But we have only just arrived at the court—and I accept it will be an important part of both our lives since you are one of the king's most loyal advisors. We must also remember that the king is the source of all patronage, and very soon,' she said, giving him a tantalising little smile, 'we may be granted the joy of pretty daughters who will one day need to marry well.'

He looked at her in surprise and found a teasing twinkle in her eyes and a saucy smile on her lips. He arched an eyebrow, shooting her a droll look. 'Good Lord! It would appear I have married an ambitious female after all.'

'I can be when it is necessary. But I am happy at Sinnington Castle and would not wish to be a courtier spending all my time at the Palace of Westminster.'

The infant named Thomas Edward St Edmond was born in early summer at Sinnington Castle after a quick and easy labour. Jane's mother and Kate were lovingly present throughout her ordeal.

Perfect in every detail, he was rosy cheeked and dark haired like his father and had the appetite of a horse. From the moment his parents beheld him they adored him. He was the centre of their lives.

'You are a perfect mother,' Guy said with satisfaction, kissing her tenderly as she nursed their son. He turned his head to look at her, his brilliant blue eyes open wide. 'As long as you don't forget all about being a wife and a lover and make me feel a miserably neglected man.'

Jane knew he was joking, for he revelled in the beauty of young Thomas. She smiled at him with drowsy contentment, seeing so much love in his serene gaze—love and gratitude—and a wicked glint of a promise of something naughtier for later. 'It would not be possible for me to do that. You know how much I love you. How much do you love me?' she asked, placing the babe in his crib. Taking his hands, she held them to her heart.

'More than life itself,' he replied, looking deep into her eyes.

'And if you had a price to put on it? What would it be?'

'You are my joy, my love. If I had to name a price, it would be a fortune—nothing less than a king's ransom.'

* * * * *